BY RACHEL LINDSAY

Miss Me with That:
Hot Takes, Helpful Tidbits,
and a Few Hard Truths

Real Love

REAL LOVE

a novel

RACHEL LINDSAY

DELL BOOKS

NEW YORK

A Dell Trade Paperback Original

Copyright © 2023 by Rachel L. Lindsay
Book club guide copyright © 2023 by Penguin Random House LLC

Published in the United States by Dell, an imprint of Random House, a division of Penguin Random House LLC, New York.

Dell is a registered trademark and the D colophon is a trademark of Penguin Random House LLC.
Random House Book Club and colophon are trademarks of Penguin Random House LLC.

ISBN 978-0-593-35712-5
Ebook ISBN 978-0-593-35711-8

Printed in the United States of America on acid-free paper

randomhousebooks.com
randomhousebookclub.com

2 4 6 8 9 7 5 3 1

This book is dedicated to:

All of those held captive to their "life plans" . . .
free yourself

All of those who are wondering what is on the other side
of the rainbow . . . go look for yourself

All of those who are ready to take flight
but are too afraid to try . . . soar

Real Love

Prologue

MOVING TO MIAMI was never on my list of things to do in life.

Sure, I used to imbibe the occasional tequila shot or two, but I had plans. *Real* plans. Like becoming a director at an investment firm, getting married, and having one child—not two, and definitely not three—before I turned thirty-five. Living someplace with a raging party scene and people who think animal print is proper business attire had never appealed to me.

But as time passed, my hair and skin adjusted to the rain and humidity, and hope settled in. Miami nights were never on my vision board, but that could be a good thing. Miami wasn't what I expected and maybe that's the exact reason it's what I needed.

Unfortunately, not even Simone Biles–level mental gymnastics could make me say the same about the ridiculous offer disrupting my lunch hour.

"Maya?" The telegenic face on the other end of my phone is drastically less enthusiastic than it was moments ago. "Are you there?"

"Yes, I'm sorry. I'm here." I hold up a finger to my impatient friend outside of my camera's view. Delilah is always cool and collected, but she's looked like she's about to come out of her skin since the second I told her who was calling.

"I'm sorry, I'm just a little—well, a lot—surprised. When I auditioned for *Real Love*, I never actually thought I'd be chosen."

"That's one of the reasons we fell in love with you, Maya, and we just know America will feel the same way." The host's eagerness is back in his voice and the smile on his face grows wider, which only makes the dread I feel grow heavier in my stomach. "You'll have to fly—"

"I'm so sorry, Paul." The people pleaser in me wants to die, but there's not a chance in hell I would ever agree to this. And if my life as a woman in investment banking has taught me anything, it's that ripping off the Band-Aid might sting for a second, but in the long run, it's much preferred over prolonging the pain. "I'm honored, but I'm going to have to pass."

I push my chair back, not completely sure Delilah isn't about to jump over the table and rip the phone from my hand. Her expression is a curious combination of shock, disbelief, and red-hot fury. It's a little scary. If I wasn't 100 percent sure this was the right decision, the shade of red rising in her cheeks might have convinced me to change my mind.

"You . . . you what?" Poor Paul looks as disappointed as my friend . . . and maybe a tidbit more angry too. I'm beginning to sense I'm the first person who has ever turned this opportunity down.

"I can't accept. I'm saying no." I fake the confidence I don't quite feel, keeping my voice as steady as possible and trying not to cower beneath Paul's glare. "Thank you for the offer, but if you liked me, then I really do feel like you'd be much better off choosing Bailey Michaels or Delilah Rivera."

Delilah's eyes narrow into slits and my life flashes before my eyes.

"Um, okay . . ." Paul's heavy breathing is the only thing

that distracts from his fire engine–red cheeks. "Listen, we know this is a huge decision. Why don't you take a few days to think this over before giving us your final answer?"

"I appreciate that, I really do, but my answer isn't going to change." I close my eyes and take a deep breath, hoping my next sentence will end this excruciating conversation. "My final answer is no."

I would say that knowing I would decline no matter what is the main reason I didn't want to go with Delilah and Bailey to audition for this ridiculous dating show in the first place, but that would indicate that I ever, in my wildest dreams—or nightmares—thought I'd actually be chosen. I mean honestly, what are the odds?

No, *really*. I wonder what they are. I'm going to try to figure out the numbers when I get off work tonight . . .

"Well then, I guess that's that." Paul cuts into my number fantasy. The edge in his voice makes me grateful this rejection is taking place over FaceTime and with thousands of miles between us. When I first became an investment banker, I lost a company an obscene amount of money and they didn't sound even remotely as pissed as Paul looks now. "Thank you for your time."

He doesn't wait for a response before my screen goes black and I'm met with dead air . . . and a very angry friend whom I can't avoid as easily.

"Please tell me that did not just happen!" Delilah, my (usually) calm and patient friend, yells so loudly it causes the poor man across from us to jump and spill his water in his lap. "It's *Real*-freaking-*Love*, Maya! You just turned down *Real Love*, the most popular dating show on television, without even considering it! What's going through your brain right now? Think about the opportunity you're passing up!"

My eyes dart around and my face heats as I realize all

eyes in the restaurant are unapologetically trained on our table of two. To be fair, I think this proves my point. If I can't handle a few people watching me, what would I do on a national television show with an audience of millions? Just the thought makes my stomach turn.

"I can't believe *you* can't believe I'm not doing this. I didn't even want to audition in the first place. I only went as 'emotional support' for Bailey after you two begged me to go with you." I grab my glass of water and take a deep sip, wishing it was vodka. "What about me says 'Yes, I'd love to make out with strangers on television for all of America to critique'? Nothing at all. Absolutely not."

I'm genuinely kind of shocked by Delilah's reaction. She is me in a Miami-born, Cuban bombshell form. She's also the only other person I know who'd rather work for thirteen hours than meet for drinks or relax on the couch. In an office full of men, we're the cream of the crop. We crush our numbers and have a plan for the future where we run the world. Leaving work for months on end to go on a dating show? No. Never. Neither of us would ever do it in a million years.

"Nothing about you says that," she says, and for a split second I think I've won the argument. "Which might be the exact reason you should do it."

Looks like I'm wrong a lot today.

"For a person revered for her logic, that's shockingly idealistic of you." I push around the now-cold pasta on my plate with my fork. "We only auditioned to keep Bailey company, and besides, she might not ever forgive me if I steal her dream from beneath her feet."

Bailey is our coworker and the third in our little work trio. Unlike Delilah and myself, she's late more than a couple of times a week and enjoys a solid happy hour more than perhaps any other living being I've ever met. She's nearly six feet of pure American beauty standards—glossy blond hair, bright blue eyes, and a slim body that works as a perfect display for everything she wears. It was her idea to audition for *Real Love* and I only gave in due to her constant pestering.

"Bailey is a big girl, she'd get over it."

"Well, you know who wouldn't? My neurosurgeon father and my professor mother." I decide to leave my little sister, who would actually freaking love this, off the list. "But also Vaughn, you know, my boyfriend?"

Vaughn is my college sweetheart and I have a feeling that like most other people on the planet, he wouldn't be thrilled with the idea of his long-term girlfriend exploring her other romantic options on national television.

"You're not married, so technically you're still single," Delilah says before sighing. I'm pretty sure that's not how it works, but she continues before I can say so. "Listen, all I'm saying is the world is freaking scary right now. You and I have been playing it safe, doing things by the book our entire lives. But what's the point of life if we're not actually living it? I know you think Vaughn is great, but why are you holding yourself back for a man who can't even get it together enough to move in with you, let alone put a ring on your finger?"

I don't know what's gotten into her. I've never heard her say anything like this before and I'm not sure what to make of it. And while I know she doesn't mean any harm, my hackles go up with the way she's talking about Vaughn.

I wave to the waiter, hoping to get their attention so we can get the bill. "Well, if they call you, then *you* can say yes."

"Maybe I will."

"I hope so." I smile to the waiter when they place our bill on the table. "I'll tune in every single week and follow all the blogs. I'll even promise not to mock you relentlessly and tell you 'I told you so' when you're looking for a new job."

And when that happens, I'll still be enjoying my six-figure salary, my long-term boyfriend, and checking off every last thing on my to-do list until I'm living the life I always planned for myself.

One Year Later

UNREALISTICALLY UNCHECKED—THE
UNOFFICIALLY OFFICIAL BLOG CONCERNING
ALL MATTERS *REAL LOVE*

Well, Lovers, our time is nigh.

The most amazing time of the year has arrived! If you're like me—which I know you are, you're here, duh—you have the drinks planned and the ingredients for a charcuterie board ready because it is premiere day for our beloved show, *Real Love*!

If you haven't been following all the drama of this year's season, don't fret, I've got you. Rumors were swirling that for the first time ever, the producers' first choice for the lead declined their offer and sent them scrambling for someone to take her place. Can you imagine turning down the opportunity to have twenty gorgeous men fawning all over you? I sure can't! But sayonara and good riddance to her because we've been blessed with—dare I say—the most beautiful, and first Latina, lead in *Real Love*'s history!

Tonight, our newest heroine, Delilah Rivera, will start the journey of a lifetime, and I for one can't wait to watch. Insiders have told me it's one of the best seasons to date and that Delilah does, in fact, find the love of her life! Meet me back here tomorrow for all my thoughts, reactions, and guesses for who the lucky guy is!

XOXO,
Stacy

1

I HIT IGNORE when my phone starts to ring . . . again.

I'm never late to anything, so I understand why everyone is calling. They're probably worried my old ladyish driving skills finally brought forth my demise against some hotshot street racer on my way to Delilah's.

Or they're wondering where I am because this party is being broadcast live on national TV. Traipsing into Delilah's living room late like I don't have a care in the world could possibly mean making a fool of myself—and/or Delilah—for all the world to see.

Not that I'd ever admit it out loud, but I've been dreading tonight for months.

Don't get me wrong, I'm over the moon for Delilah. She was one of my very first friends in Miami. She threatened to poison Mark's spinach wrap when he hushed me—actually, literally hushed me—during my first meeting at Wright, Ghoram, and Degrate. She understood me on a level nobody else ever has and has been a constant in my life . . . right until she up and moved across the country for three months to find a husband on a reality show.

The ringer on my phone goes off again. My finger hovers over the ignore button, ready to send the call to voice-mail, but at the last second, I decide to answer it. What if

Delilah finally came to her senses and took off to a small village in Mexico where nobody would ever recognize her from that one American TV show where she spent twelve weeks kissing strangers? That's news I'd want to hear in real time.

"Hello?" I say.

"Where are you? This is *live*, we can't wait for you!" Bailey's southern accent slips through in her panic. She moved to Miami from Georgia at eighteen for college and she never went back. She's a southern belle with roots in pageantry and she specializes in subtle shade, but she's very much a Florida girl now.

"Relax." I mimic the deep breathing techniques the teachers do when she drags me to yoga class with her. "I'm on my way." I leave out that I may or may not still be in my apartment. "I'll be there soon enough, but if I'm late, I'll just wait outside until one of you calls me in. I promise not to ruin Delilah's big moment with a late entrance."

This is the first time I'll see Delilah since she threw her life into a tailspin, and I'm a little nervous. What if this happily-ever-after she bet everything on takes a turn for the worse? Maybe things are great *now*, but what about in a week? A month? A year? When all that's left of this is un-employment and endless GIFs and memes plastered across the internet?

And what makes me even more nervous, the part I defi-nitely wouldn't admit out loud, is what if the person I loved so much before she left is gone? I fully understand that growth means changing and evolving as a person. But old Delilah was one of my favorite humans—what if I don't recognize this new version of her? Or worse, what if this new version of her doesn't like *me*?

"Oh my god." Bailey huffs into the phone, and from the

fading noise in the background, I know I've annoyed her into changing locations. "This isn't about you being here for her big moment. This is about you being here because she loves you and knows she wouldn't have had this opportunity or her fairy-tale ending if it weren't for you turning the opportunity down."

Even though she can't see me, I narrow my eyes in suspicion—that sounds a little too earnest for the Bailey I know. I sit on one of the pristine white stools tucked beneath my even more pristine white countertops. "And?"

"*And* you're the only person who will drink whiskey with me. I don't want to have to drink wine all night and end up snoring on her couch during a live broadcast!"

Yup.

There it is.

I'm not a drinker per se, but I do enjoy a Crown and Coke on occasion . . . and also every Thursday for happy hour and whenever someone suggests grabbing a cocktail. A girl's gotta have her signature drink.

"Ulterior motives." I *tsk* without malice. She gets so worked up it's just fun to play with her emotions. Especially when mine are already on the fritz. "But since you were so honest, I'll even go five above the speed limit and be there as fast as I can."

"Five above? Whoa there! Be careful, I don't want you getting whiplash from driving so fast."

"Smart-ass." I slide my feet into my Rothy's and grab my classic Chanel bag off the counter. "Just for that, I'm using cruise control and sticking to two miles over."

Because as much as I want to stay home and watch anything other than *Real Love* until Vaughn comes over to regale me with all the shenanigans from the Miami clubbing scene, I want to be there for my friends more.

I also want to partake in the free alcohol with Bailey.

"Please speed," Bailey begs. "I'll pay for any tickets you get *and* I'll pay for lunch on Thursday."

This is when I know she's desperate. In the words of her unapologetically southern mom, *bless her heart,* Bailey is notoriously cheap. I'm not sure she's ever offered to pay for anything over the course of our entire friendship.

This should make my exit even more urgent, but it slows my steps instead.

"Is it that bad?"

While being filmed watching a show that makes me cringe so hard I feel like I'm going to pass out was never on my to-do list, tonight is the kind of environment Bailey thrives in. Free catered food and booze, attention galore, and an excuse to dress up? I can't imagine why she sounds so desperate. She should be in her element.

"Uh . . . well . . . you know . . ." She struggles to string together a sentence. Her accent is the only thing overshadowing her nerves. "It's not bad, but I think she's nervous. She needs you here."

And when I hear that, it's like the bat signal lights up the already bright Miami night sky.

"I'll be there in ten."

Before Delilah signed up to be the lead on *Real Love,* she lived in a great studio apartment in the heart of Miami Beach. The building was amazing, and her amenities were top-notch—her pool was our favorite—but her space was minimal. She always said the size made it easier to clean and that she didn't need much room for anything other than her clothes . . . which is why pulling up to her new house in Coral Gables is a huge shock.

Cars line the street in front of her place. The large homes

with their perfectly manicured lawns are highlighted by the streetlights. I'm sure if I drove down this street during the day, the sidewalks would be filled with nannies walking together while the future leaders of Miami skip down the street blowing bubbles and running in the grass.

Now, however, camerapeople with giant battery packs are running up and down the street from RVs to Delilah's front door. The commotion and activity are a stark contrast to the quiet, almost suburban vibe this neighborhood is known for.

Just a few months ago Delilah's life was calm and organized. Now it's a freaking circus.

And I find it's one more reason I'm so happy with my decision not to do this.

I drive farther down the street until I finally find an open spot to park my car, grateful she at least chose one of the safer neighborhoods to lure me to so late at night. I'm just glad I wore my flats instead of the strappy stilettos Bailey tried to talk me into wearing. I might not know everything, but I do know there's never a reason to wear stilettos to a friend's house.

I tap out a quick text to Bailey letting her know I'm walking up and will be there in a second. I rush down the wide sidewalks, avoiding the men with long microphones who pass me with muttered apologies. I turn in to her walkway, but before I can pause to take a breath and brace for whatever the night has in store for me, I hear someone I don't know shouting my name.

"Maya? Maya Johnson?"

I nod my head yes, looking around the yard, trying to figure out who called me, when a woman with her blond hair pulled into a bun on the top of her head appears by my side. She loops her arm through mine and pulls me off the sidewalk and across the lawn, toward a tent set up at the back of the driveway.

"I've got Maya, give us three and we'll be ready," she yells into her walkie-talkie. I think somebody responds, but I can't understand what they say through the thick static.

"I'm sorry." I look around for Bailey or Delilah or anybody I know to help save me from this kidnapping, but they're nowhere to be found. They're probably afraid that if they come out, they'll also get snatched away. "We'll be ready for what? What am I going to be ready for?"

The woman escorting me doesn't respond and I can't tell if she doesn't hear me or is just straight-out ignoring me. She gives me a gentle shove onto a stool in the center of some very bright lights, throwing out orders to everyone around her. If I wasn't about to massively freak out, I'd appreciate that she's clearly the person running this show.

Normally I'm a very calm and patient person. To be a woman in a male-dominated field, it's a requirement. But all my composure disappears the second a man with pink hair, green lipstick, and lashes so long they touch his eyebrows approaches my face with a giant makeup brush and a color palette approximately four shades too light for my complexion.

I lean away from him, narrowly missing his powder-filled sneak attack.

"I'm sorry!" I repeat my earlier sentiment, just a little louder, a little more panicked this time. "But can somebody *please* tell me what is going on?"

My outburst doesn't deter him. He regains his balance and hits the intended target of my perpetually oily T-zone. At least this time, the woman with the walkie-talkie finally acknowledges that I'm speaking . . . and also may be on the verge of a nervous breakdown.

"You're going on in three"—she checks her Apple Watch—"make that two minutes. We just need to touch up your makeup so you aren't shiny and glaring on camera. Nothing much before we send you in since we have so little time."

They can make my skin as matte as they want, but I can guarantee I will still, 100 percent, be glaring on camera.

"Going on?" I repeat the words that have my stomach trying to claw its way out from my insides . . . but from which end I'm still not sure. "But . . . but . . ." The confident woman who has secured me a six-figure income before the age of thirty hitchhikes back to Iowa and suddenly I'm the trembling thirteen-year-old who ran out of my first debate and cried in the bathroom. I trip over my words and try to organize my thoughts. "I . . . thought I was just going to be . . . sitting in the background and drinking."

Walkie-Talkie, who still hasn't told me her name, looks at me like my stomach might in fact be falling out of my mouth. "Didn't Delilah tell you?" she asks without stopping. She circles behind me, shoving her hand up the back of my shirt and securing a mic pack. "Paul, the host, is going to ask you a few questions. Quick things, like how excited you are for Delilah. How you knew she would be so loved on the show since you're the one who encouraged us to offer and her to accept. That kind of thing."

Those freaking snakes.

I should've known Bailey was up to something.

I just need a drinking partner my ass.

And Delilah was in on it too! Ugh. I can't even think about it. Anger, humiliation, panic, and fear swirl around me heavier than any of the hurricanes Miami has ever seen.

Unfortunately for me, I don't have time to stew. I don't even have time to bolt. Before my brain even has time to formulate a plausible escape route, Walkie-Talkie loops her arm through mine again and makeup guy jogs beside us, swiping a new brush along my cheekbones. "Just a little blush and highlighter," he says. "To give you a little color."

I almost laugh at the absurdity of his comment. Nobody has ever taken in my deep bronze skin and thought it lacked color. But instead of laughing, I'm on the verge of tears. I'm about to make my television debut looking awful because my face was touched by someone who's probably never done makeup for a Black woman before.

The distance to the door closes and my vision begins to blur. The urge to run hits me full force, but Walkie-Talkie seems to have been expecting it. Her grip on my arm tightens as she says something that only sounds like static.

I realize that if I pass out, there's no way they can make me do this. I pray for my body to give out on me. I wish for one of those infamous Florida sinkholes to open up beneath me and swallow me whole.

But alas . . . no luck.

The door swings open and unnatural lighting momentarily blinds me as I hear my (ex-) friends cheer. When my vision adjusts, I realize cameras—from *every* angle—are pointed directly at me. A smile I'm sure looks more like the grimace of a woman birthing a ten-pound baby pulls at my lips as Delilah runs toward me.

I'm sorry, she mouths while her back is still to the cameras.

It's not a stretch to say I want to kill her for this. And even though she knows I mainly watch nineties sitcom reruns, she also knows there was a month where I binged every episode of *Dexter*. I know exactly how to dispose of a body.

I almost respond with a promise of revenge before remembering the mic clipped onto my back and bite my tongue. Instead, I force prime-time-friendly words to come through gritted teeth. "I can't believe you'd do this to me!"

She pulls me in for a hug, whispering meaningless apologies into my ear. "I'm sorry. I just knew if I told you, you wouldn't have come. And I really need you here."

My resolve for payback lessens—slightly. She's right. If I would've known I was going to be on TV . . . like really on TV, not just sitting in the background, my happy ass would be planted on my couch. There's no way I would've come.

"You owe me so huge. Like, five brunches huge."

"Deal." She squeezes me tighter before letting go and intertwining her fingers with mine and pulling me closer to my own personal version of hell . . . I mean the cameras.

Laughter off to the side of the room pulls my attention and I manage to send my dirtiest glare to Bailey. She might find this funny now, but she won't for long. Sure, technically, I might have people-pleasing tendencies that often place other people's wants and needs above my own, but I'm also an expert at grudge holding and guilt trips. Just the thought of the amount of free coffees and happy hours I'm going to get out of this causes a real smile to appear on my face . . . and just in the nick of time.

"This is her, Paul." Delilah leans against me, pulling me out of my revenge-filled fantasy. "This is Maya. The reason I was able to go on this amazing journey."

I don't know if I'm more taken aback by the fact that Delilah is so confident and unfazed in the midst of all of the chaos cluttering her living room or that I'm standing in front of a man I've seen on my television screen way more times than I'd ever admit . . . and that his teeth are making my professionally whitened ones seem dingy and dull.

"The infamous Maya!" He shouts my name like I'm not

standing inches away. His enthusiasm that translates so well on the screen is a little overwhelming in person. "We've heard so much about you. How are you?"

I open my mouth to answer, but Paul keeps talking instead.

"I'm sure viewers will love to know that you actually caused quite the commotion prior to filming." The sparkle in Paul's hazel eyes changes, and for the first time I notice the anger lingering behind them. He turns away from me and looks straight into the camera. Any semblance of relaxation fades into oblivion as I brace for what's to come. "Maya here is the first person in *Real Love*'s history to turn down our offer to be the lead."

I've hated flying ever since I realized planes could crash. Some nights when I'm struggling to find sleep, my mind thinks it's really fun to let all of my irrational fears drift to the surface. Its favorite scenario is what it would be like sitting in my seat, the oxygen masks falling from the ceiling and the plane speeding back to earth. Would I be calm? Would I scream and confess my sins? It's always been my worst nightmare. But I guess that's because my brain was never creative enough to drum up the situation I'm in now.

Good news: I don't scream. Bad news: I might pass out because even though my feet are firmly planted on the ground, the air is starting to feel really freaking thin.

"Um, yeah." Awkward laughter slips from between my lips, for all of America to hear, and it's enough to make me want to crawl into a hole and die. "That's me."

Seriously? I graduated at the top of my class. I lead meetings and work with high-powered clients every single day. And now, on national television, the best I can come up with is *that's me*? Someone kill me now.

"That *is* you," Paul says. There's no missing the sick

pleasure he's taking in torturing me. Never trust a person with teeth this white. Sociopaths, all of them. "So what is it like watching Delilah find love when this could have been you?"

"I'm so happy for her. I think everything happens for a reason." I give the first beauty pageant–quality answer that comes to mind. My face muscles start to spasm with how hard I'm forcing my smile. "This wasn't my path to love, but it is hers. And I can't wait to watch what happens along with the rest of America."

"And we know America is excited to watch Delilah on the most extraordinary season of *Real Love* yet," he says, and I have to bite back laughter. Every season is the most extraordinary in the history of the show.

"Thank you, Maya." Paul aims one last glance at me before turning his back on us and looking into the camera. "And when we get back from the commercial break, it will finally be time for you to see Delilah's adventure begin. Stay tuned."

With that uninspired sign-off, the cameras go dark, the people surrounding us scatter, and Delilah pulls me to the couch to sit next to her.

"See, already over." She takes a delicate sip of her champagne. "That wasn't too bad, was it?"

I don't tell her it was a level of torture I didn't think was possible or that I'm so anxious, I'm pretty sure I sweat through my shirt. Instead, I just nod and smile. "Nope, not too bad."

The Delilah from before she went on the show would've known I was lying. She would have called me on it the second the lie slipped through my lips. But this Delilah, she just squeezes my arm and takes another sip of her drink before her face appears on the screen in front of us.

I settle into the beautiful but slightly uncomfortable couch and watch as man after man steps out of a limo, all wowed by my stunning friend.

For two hours, we sit and watch as Delilah is showered with affection and compliments and as she flourishes with the life I was offered.

The life I never wanted.

Right?

My dearest Lovers!

Well, it's a mystery no longer!

After last night's premiere, we now know three things:

1) Delilah Rivera is not only the most beautiful woman in the world, but she's smart, funny, and cutthroat. She's not here for games and I'm freaking OBSESSED. Ten out of ten, do recommend!

2) If you meet a man named Scott, *run*! They are never any good. Scott D and Scott M were both d-bags of the highest degree and I applaud our girl Delilah for getting rid of them with a quickness we both fear and admire.

3) My sources about someone turning down the show were right on the money (as usual, you know you can trust me) and we met her last night! Maya Johnson, a coworker of Delilah's, was paraded out in front of the cameras to cheer on her friend. Now, I can't lie, I was initially hater number one, but after seeing her, I'm intrigued. She's just as beautiful as our current leading lady and clearly just as smart. I'm dying to know why she said no! Maybe watching Delilah win over our hearts will convince her to say yes to a different season?

Would you be interested in seeing more of her? Drop a comment below and check back later for my full recap of the premiere complete with spoilers galore!

XOXO,
Stacy

2

THIS COULD HAVE *been you.*

I can't get Paul's stupid words out of my head.

Even though I had two cocktails instead of my usual one, and one of the guys vying for Delilah's heart showed up on a horse, wearing chaps and singing the words to "Save a Horse, Ride a Cowboy" (she kept him, by the way), nothing could distract me from what Paul had said. His words replayed in my head throughout the night, and to my complete horror, even in my dreams.

I'm not sure it was Paul's actual words so much as what it felt like he was implying that bothered me. Seeing how truly *happy* Delilah had seemed last night, the way her cheeks warmed at the mention of her mystery man, I tried to remember the last time I looked like that. Vaughn and I are years past our honeymoon phase, but just because it doesn't feel as exciting doesn't mean it's not good. It's just real. It doesn't matter if Paul doesn't think I'm as happy as Delilah. I know the truth—I have a boyfriend I love, a job I love, and I'll feel the same kind of happiness Delilah does when I become the youngest director at my firm.

The organized and constant chaos of Wright, Ghoram, and Degrate is music to my ears. Some people like the soothing sounds of waterfalls or violins being expertly played. But me? I love the yelling across the floor and the symphony of fingers hitting keyboards. The sound of money being made—even the sound of it being lost—drowns out Paul's stupid words. I worked my ass off to get from my intern position at a small investment bank in Des Moines to one of the top investment firms in the country. And no offense to Delilah, but I think that's a lot more impressive than kissing some men on television. Of course, Delilah also put herself here—it's one of the many reasons we get on so well.

Today is supposed to be Delilah's first day back at work after taking her extended leave to film. I dart over to her cubicle but instead of her gorgeous face, I'm greeted by an empty desk chair. I know it might take her a while to get back into the swing of things, but she was always one of the first to arrive at the office before she went on *Real Love*. I've missed our early morning chats these last few months while she's been away. She may be a dirty traitor for throwing me to the wolves with the cameras last night, but I've been counting down the days until she returned. I even brought her favorite chocolate to give her as a welcome-back present.

I try not to look too disappointed as I walk to my desk and wave to the few coworkers who managed to beat me into the office today. When I reach my cubicle, it almost feels more like home than my apartment does. I lower myself into the aerodynamic chair WGD gave us all last Christmas—appreciating the way my back doesn't groan anymore when I plant myself for hours of work—and turn on the three monitors sitting on my desk. As the screens come to life, so do I. Anticipation from the promise of the unknown shoots through me as all irrelevant thoughts drift away and I plan the different ways I'll attack the day, making money for my clients, my firm, and myself.

I don't know how much time has passed when a plastic

bottle filled with juice in a very unappealing shade of green lands on my desk.

I grab it and twist off the lid, spinning to see Bailey standing next me.

"Figured you could use a little boost since I'm sure you've already been here for an hour or two and I doubt you had any breakfast."

I glance at the time on my computer. It's almost ten, so I've actually been here for closer to three hours, but I don't tell Bailey. She's a few years younger than my twenty-nine years and she's still in the phase where she spends more time indulging in the Miami nightlife than she probably should. She says it's work-life balance, but seeing how late she arrived, I think the "life" portion might be a good bit heavier than the "work" portion.

"Thanks." I smell the juice before taking a sip, the apple and lime overpowering the kale and celery I know are blended in. "My coffee fuel was starting to run low."

"I figured . . ." She lets her words trail off and I know she wants to talk about last night.

I lean back into my chair, taking another sip of the drink I love to hate and wait for her to mention it. She always seems to want me to bring things up—probably so it seems like I'm the one making a big deal out of things—but I like to wait her out. I get that she was just trying to get me there and it was in service of a friend, but I'm still annoyed she lied instead of being up-front. Maybe if I was prepared for what I was walking into, Paul's jab wouldn't have penetrated so deeply.

She fidgets a bit, twirling a piece of her long, wavy blond hair around her pale finger.

"Ugh, okay fine." She finally breaks and I fight back my smug smile. "I'm sorry about last night. Delilah made me promise not to tell you. I told her it was a bad idea, but she was so focused on surprising you that I couldn't get her to budge."

"It's fine, I guess. Just don't do it again." I talk a big game, but when someone apologizes to me, I don't have it in me to hold it over their head. "Speaking of Delilah, is she here yet?"

"I don't think she's coming in today."

"She's not?" My head jerks back. "Why?"

I guess I'll have to eat that welcome-back present myself . . .

"Not sure. Something to do with an interview in New York maybe? Honestly, I can't keep up with her anymore." Bailey is clearly less invested in our friend's return than I am. She shrugs her shoulders and takes a long sip of her juice. "You know, I thought she hated flying, but she's on a plane all the time these days. Either she got a huge prescription for Xanax or immersion therapy really works."

I don't really know what to do with this new information or the way my stomach falls as I realize my work bestie is going to be gone for even longer. So I do what I do best: avoid and deflect. "Last night was fun."

And it was . . . minus the making a minor fool of myself on television and the crushing sense of self-doubt that's been weighing me down ever since.

"Wasn't it?" Bailey slides farther into my cubicle and I know I won't be getting back to my work for at least another ten to fifteen minutes.

Bailey might not be the hardest working member of WGD, but she is a woman and she also went to Delilah's alma mater. As such, when she was hired, Delilah and I immediately stepped up to show her the ropes and help guide her down this wild career path we've chosen. Bailey is definitely different from me, but once Delilah left, we were forced to bond, and now I think we've become pretty good friends outside of work too.

Plus, Bailey is a perpetual gossip and that has its uses. I may have been here longer, but she is literally the only reason I know how to navigate the office water cooler. Thanks to her, I know Jackson is sleeping with Bianka even though he has a girlfriend of six years. She's also the reason I know Suzanne, the only female director in our office, is moving to Seattle for her husband—who Bailey also tells me only makes a portion of what Suzanne makes—and that Greg and Marcus (our bosses) have been holding a lot more closed-door meetings as of late, probably to figure out who will take her place. It's the position I've been aiming for since I first started and it might be the only thing important enough to bring Delilah back to her senses.

"What did you think of the guys Delilah let through?" She pushes some of the loose papers that have accumulated since I started working this morning to make space for her nearly nonexistent butt . . . not unlike Delilah did all those months ago when I turned down *Real Love* and she took it instead. "She *seems* happy, but I don't know. I'm not sure I trust it. I went home and looked up some of those guys and ehhhhh . . . I think she's getting played."

The part of my brain that has been concerned about this same thing leaps to life and I lean forward in my chair. "Do you think so? I've been really worried about that. I mean, she kept the cowboy. I'm not sure you can ever trust a man in chaps." My mom would be so disappointed in me for taking part in what she would consider to be the very definition of a frivolous conversation. I justify it by telling myself that even my flawless mother would indulge in this conversation if she was concerned for the well-being of her best friend.

"I know!" she whisper-shouts, even though the voices shouting around the office would be sure to drown out any gasp of disgust. "I felt bad for the poor horse."

The snort-laugh I held in last night slips free now and I'm so relieved to know I wasn't the only one with these thoughts.

"I'm sure some of it was for entertainment's sake. Delilah is one of the smartest people I know; she had to have a good reason for her choices." This is what I've told myself every time I worry more about Delilah's self-preservation more than she does. "Besides, it seems to have all worked out for her. When I asked her if she was happy, she said yes, and I don't think she was lying."

"I'm sure having the attention of the entire country and a new house in fucking Coral Gables would make anybody happy. If it works for her, then I'm happy she's happy. And I guess the dentist seemed okay, even though I'm not sure I trust blond men." She turns a conspiratorial grin my way and my stomach clenches for what I know is coming. "After all, not all of us are lucky enough to find the love of our lives in college, are we?"

I met Vaughn when I was a freshman in college and he was a sophomore. And by meeting him, I mean I stared and ogled at him from across the courtyard and went to our college football games just to see him—and admittedly a few others—run around the field in tight jerseys and even tighter pants. It wasn't until my second year at the University of Iowa, at a frat party I didn't want to go to, that Vaughn finally noticed me too. And we've been together ever since.

Even when he left school early to try to make it to the NFL.

Even when he was drafted to Miami in the third round.

Even when he suffered a catastrophic injury that ended his career before his first contract was up.

We've been through more in our ten years together than many people experience in a lifetime. When people like Bailey look at us, they see this epic love story of *Notebook* proportions that has defied all odds, but they don't see the other parts. The parts we don't talk about.

"Yeah," I quip, thinking it's about time for me to focus back on the monitors in front of me. "I don't know what I'd do if I had to navigate apps to find a date. Maybe if I was on them, then *Real Love* wouldn't have seemed like such a bad idea after all."

"You're not lying." Bailey stretches. "It is not easy out here, I wish I had a Vaughn to lean on."

"I got lucky." Our relationship isn't perfect, but is any relationship? Even my parents, who have been together for decades, have their problems. "I just wish we lived on the same schedule so we could see each other more."

"Please, that's my literal dream. See them when I need them and nothing more. You have it so good." She slides her butt off my desk. "Anyways, wanna grab lunch later or did you pack one?"

I don't want to admit to packing a lunch because I know it makes me seem even less cool and more uptight than I already am. But with rumors that my dream job is on the horizon, leaving my desk for any reason seems like an unnecessary risk. Marcus and Greg don't often wander through the office and take stock of the floor, but when they do, I want them to see that I will eat, sleep, and breathe this job.

"I packed one." I ignore the way her lips curl up. Knowing she's about to make her favorite *Golden Girls* reference, I talk a little faster, throwing out an offer I know she can't refuse. "But let's do Cipriani when Delilah gets back. My treat."

Any snarky comment she was about to make dies on her lips. Bailey is as snobby as she is cheap. It makes no sense, but I've come to just accept it . . . and also leverage it against her when I need to.

"Oh my god. Deal!" She clasps her hands together and I swear her eyes glass over. "I've been craving their braised artichoke hearts. That sounds amazing."

"Then it's a plan." I open up the drawer with my purse inside to add it to my phone's calendar as she saunters away and calls out her hellos to the rest of the office.

I pull my phone out of my purse and see I missed a call and a couple of texts from Vaughn. He usually sleeps later into the day because he works late nights attending various clubs and events he's been promoting around the city and I rarely check my texts while I'm at work, so this is super out of character for him.

I open the messages and barely conceal my groan. Of all the reasons he could text me, it's for this?

Big TV debut, huh?

So you weren't going to tell me you're famous now? Thinking maybe you owe your man dinner after all the shit I got today from the boys. You know I love your steaks, that could help make up for it!

It sounds like he's joking, but he's not. It's one of the things that frustrates me the most about him—he won't just come out and say something, he'll be passive-aggressive and disguise everything as a joke until he gets his way.

I type out a quick response with a time for dinner because I'd rather deal with this later—and there's no use in trying to talk him into a restaurant—before shoving my phone back into my drawer without waiting for a response.

I get back to work, trying to lose myself in the numbers again . . . and fight the feeling that as hard as I work to keep my life nice and comfortable and steady, something will always be waiting around the corner to knock me off course.

3

I DON'T REALLY like to cook, which makes this entire endeavor for Vaughn even more exasperating.

The restaurants near my house all know my name and orders so well that when they see me coming, they greet me like an old friend and get my food started before I even ask. And it's Tuesday, which means the Cuban place on the corner is probably wondering where I am. But just because I don't like cooking doesn't mean I'm not good at it.

Vaughn loves my cooking. So I'm making his favorite Midwestern meal of steak, potatoes, and corn on the cob instead of enjoying my usual Tuesday order of lechón con chicharrones and bacon-wrapped dates. Which also means I had to go to the grocery store and butcher after my ten-hour workday because I obviously didn't have any of this at home.

We haven't had a proper date night in a while, so I'm hoping tonight will at least spark the light that's been quietly fading lately. Nothing is *bad* between us, but . . . I don't know. Maybe we've just gotten too comfortable with each other. Like that old married couple who only exists by each other's side—except, you know, we aren't even engaged yet.

I tried to put his texts in the back of my mind, but I'm worried that beneath his usual "jokes," there might be more truth than he'd admit to. I told him about the *Real*

Love audition when I did it. He's come to a work event or two with me, so he does know Bailey and Delilah in passing, even if he doesn't know them well. He also knows *me* and that I'd rather sleep in a sewer full of rats than be on a reality television show. Actually, when I brought up the audition to him, he laughed so hard I almost got offended.

So as you can imagine, when I told him I had been offered the lead, he was as surprised as I was. I think perhaps I was hoping it would wake him up a little bit, maybe even make him a little jealous. Don't get me wrong, I wasn't playing games and I could never date an alpha male who tried to be controlling anywhere outside of the bedroom. But I hoped maybe it would take him back to our early years when we first started dating and showed each other off every chance we got.

I'm just dropping the corn into the pot of milky, buttery water when my phone starts to ring. My shoulders tense and my breath freezes. You wouldn't think dating a club promoter would be so unpredictable, but Vaughn's schedule is wild. He cancels so much I ended up just giving him a key and telling him to come over whenever—it makes life easier, and I'm not disappointed by canceled plans if we never make set plans to begin with. But if he cancels after I bought all of this food, I will be liable to commit murder . . . at least in my mind.

When I pick up my phone, my worry about becoming a hardened criminal fades.

But only by a little.

Because if there is one person on this planet who knows how to push my buttons like no other, it's my beautiful, well-intentioned, complete mess of a little sister.

"What's wrong this time, Ella?" I push the speaker button and go back to my corn.

"Damn." Ella's voice that always has an infuriating hint of laughter in it echoes throughout my apartment. "That's how you greet your beloved little sister?"

Little sister? Yes. Beloved? Maybe.

Giant pain in the ass always in need of a favor? One hundred percent.

Nobody can grate on my nerves and get away with it as much as Ella does.

Our mom—a professor of African American Studies—named us after influential Black women. Me after the great Maya Angelou, and Ella after the one and only Ella "The First Lady of Song" Fitzgerald. I've sought to honor our namesakes (and our family) by working hard to become a successful Black woman in my field. I valued my education and devoted myself to my career, blazing a trail with the greatness my parents and ancestors instilled in me.

But Ella, on the other hand? She says traditional education blocks her creativity and enforces conformity over individuality. She didn't even *apply* for college yet somehow convinced our parents to hand over her college fund so she could wander around the world, spending years in London and Spain and whatever other places she felt "called" to.

"I just know you never call for nothing and Vaughn is coming over for dinner, so it'd be easiest if we hurried this along so I don't burn the food."

"Ughhhhh." Her groan causes my phone to vibrate on my countertop. "I was hoping seeing you on *Real Love* last night and hearing you'd auditioned meant you finally came to your senses and left him. But I guess wishes don't always come true."

If wishes came true, she would've never seen me on *Real Love* . . . because it means she's going to call my parents to tattle on me, even though I'm almost thirty.

"Ella." I ignore her statement about Vaughn. I don't know if she *hates* him, but she clearly doesn't like him and hasn't for years. But considering none of her relationships have lasted longer than a weekend, I've never been too worried about her opinion on the matter. "As much as I love to hear from you, I really do have things to do. What's going on?"

"Well, my dear, sweet, wonderful sister." Her voice goes up approximately fifteen decibels, just like it did when we were kids and she was—successfully—begging Mom and Dad for something. "I'm going to be in Miami in a few weeks and I was wondering if I could stay with my favorite big sister."

"Do Mom and Dad have another child I don't know about?"

"Come on," she whines. "When's the last time we hung out? I want to spend time with you. It will be fun."

I open my stove to check on the baked potatoes, the heat smacking me straight in my face as I roll my eyes. My resolve is starting to weaken. As much as Ella makes me absolutely furious, she's right, I know I'll have fun with her. Ella was the Johnson sister everyone wanted to be friends with. She's funny, outgoing, spontaneous, and heartbreakingly beautiful. She brings out a side of people they don't know they have, and I'm no exception.

Hence the distance—literally and metaphorically—between us.

"Fine." I give in just like I always do. "But send me the exact dates you'll be here so I can plan my schedule around it."

Even across the room from my phone, her high-pitched squeal still hurts my ears. "Oh my god! Yay! We're going to have the most fun ever! I even have a friend there who works with yachts and promised to set us up for a day."

I almost ask why she didn't ask to stay at the yacht friend's house instead of my one-bedroom apartment, but the knock on my front door pulls my attention.

"Shoot!" I glance around at my kitchen and it looks like a bomb went off. "Hey, Ella." She's still talking about who knows what, but she sounds so excited that I almost feel bad interrupting her. "I have to go. But don't forget to send me your itinerary. See you soon. Love you."

I hang up the phone before she has a chance to respond and look at the clock: 7:05. Vaughn wasn't supposed to be here for another twenty-five minutes and nothing is ready.

Of freaking course. Sometimes I think his tardiness is the only thing I can rely on him for, and he can't even manage that today.

"Here I come!" I wipe my hands on the kitchen towel hanging in front of my oven and try to smooth down my messy hair before hurrying to the front door and pasting a smile on my face.

I swing the door open, and even though I'm kind of irritated with him, it doesn't take away from how fun he is to look at. He's just so, *so* handsome.

His skin looks as if a drop of the sun fell to earth and landed only on him, golden and glistening, something that has only grown truer since he left behind the dreary Iowa winters for the perpetually sunny Miami beaches. His dark brown eyes swirl with so much emotion and have a depth that pulls in everyone around him. And his body? Don't get me started. He might not have touched the turf of a football field in years, but it still screams professional athlete. He has broad shoulders, strong arms, a trim waist, and thighs that have never met a pair of pants that didn't do them justice—every inch of him screams *"Look at me!"* to anyone he passes.

So maybe things aren't quite like they used to be, but I could've done worse.

"Hi." I close the distance between us, rising on tiptoe to drop a chaste kiss on his full lips. He leans in, pushing his mouth against mine, and part of me hopes he'll wrap his arms around me and deepen the kiss. Instead, he straightens and flashes his picture-perfect smile at me.

"Smells good."

I step away, gesturing for him to come inside and hoping my smile hides my disappointment. "You're early, so it's not finished yet, but I have beer if you want some."

"A beer would be good." Vaughn's deep timbre snaps me back to the moment and I hustle back to the kitchen, nabbing him a beer and putting it on the countertop in front of him before turning back to the food.

The sound of the can opening only highlights the silence in my apartment.

"Do you want to turn on a show or music or anything?"

"And miss you seasoning the steaks like you do?" He takes a deep pull of his beer. "No, thank you."

I roll my eyes and shake my head. "You know I hate it when you stare at me in the kitchen." I remind him of the conversation we've had countless times. The only thing I hate more than cooking is having someone hovering over me when I do it. I know Vaughn doesn't realize it, but he's a backseat chef—if that's a thing—and it stresses me out. "If you end up with burned steak, remember it's on you."

Instead of coming back with a smart-ass response like I'm used to, he's unusually quiet on the other side of my kitchen island. Not only is he not asking me incessant questions about my cooking strategy, he's not even telling me endless stories from his other life as a nightclub promoter.

When he sent the text earlier, I didn't think much of it other than being slightly annoyed by having to change my plans. But as the silence stretches, I'm beginning to think I missed something.

I try to think of a reason he could be upset, but I come up empty. And after a few more minutes of listening to the faint sound of boiling corn and his can hitting the counter, I can't take it anymore. The unfamiliar tension in the room is thicker than the humidity on a rainy Florida day in August . . . that's to say, really thick.

"I hope you're hungry," I say. It's a weak attempt to break the silence, but it does the trick. "The steaks are huge."

"Oh yeah?" He asks . . . or responds? I'm honestly not sure. "I can't wait to eat them."

"Good. I went to a little butcher down the street who gets his beef from Iowa so it will be almost as good as being back home." When we first dated in college, some of my favorite date nights consisted of us spending nights in his apartment, cooking, watching movies, and completely focused on each other.

I miss it.

"The steak might be the only thing I miss about the Midwest." He turns his wrist to the side and glances at his just-bordering-on-obnoxious gold and diamond watch. "Oh shit! I forgot I have an event at Victory tonight."

"You do?" I drop my tongs on my spoon rest. "What time?"

He pulls out his phone and taps around for a bit before looking up at me. "Ten, but I'll have to be out of here by nine."

It's already 7:20, so I'm guessing this won't be quite the "date night" I was hoping for.

"Okay, well dinner will be ready in about ten minutes or

so. I just need to get the potatoes out of the oven and then I'll do the steaks." I try to keep the disappointment out of my voice, but I'm not sure I succeed.

I didn't want to admit it, but after seeing Delilah on television last night, I maybe got a little jealous.

Not jealous in a bad way. I'm *so* happy for her and I'm 1,000 percent content with my decision not to be on the show.

But the look on her face as each suitor was introduced, the way color rose in her cheeks and her smile changed for each man. The way every contestant stared in awe at her, like she was the most precious person on the planet. I want someone to look at me like that too.

I already have so much, and maybe I should be content, but I miss the butterflies and the excitement of experiencing all of the "firsts." First date. First kiss. First night together. All of the first what-ifs that drift through your mind as you lay your head on the pillow at the end of those wonderful nights in the early days of a relationship.

I wonder if I'd still be feeling like this if Vaughn was sleeping beside me every night. Don't get me wrong, I'm thrilled he found a career he's passionate about. However, his passions conflict with mine and our schedules are constantly at war these days. We're lucky to get an hour of uninterrupted time together and it's beginning to take a toll on our relationship.

"Are you sure the potatoes are going to be done? Last time they were a little raw." The passive-aggressive remark slips out of his mouth with zero regard to me or my feelings. "Did you do that trick I told you about? It's supposed to really help."

His "helpful" trick was to wrap the potatoes in foil.

Earth-shattering, I know.

"I did. And they're about ready to come out. I timed everything to be ready by 7:30."

I like to make them a different way, but because I knew it would make him happy, I used his "tip." And the proud smile tugging on the corners of his beautiful mouth proves me right.

I grab my oven mitt and take them out of the oven, placing them on my cooling rack and going immediately to my already-seasoned steaks. I put butter in the skillet, letting it sizzle before dropping in my high-quality Midwestern beef. After a quick browning on each side, I stick the skillet into the oven, watching the timer as it counts down. Vaughn might have something to say about my potatoes, but nobody, and I mean nobody, can question my steak-making method. It's tried, true, and delicious.

After pulling the steaks out of the oven, I put them on our plates, unwrap a potato for each of us, and then drop a shiny, butter-marinated piece of corn beside it.

And when I look at the clock, I'm pleased to see that it's 7:30 on the dot.

"Damn." Vaughn leans back in the chair, tossing his napkin onto his plate. "That was delicious."

"I'm glad you liked it." I grab the plate from in front of him, throwing the corncob into the trash before rinsing the plate off and sticking it into my state-of-the art (and rarely used) dishwasher.

When I sit back down at the table, Vaughn looks like he might fall asleep. But since I know our time together is coming to an end, I decide to broach the subject of *Real Love*.

While I can write an email like a boss at work or tell clients where to invest ungodly amounts of money without hesitation, when it comes to communication in my relationship I could use some help.

"So . . ." I drag out the word, not sure this is even worth bringing up. "I know we talked about *Real Love* when I auditioned, but I couldn't tell from your texts if you were really annoyed or just joking. Do you want to talk about it?"

My hands fidget beneath my dining table and I try my hardest not to pick at my freshly manicured nails.

Even though this was supposedly the reason for our dinner tonight, he still looks surprised I brought it up. "I mean, not really. We can if you want to."

I don't want to. I think this is a stupid and pointless conversation. But I think he's annoyed, even if he won't admit it to me . . . or himself.

"You know everything that happened." I shrug, giving in to ruining my nails. "I auditioned with Bailey and Delilah as a laugh, but they ended up offering me the lead. I said no right away and they offered it to Delilah. End of story."

"But that *wasn't* the end of the story." He sits up and lets out a humorless laugh. "You were on TV last night. I know you didn't take it seriously, but now I got all these people calling me telling me you were on a dating show, talking 'bout how you 'missed opportunities' to find your path to love. It made me look like an idiot in front of everyone I know."

Ooookay.

I finally understand. This is about one thing and one thing only—his ego.

"Then tell them what happened. I never took it seriously and I said no because I have a boyfriend and wasn't interested." I can't believe all of this is happening because men are worse gossips than women. I don't know if I want to laugh or cry. "I said I was happy for Delilah but I found my path to love a different way. That's all. I didn't even know I was going to be on TV. It was an ambush."

"An ambush?" He pushes his lips together the way he always does when he's fighting back a smile. "How'd they manage that?"

Seeing his expression change and hearing his tone lighten, all of the cords that I didn't even realize were wound so tight release. Vaughn and I might not have the hottest fire between us right now, but this is what we *do* have. Years of inside jokes and familiarity. He knows me better than almost anyone.

"Oh my god. You won't even believe it. You know how much I hate—" I start as his ringer, which is never on silent, blasts through the room. You'd think he was an ER doctor or something the way he was glued to his phone.

He doesn't wait for me to finish before reaching into his pocket and grabbing what almost feels like another person in our relationship.

"Shit, sorry." His jaw clenches and his eyes narrow on the screen. "I gotta get this really fast."

I know the drill, so I aim a bright smile that hides my disappointment at him as he leaves the room without even a regretful glance my way.

I sit at the table, looking at the empty seat in front of me for a moment before getting up to start cleaning my kitchen. His work calls can last minutes or hours. I learned a while ago not to sit around and wait to find out which it would be.

I'm placing my pans in the sink when he comes back into the room.

"Sorry about that." He walks straight to me. "That was Kevin. He needs me at the club earlier than he thought, so I've got to go."

"You're leaving now?"

"It's work, babe." He leans down and gives me a kiss that feels more robotic than romantic, but it doesn't seem to faze him like it does me. "Can I call you when I get home?"

"I'll call you tomorrow. I have another early morning at the office." This is one of those times where I really resent the differences in our schedules.

"Thanks for dinner and sorry for letting that TV stuff get to me." He tucks my hand in his as he walks to my front door. "This was nice though; we should go on a real date one day." I'm not sure he really means it but I jump on the opportunity.

"I'd love that," I say. "Let me know what day works for you. I'll clear my schedule."

"And I'll plan it this time since you did all the cooking tonight." He drops a kiss on my cheek, his brown eyes sparkling. "Talk tomorrow?"

"Yes." I nod. "I can't wait."

I wave goodbye, watching him for a few seconds before locking the door behind him. Tonight might not have been everything I hoped it would be, but it did give me an idea.

Instead of sitting on the couch and watching some trash TV, I run and grab my phone. I hesitate before gathering up the courage and sending a quick message to Bailey and Delilah.

Vaughn just left and I have an idea. Are you both free this weekend? Brunch and shopping? Your girl needs to spice up her relationship and I think you two are my only hope.

I've only just hit send when my phone vibrates in my hand with a response. Not surprisingly—since Delilah is notoriously terrible at responding to text messages in a timely manner—it's Bailey's name that I see.

Shopping and brunch? Those are my favorite two words! Count me in! And when you say spice, how spicy are we talking on a scale from 1 to 10, 1 being rose petals on the bed, 10 being erotica-level sex dungeon? Also, proud of you for texting me on a weeknight about something other than work. Good for you 😜

Upon reading the words "sex dungeon," I instantly rethink my plans.

First of all, I've only texted you about work a few times. Second, on that scale I think I'm probably a solid 4.5. I'm thinking more romance than kink.

As soon as I hit send, the text I wasn't expecting until tomorrow comes through from Delilah.

I have a couple early morning interviews on Saturday, but I'm free around noon. If that's not too late, I was at The Standard for press the other day and met someone who said they'd be happy to set us up. We could eat and maybe have a massage? And 4.5 is too low, meet us at a 6 or no deal.

Wow. So this is what life is like for people living the high life? Brunch and massages at one of the most popular places in Miami on a whim? I guess there has to be some kind of benefit for letting the world witness your love life. And if I get to reap some of the rewards without having to kiss a bunch of strangers? Well then, I'm feeling even more confident than ever before about turning down the spot.

Fine. I'll raise it to a 6 but only if facials can be thrown in. You did ambush me on television, so it feels like a solid compromise.

It's only a matter of seconds before my phone dings with Delilah's one-word response of "Deal" and only a few more seconds before Bailey's text solely consisting of champagne and heart emojis comes through. And while I can't be sure what the future holds, I fall asleep excited by the vast possibilities of tomorrow.

4

I REGRET EVERYTHING.

I regret moving to Miami. I regret the leopard print bathing suit I bought last summer. I regret telling my mom that I was the one who took her last soda when she already thought it was Ella.

But most of all, I regret befriending my coworkers and not living my life as a lone wolf.

"A laminated folder? A checklist for 'couple goals'? Seriously?" I sneer at a gloating Bailey from across the table as I flip through the folder she brought while we wait for our frosés to arrive. "And how much longer until Delilah gets here?"

"Geeeez. So touchy today, aren't you?" She pushes her oversized sunglasses to the top of her head. "Delilah's famous now, tardiness comes with the package. She just wrangled, what, thirty-five guys? She's going to be exhausted for at least a few weeks."

I roll my eyes and revert back to my moody teen self, refusing to look at her. "Whatever."

The carefree bliss I felt as I drifted to sleep after texting them faded with my dreams and I woke up feeling the full magnitude of what I'd done.

I wouldn't call myself a secretive person, but I do keep my relationship pretty close to the vest. Even though Delilah and Bailey have met Vaughn before, it was all surface level. They know how long we've been dating and the basic details of our relationship, but that's where it ends. I grew up with the women in my family preaching about keeping outsiders from diving into your relationships. Now I keep hearing my mom and aunt in my mind, telling me I'm making a huge mistake. I almost canceled, but when Delilah came to work looking all beautiful and glowy and asking for my time and location of birth, I was so thrown off I couldn't back out.

So now not only am I going to have to talk about my relationship, I'm also stuck going to a group astrology reading. As if I need to hear the universe is rigged against me and my relationship is doomed to fail.

Not that I believe in any of that nonsense or anything . . .

"You're a toddler." Bailey interrupts my valiant attempt at pouting. "You asked for our help and Delilah and I have a plan. Plus, the longer you try the silent treatment on me, the more I'm going to make you beg for forgiveness."

I hate that I know she's not exaggerating.

One time a coworker blamed Bailey for missing a meeting, saying she never scheduled it. He even took it to our bosses to complain. Bailey responded by creating a Power-Point presentation showing the time stamps of not only her original email, but the follow-up ones and quotes from coworkers confirming that she has excellent communication skills. Judd was so embarrassed I thought he was going to quit on the spot.

I don't want to stereotype and say her dramatics stem from her southern roots, but she is the only Georgia peach I know and she is also the most dramatic person I've ever come across. Coincidence? Who's to say?

"Fine, I give in. But if anything on your list backfires, I

hold the ability to leverage it over your head until the end of time."

Okay . . . So maybe the petty and dramatic traits aren't solely a Bailey problem . . .

She shrugs and puts her sunglasses back on, not at all fazed by my impending nervous breakdown. "Fine with me."

The restaurant is outside and on the ocean. White chairs are the perfect contrast to the bright blue water. Umbrellas hover overhead so while everyone is still wearing their sunglasses, they don't have to. Which is why, like in most Miami places, you can never tell what or whom anyone is looking at. So it's weird when, almost at once, the energy seems to shift. The chatter ceases for a moment before a cascade of hushed conversations fills every corner. Even the sounds of the ocean waves seem muted.

I've been in Miami for a few years now, but I have yet to see a celebrity out in the wild. Hope bubbles inside of me as I turn around, hoping Rihanna or Beyoncé has decided to grace us with their glorious presence. But instead, I see Delilah, and a hopeful bubble bursts like a water balloon that hits the ground and sits there for a few minutes before its anticlimactic pop.

"Oh." I slump down into my seat when she reaches us. "It's just you."

"Ummm . . . Rude?" She places a shopping bag on the ground and holds down the back of her skirt as she pulls out her ultramodern chair. "How about, 'My dearest friend, Delilah, it's so nice to see your beautiful face'?"

"Sorry." It's half-hearted because my secret stan self really had its heart set on a pop goddess. "It is good to see your face, but I thought you were Beyoncé the way people got so excited when you came in."

I would've even settled for a DJ Khaled sighting at this point.

"That's fair. Anybody is a letdown compared to Queen Bey." She settles in and drops her arms onto the table. "But even though I'm not Beyoncé, did you still order me a drink?"

"One metabolic lemonade. Extra cayenne. Extra hot . . . just like you." Bailey recites Delilah's usual drink order.

She may be joking about the "extra hot like Delilah" bit, but she's not lying. Delilah is stunning. One of those people you're sure has had massive amounts of work done because it's just not fair that God blessed one person so heavily. Her Cuban roots give her permanently tan skin and she always looks as if she's dusted in gold powder. Which she's not, because I asked . . . more than once. Her thick black hair is glossy and sleek even though she uses drugstore shampoo and conditioner. Her eyes look like the darkest whiskey with just a touch of honey swirled in. And her body . . .

Honestly? If I didn't love her, I'd hate her.

Never on a diet, she somehow looks as if she has a corset cinched around her tiny waist. Her butt makes my pretty generous backside look lacking. And while I've been known to refer to my breasts as "fashion boobs," her cups runneth over. Literally and metaphorically.

It's actually just fucking rude.

It's one of the reasons I was a little surprised when she was chosen as the lead for *Real Love*. Of the three of us, Bailey is the "traditional" beauty. She's very pretty and has a face you're sure you've seen before. But Delilah? Delilah's beauty can't be summed up in one word. It's intimidating how stunning she is. She could never be described as the girl next door because nothing about her, from the fullness of her lips to the sharpness of her cheekbones, is relatable.

And that's just the outside junk. On the inside, she's pretty good too. As clichéd as it sounds, she would give the shirt off her back to someone in need. And I'm not just saying that either. I was with her when she did it once. Took off her rain jacket and gave it to an older woman who was walking down the street when a rainstorm hit out of nowhere.

Which is why, no matter how uncomfortable it makes me, I understand why everyone is staring at us right now.

"Thank you." Delilah doesn't seem to even notice the way heads are turned and sunglass-covered eyes are no doubt tracking her every move. "I'll buy the next round."

Bailey leans in, and in the most un-Bailey-like fashion, drops her eternally loud voice to a whisper. "Do we think everyone is staring because Dee is on *Real Love*, or because they heard someone actually ordered that gross lemonade?"

"For real," I whisper back, trying but probably failing at being discreet. "I didn't even know this many people watched the show."

"This is the show's fourteenth season. Of course a lot of people watch, otherwise it would've been canceled ages ago." Delilah rolls her eyes so hard, I swear I can hear them hitting her skull. "And, Bailey, you're so full of crap. You love this lemonade, you're the one who introduced it to me!"

"Are you calling me a liar?" Bailey holds a hand to her chest. "Well I have never!"

"Please." Delilah leans back into her seat and I don't even have to look at her to know she's wearing a shit-eating grin. "With the way you troll our coworkers, I know you've been called much worse."

If I'm honest with myself, maybe part of the reason I was so quick to welcome Bailey into my life is because she kind of reminded me of the girl from high school who you wanted to be friends with, but was always too cool for you. She's a blast to be around and so funny, but nice might not be the description most people would use for her. There have been lunches where she has spent the entire duration going off on someone and made my heart ache for her enemies. As a person who doesn't do conflict well, I vowed a long time ago to stay in her good graces. Hence why she was able to convince me to audition for a dating show.

"Speaking of much worse—" Bailey's segue causes my stomach to flip. "How are we going to save Maya's relationship?"

"First of all, rude," I say, sticking up for myself. "Second of all, it doesn't need 'saving.' It's not bad . . . just a little boring."

"Woof." Delilah's full lips form a frown. "Boring is perhaps the saddest adjective to describe a relationship that I've ever heard."

"One could also say it's safe. I like safe." I'm the polar opposite of an adrenaline junkie. I have more irrational fears than anyone I know. These fears include—but are not limited to—parking garages, squirrels, outer space, and being struck by lightning while indoors.

Plus, Vaughn and I worked really hard to restore the safety in our relationship. I'm proud of us. I just want to make things a little more exciting and it's all the fault of the two people sitting in front of me. If they would've been normal humans who don't apply for a dating show, we'd all still be enjoying our jobs, living regular lives, and being perfectly content in our boring relationships.

Stupid Delilah following through with her threats of taking my place and choosing to date a man who wears chaps. The audacity!

"Sorry, Maya, but 'safe' is not the comeback you think it is." Bailey's tone says she's sympathetic, but the smile on her face says otherwise. "Safe might be the only word sadder than boring."

I don't get a chance to reply to this outrageous claim because a man in a crisp button-down and thick black-rimmed glasses approaches our table with a tray holding two frosés, a nasty lemonade, and three orders of avocado toast—we are millennials after all. I've never been more thrilled to see the manifestation of our basicness appear before me . . . ever. Because even though I think Delilah and Bailey love to torture me, nothing compares to their love of food.

We sit in semisilence, mindlessly chatting about what a nice day it is and how needed a massage is until our food is gone.

"So," I lean back in my seat, happy to notice that our fellow patrons have grown bored of Delilah and we're no longer being watched. "What's in the bag?"

"Well." Delilah drains the last bit of her drink and reaches for the nondescript bag she placed on the ground when she first arrived. "Bailey and I talked and we figured if you wanted spice, you might need a few new things."

Usually I love a surprise gift, but when Bailey tosses her napkin onto her plate and aims a movie-villain evil smile my way, anxiety unfurls throughout my veins.

"Oh god." I groan, sliding down my chair and scouting the nearest exit. "What did you two do?"

"Stop being so dramatic." Bailey reaches across the table, snatching the bag from Delilah and then shoving it in front of me. "You wanted spice, we're providing it."

Visions of whips and chains and sex toys flash in my brain as bright as the camera phones aimed our way will when I reveal the contents of the "present" Delilah and Bailey are making me open.

Delilah reads the fear that must be written across my

face. "Don't worry, we respect that you're a little more con-
servative with this kind of thing and didn't get anything
too obscene."

Shocking nobody, they don't provide the reassurance I
was hoping for. But it's clear I'm not going to escape this
table without opening this present, and since I really want
the massage, it's now or never.

I reach into the bag and thank god for the melanin hiding the flush burning my cheeks.

"Oh my god." I hold up the black lace lingerie set before
letting the barely there scrap of fabric fall back into the bag.
"Is that supposed to fit me?"

"It is, and Vaughn is going to *flip*." Bailey's southern accent slips out as her voice carries across the patio. "Isn't it
the sexiest thing you've ever seen?"

Considering we're in public, I didn't examine it closely.
But even so, it's the sexiest thing I've ever seen. "It definitely is. Thank you for doing this for me."

Even though the aftereffects of embarrassment still have
my skin tingling, I can't deny how grateful I am for these
two women.

I just hope that when I put it on for Vaughn, he'll be
equally as appreciative . . . for once.

Greetings Lovers!

In preparation for tomorrow, I have some truly delightful gossip to report to you about our lovely Delilah!

I was sent a few pictures from one of our Miami Lovers. Delilah was out and about with her friends over the weekend. They said she looked like a golden statue and managed to be even more beautiful in person. Not sure that's possible, but I don't want to call them a liar because that'd be rude. Delilah sipped on a lemonade while her friends indulged in a little early day drinking and munched on avocado toast. What can I say? She's a girl after my millennial heart.

In other news, my sources are telling me this week's episode of *Real Love* is a total doozy. Apparently, a certain hunky suitor goes out on a limb by pulling Delilah away on a group date. I'm hearing he created his own one-on-one date within a group date that didn't win him any favors with his competitors but made Delilah's heart flutter. I'm not sure if this changes things in the long run, but I love a cold suitor who isn't afraid to make big moves. The guys clearly see what a catch Delilah is and they are not holding punches . . . or kisses.

No matter what, I'm just glad Delilah Rivera, queen of our hearts, is living her best life and being spoiled rotten. That's all we want for her . . . plus maybe a little on-screen chemistry and drama along the way. We're not asking for too much.

XOXO,
Stacy

5

ARMED WITH UNDERWEAR that costs almost half of my mortgage, I fake an air of confidence as I sit at the table waiting for Vaughn. Like I said, promptness has never been his thing.

He doesn't work Monday nights, so to kick-start my "bring on the romance" plan, I booked a table at what Google told me was one of the most romantic restaurants in Miami.

Luckily for me, Google did not lie.

The warm Miami air caresses my shoulder as I readjust the strap of my dress that's showing more skin than I've ever shown in public. I watch the French doors from our table for two in the most beautiful garden I've seen outside of a movie set in the English countryside, hoping to see Vaughn step through them at any moment. The flames of the candles in the middle of the table flicker and cast a warm glow as I sip on the glass of wine the waiter recommended. It's great, but I wish I would've just ordered the Crown and Coke I really wanted.

I check the time once more and it's now twenty minutes past our reservation time. I'm not sure whether I should call Vaughn or give him five more minutes.

This place *is* hard to find. Maybe he got lost?

My fingers twitch around the clear phone case before I tuck it away in my purse and decide to wait it out.

At least this way I can order the appetizers by myself—Vaughn never wants to try anything new or exciting.

I make eye contact with the waiter, who's never far away, and ignore the flare of pity in his eyes as he approaches.

"How may I help you, ma'am?"

I hate, abhor, *loathe* being called ma'am. My grandma is ma'am. My mom is ma'am. But me? In this dress? I am most certainly *not* ma'am.

"Can I get the spread trio and the grilled octopus for the table, please?"

His eyes tense at the corners and I can only imagine what he's thinking, but like the professional he must be to work at a place like this, he makes sure no further indication of sad scenarios running through his mind are visible on his face.

"Of course." His smile shines bright even in the dim light. "I'll go put that in right away."

He gives me a little bow—which is as lovely as it is off-putting—before turning on his heels, heading inside, and leaving me with my thoughts once again.

My mind isn't always the friendliest environment, but it's truly acting a fool right now. Part of me is worried Vaughn forgot about tonight and I am actually being stood up—it wouldn't be the first time. Another section of my brain still can't believe how much the lingerie I'm wearing cost. And the rest is stuck thinking about Delilah, something that has become much too common over the past few weeks.

Even though she's finally showing up at work again, it's like part of her is still missing. She's making mistakes she never made before, coming in late, and leaving early.

It's clear to anyone that her priorities have changed, but I didn't realize how much until I asked her about her plans for the promotion and she told me she wasn't sure she even wants it anymore. The announcement should've thrilled me; after all, Delilah is my biggest competition, but instead it's knocked me off balance. Like somehow her making such a drastic shift says more about my life than hers. I knew Delilah going on the show would change some things, but not everything.

I shift my focus to the single long-stem rose in the middle of the table and try to clear my mind. The rose is so delicate it almost doesn't look real. Sometimes it blows my mind that this kind of beauty just exists in the world. Roses don't have to diet and exercise and coat themselves with makeup. They just *are*.

I don't know how long I stare at the rose in deep, philosophical thought, but I tear my gaze away just in time to see Vaughn walk through the open door. He's no doubt charming the maître d' as he smiles wide and claps the stranger on the shoulder like an old friend.

"You would not believe what a long day I've had." He pulls out his chair and sits without so much as a kiss on the cheek. "Then Vinny called me back into his office right as I was leaving and talked my ear off. And you know what traffic is like around here."

Wow, okay, so we're not even going to apologize for being late or ask me how my day was? Not exactly the start I was hoping for, but I take a deep breath—we can still recover from here.

"Miami traffic is an ordeal." I unwrap my silverware and place my napkin in my lap. "I took an Uber just so I didn't have to deal with parking."

He pulls his phone out of his back pocket and doesn't

take his eyes off the screen. "Good call. Driving isn't your forte."

I don't know what I feel more annoyed with, his constant insistence that I'm a terrible driver—which I am not! I just don't drive like I'm street racing—or that he's already on his phone.

Delilah mentioned that when she's with her new mystery man, they aren't allowed to have their phones. I thought that sounded slightly unhinged when she first told us, but now I'm thinking they might be onto something. I can't remember the last time Vaughn and I had a night together that wasn't interrupted by ringing phones or text messages or social media push notifications.

"Hey." I reach across the table and put my hand over his phone. "Do you think we can maybe have dinner without our phones? Just tonight."

"Yeah, sure." The words are light and airy, but the tension around his eyes and mouth shows he's none too pleased with this idea.

"Thank you." I move my hand to squeeze his. "I just feel like we're a little disconnected lately. With our schedules being what they are we don't get enough quality time together."

"I think that's a great idea." He puts his phone away and his long, calloused fingers curl around the delicate menu. "You really do look beautiful tonight."

I appreciate him saying it even though it feels like he's hardly looked at me since he got here. It feels more like an afterthought than a genuine compliment.

While he said everything was great when he left my house last week, we haven't talked much since. The date he said he'd plan fell through when he double-booked two clubs.

"This old thing? Thank you. I wanted to look nice." If he thinks this dress is good, he's going to flip when he sees what's beneath it.

"This is nice, babe." He reaches his hand across the table and interlaces his fingers with mine. His mega smile softens a little bit and he reminds me more of the Vaughn I met back in Iowa than the club promoter I'm so used to these days. "We should do it more often."

Our waiter clears his throat, startling us both as he sets the appetizers on the table, forcing us to separate our hold on each other.

"Can I get you anything else at the moment?" He seems so happy, and I don't know if it's because he's relieved I didn't get stood up or because I didn't get stood up *and* I'm not messing with his tips for the night.

"I'll have a tequila soda," Vaughn says.

"Yes, sir, I'll have that out for you shortly," he says before he disappears once more.

"What is this?" Vaughn asks when the waiter is out of sight. "You order the weirdest food."

"Just because you're not used to something doesn't make it weird." I try not to roll my eyes. Vaughn has the palate of a toddler and it makes me irrationally angry. We've been dealing with this for years—he tries to yuck my yum, eventually gives in and tries the food, and then likes it. If it wasn't for me, he'd be the kind of person who only eats meat and potatoes like some sort of Midwestern caveman. But no matter how many times we relive this scenario, he never ceases to complain about everything I order. Which is why I was only too happy to order before he got here.

He doesn't say anything as he scoops one of the spreads *and* the octopus onto his plate. I keep my mouth shut because I refuse to start a fight tonight, certainly not over something as unimportant as food. Instead I remember why I'm here. This might not be the romantic dinner of my dreams, but we still have the after-dinner festivities to look forward to.

Fun fact, if you don't want to be annoyed by your partner, three glasses of wine *really* helps. Two is not enough, and four is too many. Years of perfecting this has taught me the magic number is three. It's the sweet spot.

I push open the door to my place, holding on to Vaughn's hand as I pull him into my apartment. My skin feels electric and my mind is feeling fizzy in the best way possible thanks to those three glasses of wine.

"You have to sit on the couch for a second." My words are slower than normal, but I can't actually blame that on alcohol. I'm so nervous about step two of my plan my brain is on the verge of malfunctioning. "I have a little surprise for you."

"Oh, do you now?" He pulls me into his hard chest and wraps his arms around me. "What is it?"

"I can't tell you." I let my head fall onto him and I revel in this feeling. *This* is what I was hoping for. "That'd ruin the surprise."

When we first started dating, we'd stand like this all the time. In our dorm rooms, we'd hold tight to each other, dreaming of the future but grounded in the moment. And when we'd leave, he'd touch me for any or no reason at all, like it physically pained him to keep his hands off me.

Life was so much easier back then.

Before the injuries. Before the jobs. Before the mistakes.

Even though I don't want to, I push away from him, trying to latch on to the liquid courage pumping through my veins so I don't lose my nerve. I keep my steps slow and measured as we move through the dark open space of my apartment. The space I've kept mostly empty in the hopes that we'd find a place together soon. Of course, I've been hoping for that for years now.

When I first moved to Miami, I lived with Vaughn for a couple of months. It seemed logical to stay with him instead of living in a hotel or renting a place I'd never seen before.

Let's just say it was quite the learning experience.

Our schedules clashed time and time again until it began to take a real toll on our relationship. I'd get snappy when he would wake me up before my alarm. He'd get frustrated when I didn't have time to cook and do house crap. In the end, we decided it would be better if we both had our own places until we really settled into our careers.

But now we're both in more comfortable, more stable parts of our careers. I've really been wanting to take the next step in our relationship for a while now.

And maybe tonight will help move us in that direction.

If I can just make everything perfect . . .

"Sit right here." I push him onto the couch and he doesn't hesitate before grabbing my remote and turning on ESPN.

Because nothing says romance like throwback football games.

Thankfully he doesn't see me roll my eyes as I slip into my room.

I may have gone a little overboard with re-creating my Pinterest inspiration board for tonight. I bought a candle or fifty and set them up in the bedroom before I left for dinner. I rush around lighting them all only slightly concerned about setting off my fire alarm. I grab the box of rose petals I ordered online and scatter them across my bedspread and the floor before running into the bathroom to freshen up.

I peel off my dress, put on the suspenders and thigh-highs Delilah and Bailey said were a mandatory part of the outfit, and stare at the stranger in the mirror.

"Congratulations, Maya. Are you comfortable? No. Are you confident? Not really." I start giving myself perhaps the worst pep talk in the history of pep talks. "But you're going to fake it until you fucking make it. If Delilah can go on national television and prance around in a bikini, you can pretend to be a goddamn sexpot in front of your boyfriend of for-freaking-ever. You will *not* waste this lingerie, so get it together! You've got this!"

I take a deep breath, feeling surprisingly pumped up. I smooth my hair down, apply another layer of lipstick, and spritz one pump of perfume on my wrist.

I can do this.

I'm going to rock Vaughn's fucking world. He's going to realize I am everything he's ever wanted. This is the first step to the next level of our relationship, showing that I can mix it up and surprise him even after so many years together. After tonight, he's never going to want me to leave his side.

I take my time walking back into the living room. I want to portray calm, seductive energy, not the chaotic, unhinged energy I really feel.

I pull the door open like I've seen in movies, stepping into the living room in nothing but the barely there matching lace set. "Vaughn," I say in a singsong voice. "I'm ready for you."

I already feel fucking ridiculous and that feeling sky-rockets when he doesn't immediately turn around and ogle me. In fact, he doesn't turn around at all.

Seriously?

"Vaughn," I repeat, the annoyance in my voice unmistakable.

Again, nothing.

My mom always said one of my worst traits was my insistence that sighing is a viable form of communication. But the sigh I emit in this moment says everything words could never.

I stomp into my living room and come to a stop in front of my couch where Vaughn is sleeping like a goddamn baby.

The *audacity* of this man. I was in my room for maybe fifteen minutes.

"Vaughn!" I yell this time, because who has the patience for this? Not me, that's for sure. "Wake up!"

I shove his shoulder and his eyes flicker open.

"Ow." He groans and rubs his shoulder. "What was that for?"

"Because you were asleep and I have a surprise for you, remember?" I know it's wrong to strangle a person, but *wow* do I want to choke this man right now.

"Fine." He yawns and stretches his arms over his head before he takes his time sitting up. "What's the surprise?"

Any of the motivation I was feeling after my pep talk to myself dissipates instantly into the air around me. I want to run into my room, hide under the covers, and never show my face again.

"This!" I motion to my practically naked body. "This is the surprise!"

If this outfit can't get his attention, then I really don't know what we're doing here.

"Oh." He blinks away his sleep. "You look nice. Is it new?"

Oh?

I look nice?

IS IT NEW?

I'm going to go back into my room and knock over all of my candles because I'm ready to burn it all down.

"Yes," I say through gritted teeth. "It's very new. I got it just for tonight so we could have a nice, romantic evening. You know, like real couples tend to do?"

"Whoa. Calm down." He holds his hands in front of his chest. "I said you look nice. I'm sorry I fell asleep, but I don't think that warrants this attitude. You know my sleep schedule is weird from work."

I wonder if in the whole history of the world there's ever been a time where a man telling a woman to calm down has actually made her calm down.

I'm thinking that's a hard no.

"This isn't *attitude*, this is anger." *It's hurt.* I grab the throw blanket folded over the arm of my couch and wrap it around myself before sitting next to him since I can't disappear or turn back time. "I put a lot of effort into planning our date tonight even though you promised you'd plan this one. I spent ages picking the perfect restaurant, put on lingerie I'm wildly uncomfortable in, scattered rose petals all over the place, and my room has so many candles lit it's definitely a fire hazard."

"I said I'm sorry, what else do you want from me?" He sounds exhausted, but I have a sneaking suspicion it isn't because I woke him up. "Why are you making such a big deal out of this? I mean, expensive restaurants and candles? That's not who *we* are. That's definitely not who *I* am."

He's not wrong. This isn't who we are, but I'm not sure if either of us even knows who we actually are. We met as broke college kids and now we're successful adults. But somehow, even though we've grown, our relationship still feels stuck in the dorms we've long escaped.

"I just really wanted a special night to help us find each

other again." I consider my next words, unsure I should say them out loud. "Don't you feel like we're drifting apart lately? I feel like there's a lot of distance between us. Sometimes I don't even feel like I'm in a relationship at all."

"Wow. Not in a relationship? This is just what happens when two people have been together as long as we have." He adjusts his long legs and shifts so he's looking directly at me. "So are you saying that because I'm not into this kind of thing I'm not a good boyfriend? Because I'll never want to do the fancy restaurants your family is used to, I'll never light candles, and I might not realize when you go shopping for new underwear. And I don't think a good girlfriend would try to change me into that person."

"I'm not trying to change you," I argue back, furious that my voice is thick with unshed tears. "I just want us to prioritize each other sometimes. Have nights we can put away our phones and not think about work. I want us to show the other that we care, that we do actually want to share our whole lives with each other, not just pencil us into our schedules."

His eyes go soft, and for a moment I think I finally got through to him, but they harden again. "You know how much I struggled to bounce back after football. Being a club promoter isn't something I want to do forever, but it's what I need to do to make connections in this industry. That's where my focus is right now and I thought you were good with that, but now I'm not so sure. I can't give more than I've been giving, and it's not fair of you to ask me to do that. It's actually pretty selfish of you."

His words knock the breath out of me. I've been called quite a few things before, but never selfish. It almost feels like he's intentionally trying to hurt me now.

"I'm not asking you to ignore your career." This is not

where I thought this evening was going to go and I have
no idea how to fix it. "I would never ask you that. I just—"

"You just want to feel like the priority and . . ." He takes
a deep breath and my vision blurs. "I can't make that promise. I love you, Maya. But maybe you're not the person I
need. Maybe this isn't working anymore."

His words slice through me like an axe and pain radiates
into every single part of my body. The tears I've been fighting fall down my face. I try to come up with an argument
about how wrong he is, convince him that we're meant to
be together. But I'm angry and heartbroken and mortified
and all of the emotion is clogging my brain. The logic I
thrive on is nowhere to be found.

"So what? Because I wanted to have a nice night and
make an effort and surprise you, you want to throw us away?
After ten years, we're breaking up?" I pull my hand from
his, wiping away the stupid, traitorous tears. "Just like
that?"

"I think so." He reaches his hand out for mine, but I pull
it away. His touch might break me. "I'm not saying this
will be forever, but I don't think this is working right now.
I need to keep my head down and focus on work. I think it
will better for both of us."

I know Vaughn is trying to make me feel better, but if
there's one thing that pisses me off more than anything
else in the world, it's a man telling me he knows what's best
for me.

"So you get the final say in what's best for me without
even consulting me about what I might want or need?" My
sadness shrinks beneath my anger.

"This relationship isn't what I need right now and it
doesn't seem to be what you need either," he says, and it's as
if I didn't speak at all. "We've been through so much. We've

spent our entire twenties together. But right now, I need space away from it. I need to take some time and figure out what I want before I can decide if I want to move forward in a relationship with you."

I open my mouth to tell him that after ten years together, he should already know. He shouldn't need to figure anything out and he really shouldn't make these decisions for me. But I don't. It's pointless. Once Vaughn has an idea, nothing and nobody can talk sense into him, and it's clear what I want isn't something he's at all worried about.

I pull the blanket tighter around my body, horrified that I'm still half naked, and nod. He takes that for what it is, and even though I don't want him to touch me, I don't pull away when he leans over and places a soft kiss on my cheek.

He stands up, his long, lean body slowly rising from my couch, and every muscle in my body begins to scream for me to chase after him, to fight harder and tell him this is wrong. To beg him to stay and prove that he doesn't need "space."

Instead, I sit frozen on my couch, watching as he walks out of my door without so much as a backward glance. I don't know how long he's been gone before I finally get up, but I do know it's been long enough that the smell from those obnoxious candles has permeated every nook and cranny of my apartment.

Before I go to my room and face the rose petals that are going to mock me, I walk to the fridge and pull out the bottle of champagne I placed in there after work. I pop the cork, and ignoring the flutes on the counter, lift the bottle straight to my mouth. I carry the bottle with me to the bathroom, taking deep gulps as I impatiently wait for my bathtub to fill with the bubbles I bought for tonight.

Just as the water is nearing the edge, I hear my phone ringing from the other room.

Now I'm not proud of this, but for a moment the thought of Vaughn calling because he's realized what a gargantuan mistake he's made has me running to my phone. Which is why seeing my sister's name flashing on the screen feels like I was punched in the gut for the second time tonight.

"How can I help you?" I don't mean to be so short with her, but I don't have the energy to bother with pleasantries at the moment.

There's silence on the other end for a second too long and I almost hang up when I hear her voice loud and clear. "What's wrong and what did Ralph do to cause it?"

I couldn't hold in the exasperated sigh even if I tried. I just can't. Not tonight and *definitely* not with Ella. She's never liked Vaughn, and for years has demonstrated this by calling him by his first name, Ralph, which he absolutely loathes.

"Nothing. I'm fine, but do you need something?"

"You are *so* not fine," Ella, my beautiful but relentless and socially clueless sister, says. "You sound like you've been crying. You never cry. Why were you crying?"

"I wasn't crying. Everything is fine. I'm fine." I overcompensate, sounding even more guilty now. "Vaughn and I got into a little argument, but everything's fine."

Ella would dance on tables if she knew what had just happened between me and Vaughn. To say she's not his biggest fan is a massive understatement. Which is exactly why I can't tell her. This can't be one more thing she adds to her arsenal of reasons she thinks we shouldn't be together.

"I've never heard a person say the word 'fine' so many times in my life, but I can tell you don't want to talk about it so I'll drop it." The *for now* at the end of the sentence is left unsaid, but I know it's there. Ella never truly drops anything. "But if you need to talk, I'm always here for you."

The genuine concern in her usually bubbly and silly

voice absorbs some of my anger and sadness. But without either of those to hold on to, I'm left depleted and utterly exhausted.

"I know, thank you. I think I'm just tired, it was a long day." This is not a lie. Today might've defied the laws of time as the longest day ever in the history of the world. "Did you need something?"

She hesitates for a second before answering, which, even though it's not like my hotheaded sister, I appreciate. "It's not important. You rest, I'll catch up with you next week."

"Thank you. Talk soon."

"You know it," she says, and the worry I sensed from her earlier is gone.

I can't tell if her farewell was a threat or a promise, but all I know is I'm too tired to figure it out or care.

I turn my phone off and decide against the bath. I go into my room and blow out all of the candles before climbing into my bed with my makeup still on and without even wrapping my hair. I just need to hurry up and sleep so today can be over and it can be tomorrow.

Tomorrow will be better.

Tomorrow *has* to be better.

6

IN NEWS I'M sure won't surprise anyone, my problems did not, in fact, disappear by the time my alarm clock went off this morning.

If anything, they quadrupled, because not only did I not have any messages from Vaughn, but I had a reminder on my phone for plans with Delilah and Bailey to watch another stupid episode of *Real Love*.

And the only thing more miserable than wallowing in self-pity all by my lonesome is having to pretend not to wallow while being around other people who are so obnoxiously happy you want to punch them in the throat.

"Oh my god!" Delilah flops down beside me on the couch, her too-full cocktail coming *this* close to spilling all over her new couch and my favorite pair of Ann Taylor slacks. "I can't wait until I can finally tell you everything that's happened these last few months. I'm going to owe you for eternity."

An eternity's worth of gratitude? I know she's not trying to rub her newfound bliss in my face, but I can't help the way it gets beneath my skin and stings my already-raw feelings. I'd happily take payment in the form of never having to come to another one of these freaking parties.

"You'll never owe me for this. I'm just glad you're

happy." And I am . . . I'll probably just be a little happier when I'm not reeling from my own disastrous breakup.

"I've really never been happier." Her voice drops to a whisper despite Bailey being in the other room. "I used to think getting the promotion or checking off enough things on my to-do list would finally make me feel content and secure, but these last few months I realized I was looking at everything the wrong way. I was chasing accomplishments instead of focusing on how I wanted to feel. Without you pushing me toward this, I'd still be looking for happiness in external validation instead of finding it in myself."

I blink a couple of times, waiting to be sure she's being serious and not mocking me with the inside of an inspirational card, but before I can think of a response not dripping with sarcasm, Bailey interrupts with her usual impeccable timing.

"Is Maya finally divulging the details of her date with Vaughn? Was he surprised? Did he love the lingerie? Tell us everything!"

Thanks to an abundance of meetings at work, I was able to avoid this question until now. I hoped Delilah and Bailey would be too busy to think about it tonight, but I'm never that lucky.

"It was great!" I lie like a person who lies to their friends. I tell myself I'm only doing it because we're here for Delilah and it would be selfish to turn the attention on me, but if I'm being honest—if only with myself—I'm completely embarrassed and I need a little longer to deal with it on my own before I can recount it out loud, even to my closest friends. "We went to this fantastic little restaurant and then back to my place. To say he was surprised would be an understatement. He nearly passed out from it all. I think that night really changed our relationship."

The best liars lie in technicalities and that's exactly what I'm doing.

Oh god.

I am a liar!

"I knew he was going to love it." Delilah claps. "I think it's great that you're taking the time to prioritize your relationship. I know you love work, but I promise, your relationship is so much more important."

"Well, I don't have a relationship," Bailey chimes in. "But I am definitely on team 'have a life outside of work.' We're too young and fun to let finance rule our lives." At the thought alone, she breaks into a full-body shiver.

Not that Bailey's dramatic or anything.

Luckily, before I'm forced to lie some more about my perfect relationship, Delilah's face appears on TV. "Oh! It's starting!"

Saved by *Real Love*. Never thought I'd say that.

I can tell Delilah wants more details about my weekend, but Bailey—bless her heart—only cares about something as long as it benefits her. She tends to be self-absorbed and very quickly loses interest in anything that doesn't immediately concern her. It can be really annoying sometimes, but in this moment, I couldn't be more grateful.

"Oh yay!" Bailey shouts even though we're right next to her. "This week's episode looks so good!"

On the screen, the men are all gathered in the living room of the mansion they're sharing. Handsome guys of all races, religions, and sizes crowd the couches. Some are lazing on the thick rugs covering the floors, while others are standing around, probably wondering how in the hell they ended up in a situation like this. They're all discussing the many reasons Delilah is the woman of their dreams when a knock on the door pulls their attention from the contrived conversation and, like overexcited puppies, they race toward the sound. The fastest to the door swings it open, ripping the date card away from the messenger (points lost for manners, Greg!), and holding the card over his head like he just received the map to Excalibur.

His recites an intimidating number of names before reading the clue: "Milk does a body good. —Delilah."

Instead of faces that should look terrified and/or regretful, the camera pans over expressions of pure determination and glee as they throw their fists into the air and chant like maniacs. As if the possibility of naked alligator wrestling isn't even in the realm of possibilities even though the producers clearly have a sadistic streak.

I am, once again, very glad I did not decide to try to pick a suitor from this pack of fools.

But before I can revel in their lack of survival instincts— or at least pride—the show comes to a sudden halt as Bailey pauses it, wielding the remote like a weapon.

"That was a weird clue, but honestly I don't even care about these dates." She's off the couch and hovering over Delilah like some kind of gossipy archangel. "Just *please* tell me you don't pick Anthony."

"My lips are sealed." Delilah does a zipper mode in front of her pink-painted lips. "You'll have to wait and see just like everyone else."

"Oh, don't give me that media training bullshit answer!" Bailey leans in closer, not backing off in the slightest. "I get total 'only there for TV' vibes from him. I don't trust him."

Now, I know I'm not a reality TV connoisseur or anything, so maybe I'm missing the red flags that go beyond the initial red flag of signing up for a reality dating show in general, but I don't know what she's talking about. Anthony is actually one of my favorites. He's a little too handsome for his own good, but still not as good-looking as Delilah.

He's a lawyer—which could also be a red flag, but I'm in finance, so who am I to talk?—but not a corporate one. He's a civil rights attorney who specializes in underprivileged communities working with children of color who are arrested for minor offenses and held without bail or a trial date for years. So yeah . . . he's all good in my book. Top-tier actually, so I don't know what she's objecting to.

"I like him," I say. I just want to get back to the damn show so I can go home sooner.

"How?" Bailey's voice increases by what feels like hundreds of decibels. "He's *so* transparent. No way a guy like him would be competing for Delilah without ulterior motives."

I know Bailey doesn't mean any harm, but I'm not sure she thought about those words before she said them. Out of the corner of my eye, I see Delilah's megawatt smile falter a bit as she sinks farther into the supersoft cushions of her couch.

"Hard disagree. Delilah is all the motive anybody needs to be on this show. Plus, he's already said he hopes he can put more of a spotlight on the injustices he's fighting. I think he's been one of the most up-front about his motives." I never thought I'd be defending the honor of a dating show contestant that wasn't Delilah, but if last night taught me anything, it's that not everything goes according to plan. "But also, it was *your* grand idea to have us all go to the auditions in the first place. If you thought all the good ones had bad intentions, why would you want to go on there at all?"

"Because I thought it would be fun, or maybe I could become an influencer and have a fun job instead of our boring one." Bailey narrows her eyes my direction and her cheeks go red. I normally hate confrontation, so I don't think she knows how to respond to me disagreeing with her. "But are you saying because this was my idea I'm not allowed to have opinions or worry about our friend?"

That feels like a reach.

"Never said anything close to that. I disagreed, that's all." I pull the remote out of her hand, beyond ready for this conversation to be over. "Anthony is one of my favorites, but even if he wasn't, I'm going to trust Delilah's judgment to pick the person best for her."

For a spilt second, Bailey looks like she's going to argue some more. Thankfully, though, she just mutters "whatever" and sits back down.

"Well, if it makes either one of you happy, you're going to die when you see this date." Delilah tries to lighten the mood. "The producers had to spend a good bit of time convincing me to do it. It's fully unhinged."

I hit play and it's only a matter of moments before we see Delilah in a tight white tank top, short (and I mean short) overalls, and rubber boots standing in front of the most picturesque farm I've ever seen. I'd imagine if farmer porn was a thing, it would look just like this.

The men must have all received the same memo, because when they file out of the limo, they're all wearing some combination of boots, flannel, and well-worn denim.

And I, for one, *hate* how into the look I am.

And it's a feeling that only intensifies when they start feeding baby goats!

Listen, I don't knock anybody for their kink, but never did I think men in denim bottle-feeding goats would be mine. But live and learn and all that jazz, I guess.

"What. Is. Happening?" Bailey is staring at the screen slack-jawed. "And why do I like it so much?"

I am about to agree when things take a sudden and drastic turn for the worse.

"No!" I cover my face with my hands and watch the nightmare unfold through my fingers. "Delilah!"

"I know!" She's gasping for air and I don't know if she's laughing at the disaster on the screen or our reactions. "It wasn't my idea!"

What started as a well-planned day to gawk at wholesome, hot guys meeting baby farm animals quickly devolved into chaos when Jaxon went to milk the cow but did it too quickly and ended up getting kicked so hard, they had to call in medics. Then they moved on to the chickens, who clearly did not like the addition of so many people and started running around and pooping everywhere . . . including the adorable outfit our poor friend Delilah looked so cute in. It was like a sea of white, which made Mike gag, and his gagging caused Trevor (or Terry? How Delilah keeps their names straight is a mystery) to throw up. By the end of the date, they all had this vaguely haunted look on their faces, like they might all need intense therapy to recover.

I've never witnessed anything so gloriously horrendous in my entire life.

It's a masterpiece.

"Yeah . . . so I'm thinking maybe a day at the farm isn't the best date idea after all," TV Delilah says as the camera zooms in on her dirt-speckled face before cutting to commercial.

Usually when the breaks come around, we grab a refill or run to the bathroom, but this time, neither Bailey nor I move. We're frozen in our seats, staring at the toothpaste commercial, trying to figure out what in the world one says after watching their friend and her multiple boyfriends get covered in poop for almost five straight minutes.

"Wow. So . . . That was . . . wow." That's my very helpful and well-thought-out contribution.

"I've changed my mind about Anthony," Bailey says, managing to string together a complete sentence. "If a person who gets chased by a pig and pooped on by a chicken still looks at you like you're the most gorgeous woman in the world, then they pass any test." She stands up and straightens her skirt, which might be too short for a casual night at a friend's house. "Now if you don't mind, I'm going to need a shot of tequila or two after seeing that date."

And even though tequila is usually the thing putting me on the floor at the end of the night, it's now what snaps me out of my farm-induced haze and into the kitchen.

We crowd around Delilah's gorgeous marble island as I slice limes while Bailey pours the largest shots I've ever seen.

Delilah raises hers in the air and we follow along as she offers a toast. "Here's to terrible dates, good tequila, and best friends. Thank you for supporting me throughout this journey."

I slam the shot, trying not to think about the hangover I'll have tomorrow and instead focus on enjoying a night in with my friends.

Because even if they are obnoxiously happy, it doesn't mean life doesn't shit on them sometimes too.

If you're like me, you went to sleep reveling in the thoughts of Anthony feeding the baby cow and Jaxon holding the baby ducks. It was a farmhouse fantasy and I will not be shamed for loving it. This episode will go down in *Real Love* history as one of the best episodes to ever air. Did it get messy? Yes, but that was part of what was so amazing about it.

I think our girl Delilah really came into her own last night. Even though she was thrown for a loop on that date, she commanded the room and I think we're seeing her learn how to trust the process. Even in the midst of chaos she was impressively in charge of not only herself, but her group of men. I have no idea how she did it, but I bow down.

At the elimination ceremony, was anybody else surprised William received champagne? We're three episodes in and I still forget he exists. Three men went home last night, and even though I'm sad the hotness that is Ryder will no longer grace my television screen, I think it was the right decision for Delilah.

All in all, it was an A-plus-plus night, which is why I was so, so shocked to get this juicy gossip from my inside source. Apparently, the honeymoon is over for Delilah. People around her have pointed out things about her frontrunner that she didn't notice before. Even though I've already had a few favorites, we're hearing that a certain blond dentist isn't as well-intentioned as we were initially led to believe. Delilah has been hearing some nasty rumors, and if he really was her choice, she's got to be feeling pretty nervous right about now.

XOXO,
Stacy

7

DRINKING TEQUILA ON a work night is a terrible idea. Especially when you're approaching thirty. When I was in college, I wasn't exactly a party girl. However, if for some reason I did decide to go wild one night, I could still wake up the next day and function.

Not so much now.

I didn't even get drunk last night and I *still* woke up with a headache from hell. I took two Advil at lunch and they didn't even help. I think this might be nature's very passive-aggressive way of informing me that I am, in fact, officially old.

Rude.

I did my best to hide from everyone today as I counted down the hours until I could go home—not including Delilah, since she called out of work again—but unfortunately for me, there is one person in my life I can never avoid: my mom.

When I moved to Miami, my mom insisted we have at least one set day a month where we talk on the phone. I suggested Saturday mornings, but she vetoed that and insisted on Tuesday at five. I don't have any proof, but I think she chose Tuesday just to get on my nerves. She knows I hate leaving work early, so it was a test to see if I would prioritize her. Which, of course, I did.

People pleaser Maya strikes again.

I pull out of the parking garage and hit her contact in my phone. The ringtone blares through my small car and just like always, she answers on the third ring.

"Good afternoon, Maya." Her smooth voice fills the space around me. "How was your day?"

"It was good." I give her the standard answer. Work is always good. "My coworker is finally coming back so that's been nice. My workload is getting a little lighter."

"Not too light I hope." I hear the phone rustle and imagine her leaving wherever she is, her long legs gracefully moving throughout the house until she's sitting in her favorite chair by the window in her bedroom. "I know you said there might be an opportunity for a promotion soon. You don't want them to think you're not capable."

As a professor, Deborah Johnson knows how to both motivate and chastise me. I always feel like I'm walking on a tightrope around her. It's a balancing act between not needing her approval and wanting it desperately.

"My light load is still heavier than everyone else's I work with," I reassure her.

"Good." She's as terse as ever, never taking an extra minute to compliment me on my accomplishments or drive. It's what's expected of me, and meeting expectations is the bare minimum, not a reason for celebration. "Now, I spoke to Judith last night and she told me that you and Vaughn have separated? What is this about?"

Seriously?

I knew our moms were friendly, but for some reason I didn't think they were *this* friendly!

To be fair, I don't think they actually are. As much as I love Vaughn's mom, she's a bit of a gossip. Plus, she loves me. She was probably not thrilled to hear the news and started scouting around to try to see if she could fix it.

"We just needed some time and space to regroup," I say, trying to explain even though I know it's not going to be good enough. "We're both focused on work and our schedules clash. I need to know he's capable of making our relationship a priority."

"Oh, Maya." She sighs, and the sound of her disappointment makes the recycled air in my car turn heavy. "Don't be silly."

"I'm not being silly, he's being silly." Less than five minutes on the phone with my mother and I revert back to the insecure, whiny teenage girl who my mom has only ever seen as a silly little child. "I have a busy job too, and I don't think I'm being unreasonable to want my partner to want to spend some time with me without my having to nag him about it."

"This is what I warned you about when you first started seeing Vaughn. Do you remember?" She doesn't wait for me to answer because she knows I do. She reminds me of this conversation at least every six months. "I told you to think long and hard about dating an athlete. I warned you that not only is football an unsteady and volatile career, but the end would come sooner rather than later and you needed to be prepared to stand by him as he found a real career."

"I have stood by him and I have been completely supportive." More than supportive, actually. I was the person who stayed with him after he blew his knee out during his third season in the NFL. I was there when they told him he'd never play again. I stood by him through tears and rage. I was steady in my encouragement, cheering him on as he hopped from one career to another until he finally found one he loved. All I wanted was a goddamn date night and that's not too much to ask. "This isn't about me supporting him. It's about him not prioritizing our relationship and I don't think that's my fault."

I'm wasting my breath. My mom will never understand because my parents are the epitome of Black love.

They met in college, where my dad was studying to become a doctor and my mom was a history major. The story is it was love at first sight. They spotted each other across the crowded square, walked toward each other as if in slow motion, and have been together ever since. I'm not sure I've ever even seen them fight.

"Maybe that's so," she says. "But you still need to figure things out. You're nearly thirty, Maya. This is not the time to start over. This is where you lay your foot on the gas and really take off. Not start hanging around with reality show stars and losing everything you've worked for."

Any comeback I was planning dies on my tongue.

Twenty-nine years and I've never won a single argument with my mother. I think the record is something like:

Mom: 2,841,596
Maya: 0

You'd think I'd have learned by now.

"Delilah was my friend before she was a reality star." It's a terrible comeback, but it's all I have. "I don't know what she has to do with this."

"You don't know what your appearance on national television, during which you revealed that you inquired about participating in a dating show while having a long-term boyfriend at home, has to do with this?" Her laughter flows through my speakers, but it's devoid of all humor. "Now, Maya, I know I didn't raise a fool. Whether you want to admit it or not, you invited drama into your life. I cannot understand why, but now you must deal with it."

I consider explaining that I only applied to support my friends and that Vaughn was aware of every step the entire way, but I know it won't help. Only one thing will get her off my back and it's time to tap out and let her do her thing.

"You're right." I say her favorite words. "What should I do to fix it?"

I clutch my steering wheel as I hear the smile in her voice.

"Remember to avoid the three D's—you never want to be desperate, delusional, or disappointing." She recites her favorite mantra with practiced ease. "You'll need to give Vaughn the space he asked for until he comes to his senses. Let him know you'll be there when he's ready to talk and then keep your head down and focus on work. Take this time before you two get serious to achieve professional goals that might need to be put on the back burner if you become busy planning a wedding."

I'm worried my molars are going to crumble with how tightly my jaw is clenched as I turn in to my designated parking spot beneath my building.

"Okay, Mom. I'll try." Focusing on work is never bad advice and I do agree with giving Vaughn space. "Thank you."

"Of course, dear. You know I just want what's best for you," she says, and I know she means it.

We might not agree all the time, but I've never doubted that she wants to see me successful and happy in life.

"Okay, well I'm about to get in my elevator, but let's talk again soon?" Not too soon, hopefully. I love my mom, but I'll need a solid seven to fourteen days to recuperate from this conversation. "Love you."

"Love you too."

We hang up and I collapse against the elevator wall, listening to the calming music as it climbs to my floor. That conversation drained me. I decide to skip the gym tonight and order takeout and have a long, long bath instead.

I'm thinking of the extra samosas I'm going to order when I push open my door and my plans to relax go up in smoke.

"Hey, sis," Ella shouts from her spot on my couch. "I thought you'd never get here."

And I thought my mom provided me with enough family time to last the week.

Joke's on me.

8

"ELLA?" I STAND frozen in my entryway. "What are you doing here?"

Don't get me wrong, I love my little sister. She's the only person I've ever been in a fight for. I was in fourth grade and I saw her crying on the playground because some boy was teasing her about her wild curls (that I always envied). I shoved the little shit, and when he tried to fight back, I punched him in the stomach.

I was grounded for a month and Ella snuck me candy every single day until I was free.

But as with life, there is duality to everything. And as much as I love her, she is the antithesis of everything I am, and sometimes I wonder if she was placed on earth to test me.

"What? No 'nice to see you, how have you been, Ella'?" She stands up, her long, graceful body making even getting off the couch look like a dance. "Aren't you glad to see me?"

"Of course I'm happy to see you." I slip off my heels by the door, neatly placing them beside each other, trying to ignore the fact that Ella's own shoes are tossed haphazardly across the floor. "I just thought you weren't coming for a few more weeks. A heads-up would've been nice."

"And ruin the surprise? Where's the fun in that?" She glides across the floor and slams into me at full speed, wrapping her thin arms around my not-as-thin frame.

"Can't breathe!" I try to peel her off me before giving up and slouching into her grip. "I forgot how freakishly strong you are."

It's the dancer's body. She seems so thin and delicate, frail even, like the lace of the ballerina costumes she used to wear. But beneath her long limbs and flawless skin are thick, corded muscles from her fingertips down to her toes. I may look fit with my thick thighs and tiny waist, but I don't stand a chance against Ella.

"Don't you love it?" She smacks her lips on my cheeks. "I can fight Ralph for you if you want."

"Why would you even say that? I don't need—or want—you to fight anyone." I always do my best to keep my real feelings under lock when Ella is around, but I swear she only says things she knows will get a rise out of me.

Like wanting to fight my former professional athlete boyfriend.

"Fine." She sounds disappointed as she drops her arms and allows my ribs—and lungs—to finally expand again. "But if you change your mind, I'll be in your living room so I'll be easy to find."

"Seriously though." I follow her as she makes her way back to my couch. "What are you doing here? You said you were coming in a few weeks, not days. I wasn't ready for you."

I needed time to build up my mental fortress and maybe call my old therapist for a session or two.

"Yeah, that was before I called and you sounded like you were about to have a nervous breakdown because your douchebag boyfriend treated you like garbage again." She grabs the remote and mutes the woman screaming across the table from another woman. "What was I supposed to do? Just sit there and let Mom tell you to make it work no matter what? Or wait while you excuse his bullshit all over again? I don't think so."

"You don't even know what happened." Again, she has never even *been* in a relationship! The fact that she thinks she can offer me advice better than our Mom—who's been in a successful marriage for over thirty years—is almost as funny as it is insulting. "And what do you mean I'll 'excuse' him all over again? I don't do that! We both made mistakes early in our relationship, but we've grown since then."

See?

This is why I need prep time. I've been in her presence for mere minutes and I'm already yelling. There isn't a person on this planet who can get me as worked up as Ella Louise Johnson.

"He cheated and then you stepped out for revenge. I know they say two wrongs don't make a right or whatever"—she rolls her eyes—"but in this case your wrong was definitely right."

"Why do you do this to me?" I could maybe handle this like a rational adult if I hadn't just expended all my energy dealing with my mom. "You can't just show up at my place willy-nilly, three weeks early, and give me shit. It doesn't work like that."

"Did you really just say willy-nilly?" She starts to laugh. "Who are you? Aunt Rose?"

For some reason, this enrages me. Who does she think she is? Plus, I love her, but Aunt Rose is awful! Out of everyone in our family, that's who she compares me to?

"Do you think you were born with this amount of audacity, or did you acquire it while you pranced across the world with no responsibilities whatsoever? You would think you'd feel the teeniest bit of guilt for the amount I've had to cover for you and clean up your messes as you've frolicked around without a care in the world for the last seven years."

I often wonder if we are actually part of the same family. Ella and I were never held to the same standards growing up. I know it's not her fault, but sometimes my resentment about it creeps to the surface.

"That's crap." She unmutes the TV and looks away from me, suddenly ready to disengage now that I'm looking at her life instead of mine. "You've never had to clean up my mess."

If I hadn't just been reminded how strong she was, I'd jump on her and pull her hair like I did when we were little and I still had a chance to beat her in a fight.

"Are you kidding me right now? What about the time you were dating Devon Williams and ghosted him after you set me up with his cousin? I was the one stuck on a date without you, explaining your 'busy' schedule. Or the time you quit the internship Dad set up for you without giving notice? Because you decided to audition for that wild-ass off-Broadway show you saw on the internet? I had to cancel a trip to Mexico and do your work while also trying to focus on school." I could go on for ages, but decide to stop before my head explodes. "You always do whatever the hell you want, and whatever, that's fine I guess. It's your life. But the least you could do is acknowledge what I've done to clean up after you."

At twenty-six years old, Ella has experienced many things, but being a responsible adult who can hold on to a job isn't one of them.

"Oh please." She shifts on the couch to face me. The happy-go-lucky smile always lighting her face is gone and my anger is mirrored back at me through our mother's chestnut eyes. "You've always been so worried about being perfect for Mom, you never even saw me."

I don't know what surprises me more. That my sister actually does have a temper or what she's accusing me of.

Any other day, any other time, I could've handled this like a mature and rational adult. But she caught me on an off day, and unluckily for her, she's catching the brunt of the frustration that's been building in me for weeks. Maybe even months. I don't mean to unload on her, but now that I've started, it's like an avalanche I can't stop. This has been piling up for years because I've never given myself the grace to have a release. I swallow my feelings and stuff them deep down, hoping they'll disappear and I can pretend they never existed. But that never works.

"Of course I saw you, we *all* saw you! How could anyone miss you when you were the center of the universe and the rest of us were just your accessories?"

"Oh my god. Is she serious?" Ella shakes her head and starts talking to the ceiling like I'm not even here. "She can't be serious. Working in a soul-sucking corporate job has finally taken its toll. She's lost her mind."

If I was even slightly in touch with reality at the moment, I'd probably laugh at her over-the-top dramatics. But I'm pissed, and her over-the-top dramatics reinforce how true I feel everything I said was. Even in this very moment, she's still just being Ella. She's still just making it about her.

So I do the super adult thing.

I grab the oversized throw pillow that came with my couch, lift it over my head—for maximum impact, of course—and hit her as hard as I can.

Because you know . . . maturity and growth and shit like that.

"Ow!" She screams and I know I woke up the beast. "What the hell, Maya!"

Before she can regain her balance and retaliate, I hop off the couch and run toward my room. The stupid hardwood floors are like ice beneath my opaque tights and cause me to lose precious seconds off my minuscule lead. I slide into my room, fighting against momentum to shove the door in her face. Unfortunately for me, her long legs and quick reaction time are too much for me to compete with and she comes barreling into my room, tackling me to the floor like a maniac.

Which I guess is sort of fair since I did hit her first.

Well, well, well. If it isn't the consequences of my own actions.

Her long legs straddle my waist, slapping my arms. "What's wrong with you?"

"Get off me, you monster!" I buck my body as hard as I can to try to get her off me, but she's like a rodeo pro! My little body doesn't stand a chance.

I really need to learn to pick my battles better.

"I'm!" *Smack*. "Not!" *Smack*. "The!" *Smack*. "Monster!" *Smack*. "Here!" *Smack. Smack. Pinch.*

"Owww!" I screech, giving up my fight and moving to rub the sensitive skin on the underside of my arm. *Now she's just fighting dirty.* "Holy crap! You just freaking pinched me!

"And I'll do it again," she says without any remorse whatsoever.

"You know"—I stop trying to see if she broke any skin and look her dead in her wild eyes—"I was wrong, you aren't a monster."

"Thank you very much." She seems pleased at my words and loosens her thighs on the sides of my body, giving me the opening I was looking for.

I push my heels into the floor, recalling every Pilates and yoga class I've ever attended, and thrust my hips forward, turning both our bodies until she's on the floor and I'm straddling her. Her eyes are wide and the look of shock on her face is one of the most glorious sights I've ever seen. "You're not just a monster, you're a life-ruining, soul-sucking vampire!"

I think about executing my pinching revenge when I remember that Ella, my dear, sweet, horrible little sister, has always been unbearably ticklish on her sides and change tactics.

"Oh no." She shakes her head, correctly reading the look on my face. "Don't you dare."

I channel our childhood and lift my hands into the air, curling my fingers into claws à la Jim Carrey in *Liar Liar*.

"No!" Her screams rattle my hurricane-proof windows.

I'm convinced that my neighbors will soon be calling the cops, but I can't stop, won't stop. Not when I'm this close to victory. I inch my hands closer to her waist, thrilled with seeing the fear in her eyes up close. Maybe being a sociopath runs in the family? I should not be enjoying this so much.

"Maya. For real. Don't." I'm not touching her yet, but the phantom tickles have already hit and she's scream-laughing. "I drank two of your sparkling waters while I was waiting for you. If you do this, I'm going to pee."

As far as deterrents go, this is definitely the best one she could've come up with. Do I want to torture her at the expense of my favorite rug?

I consider her words before extending one hand. "Truce?"

She hesitates for a moment and I revert back to my tickling position.

"Truce! Truce!" she says, grabbing my hand and shaking as hard as she can.

I roll off her and lie on my fluffy rug, knowing I made a good deal. We're both silent for a few minutes as we stare up at my ceiling, trying to catch our breath.

"So . . ." Ella speaks first . . . because she's Ella and of course she does. "Wanna tell me what's bothering you?"

My entire life, Ella has driven me to the point of violence. But even in the height of it, I can never stay mad at her. Nobody can. Which is why she's the only person I know who can get away with half of the crap she pulls.

I lift my arm and tick off the reasons as I list them. "I'm anxious about a promotion opportunity coming up at work. My best friend is almost unrecognizable and I'm getting a little lonely. And, even though I know I'm going to regret telling you this, Vaughn and I are going through a little . . . hiccup."

"Well first . . ." She rolls onto her side and looks serious for once. "I don't know why you'd be stressed about work. You're the most determined, capable human I know. If there's something you want, the only people that need to be concerned are the ones considering getting in your way. Next, what friend? Have you ever thought this could be a good thing? Changes mean growth and different isn't always bad. Maybe try new things together, you might find you like getting out of your comfort zone. Finally, you know how I feel about that d-bag and I don't want to end up wrestling again because I hurt your feelings by telling you the truth."

I usually let all of Ella's "advice" go in one ear and out the other. But for some reason, as I lie on the floor, my lungs still burning after fighting like an eight-year-old, my problems seem more manageable. Ella's life is the opposite of what I want, but for reasons I can't explain, my stupid, useless heart is latching on to her words.

"You make everything seem so simple." I both hate and envy that about her.

"Because it *is* simple." She shoves off the ground and looks down her nose at me . . . a surprising reversal of the normal structure of our relationship. "You make everything so much harder than it needs to be. You already know the answer to most of the stuff you're worried about, but for some reason I'll never understand, you don't trust yourself."

"I trust myself." Kind of.

Maybe.

No.

Not at all.

"Oh please." Her eyes roll like they always used to when Dad would lecture her on the importance of education. "If you trusted yourself, would you still be pretending like it's your life's dream to work in finance? Would you still be dating Ralph? No. You'd be out there, doing what you actually love and spending time with people who truly deserve your attention."

Honestly? It's a little rude that she doesn't even grant me the common courtesy of pretending like she believes I have everything I want.

"I *do* love my job!" I'm confused to find myself defending my life choices to the person I never thought I'd have to defend them to. "And I love Vaughn."

"You don't love your job, you're just good at it. There's a difference. You're good at numbers and they're safe and reliable and make you feel comfortable. But you *loved* working on the morning show in high school until that bitch Ramona gave you a hard time about it. Then all of a sudden you were all about mathletes and helping Dad with taxes like a total weirdo."

Wow! Attack much?

I don't know whether I want to laugh or go for round two of wrestling. "You're actually certifiable."

I force myself from my spot on the floor and make it to my feet. My stomach growls, reminding me of my plan for samosas, tikka masala, and more naan than is probably healthy for a single person to consume.

"Oh, look, you're running away. What a shocking and unusual turn of events!" Her heavy sarcasm follows me across my apartment as I find my phone.

"I'm ordering Indian food. Want anything?" I don't give her the pleasure of an outward reaction to her false assessment of my life. "Their tikka masala is the best, but I also really like the shrimp saag."

"I'm not eating meat right now. It's so bad for the environment," she says like she's not a person who flies all the time, drove a car for years that failed emissions on the reg, and always has a bottle of Smartwater in her hand. "But I'll have saag paneer and veggie samosas."

She rests her hip against my counter, staring hard as I call and place our dinner order.

"Why are you looking at me like that?" I ask once I hang up. "Only you could manage to look so judgmental when someone else is buying you dinner."

"I just realized something about you," she says, but doesn't expand.

I know I shouldn't ask.

I don't care nor do I want to know.

I should just shrug, wash my face, and find something to watch while we wait thirty to forty-five minutes for our dinner to arrive.

That would be the smart, self-preserving thing to do . . .

"What did you realize about me?"

What can I say? I'm a glutton for punishment.

"I always thought you did everything Mom wanted because you were trying to prove that you were better than me." She drops her voice to a quiet whisper. "But now I know that was wrong. I scared you. The way I attack life freaks you out. I'm the mirror to the life you wanted but you were afraid to have. So you've chased Mom's approval instead, hoping she could validate your decisions. You've hoped she would tell you that you're perfect and in turn, it would turn your fear and regret into passion."

Okay.

Does she think she's a licensed therapist or something now? What gives her the right to say that to me?

"Do you feel better now?" I should've gone to the bathroom when I had the chance. "Maybe you don't understand this, but just because I tried out a hobby for a minute in high school and then quit it doesn't mean I abandoned my lifelong dream."

"Please! You act like we didn't share a room and I didn't snoop in all of your journals where you'd write about becoming the next Oprah or Barbara Walters." She pushes off the counter and gets in my space again. "You stopped because you were afraid. In finance, there's a right and wrong answer. You can be right and it's not subjective. You don't know how to put yourself out there, even if it could mean bringing you actual happiness. Maybe *especially* if it could mean bringing you actual happiness."

Our high school did have the best broadcast journalism program in the state and my fourteen-year-old self worked her butt off to become an anchor by the end of sophomore year. Ella's right, I did love it. It was a blast.

But so was treasure hunting in the backyard when I was a kid. That doesn't mean I'm supposed to be Indiana Jones.

"Okay, Ella. Do you feel better now?" I don't want to let

her pull me in again, but even though I know I'm going to regret this later, I can't stop myself. "Is this what's been on your mind? Why you had to come here? To tell me about this alternative reality in which I'm massively unhappy so you don't feel like the screw-up in the family?"

I see the way my words cause her to flinch and her big, chestnut eyes dull just a bit, but I don't apologize.

I don't even acknowledge her.

Instead I do what I should've done when I walked in and saw her in my space. I go to my room, lock the door, and remember what my mom told me to do. I make a list of everything I need to get done at work, update my schedule, and then I text Vaughn.

And I do it all while pretending I'm not the worst sister in the entire world.

9

NEVER HAS THE delightful, flavorful treat that is Indian food been so tense and awkward.

I ate by myself at the table while Ella sat at the counter, muttering beneath her breath and aggressively crunching into her samosa.

Also, Vaughn didn't text me back. I expected that, but it always sucks to be ignored after putting yourself out there.

I set my alarm to wake me bright and early in order to avoid dealing with Ella before work. I have too much on the line to start my days distracted and frustrated. Which is why I was so shocked when my sister, who is notorious for sleeping until noon, was dressed and had coffee waiting when I opened my bedroom door this morning. If that was her way of apologizing for last night, I wasn't going to complain about it.

I should've known she was up to no good—she's always up to no good—but instead, I let her puppy dog eyes and exquisite espresso-making skills sucker me. I was so hypnotized by her apparent change of attitude that when she asked if I could drop her by the harbor to meet a friend on my way to work, I didn't even question it.

With Ella's hippie lifestyle and assortment of equally go-with-the-flow friends, I figured I'd be dropping her off at someone's little self-repaired sailboat they were taking around the world. But when she asked me to drop her at a big, gorgeous private yacht and asked if I wanted to say hello to her friend in the crew quickly, I figured I might as well take the opportunity to actually see one of these boats that I drove past in the harbor every day. Besides, it would be rude to say no, right? And as I stood on the bow of the yacht with my eyes closed, soaking in the warm sun and breathing in the fresh, ocean-salted air, thinking I'd finally come to understand the appeal of owning a boat, I didn't even notice as we moved farther and farther away from the dock until it was rapidly shrinking in the distance.

"Ella!" I startle the poor seagulls flying above us. "What the hell?"

"Whoa, sis." She steps out of the cabin holding a towel and her sunglasses. The dress she was wearing has been abandoned, replaced with a very tiny string bikini. "You kiss Mom with that mouth?"

She's got the filthiest mouth out of everyone in our family besides our Uncle Cliff, but he doesn't count because he's eighty-six and mumbles so much that you can't really make out the bad from the good. But of course this is just another thing for Ella to make light of. God forbid she takes anything seriously, especially my anger or, you know, my freaking career.

"Don't even start with me!" My face starts to heat and I don't know if it's from the sun or from anger. I dig my phone out of my purse and nearly throw it into the ocean when I see I don't have any service. "I can't just not show up at work!"

She shrugs and puts on her ridiculously oversized sunglasses. "You did swim team that one summer, you could always swim back if you really want to."

"If I didn't think Mom and Dad would be really sad about you being lost at sea, I'd throw you overboard right now."

I told Mom she didn't need any more kids. I was content being an only child, but she was convinced we needed to be a family of four. Seeing as she nailed procreation on the first attempt, I'll never understand why she decided to roll the dice a second time.

"I have a friend on board." She spreads the towel on the bow of the boat and stretches her long, lean body on it. "He'd save me."

The only thing more infuriating than her having a comeback to absolutely everything is the way she just casually looks like a supermodel. I'm fine living in Miami. The food is great, the art is phenomenal, but the constant pressure I feel to be beach ready stresses me out. Delilah says it's all in my head, but I always feel as if every dimple and stretch mark on my body is highlighted beneath the omnipresent sunshine. I avoid getting into a bathing suit at all costs, whereas Ella would live in one if given the opportunity.

"Grandma would turn in her grave if she saw you in that sorry excuse for a bathing suit." I unbutton my blazer and toss it to the floor—it's dry-clean only, but beads of sweat are already starting to drip down my back. Sexy. "What's the point of it? You might as well be nude."

"I like it, that's the point, Judgy Judy." She looks up at me, but all I see is my own sad, sweaty reflection in the lenses of her sunglasses.

"Whatever." I shove her to the side so I can slide onto the oversized towel with her. "The color does look really good on you."

"See!" She nudges me back with her shoulder. "Your cold heart is already starting to thaw now that you're in the sunshine here. I know you claim to love work, but you have to admit this is a much better way to spend your day."

She's not wrong, but I have this medical thing where I'm physically incapable of telling her that. "I guess it's okay," I say instead. "It would've been nice to give me a heads-up so I could've called out though."

"Oh yes. Like you would've come willingly if I asked." Sarcasm drips off her words.

She's not wrong.

My apartment overlooks the ocean. Sometimes at night I'll leave my phone inside, make myself a Crown and Coke, and sit on my balcony watching the boats. Most of the time it all just seems obnoxious—I can imagine the greasy men scrounging for change to rent an overpriced yacht for a day. I'm sure they wear their favorite silk shirts that they think look so "Miami," but really just look so ridiculous. The co-workers I avoid like the plague are their idols and they pretend to be some rich finance bros and lure a group of poor, unsuspecting women in town for a girls trip onto the boat. In the end, there's an excess of alcohol, drugs, and regret. Lots and lots of regret.

Or, worse than the fakers, there are the actual rich men who buy big, obnoxious, ridiculously expensive things to overcompensate for something a little . . . *smaller*.

Both are gross and both are the reason, even though I've resided in Miami for years and my friends have gone out on boats multiple times, this is my very first time enjoying a leisurely day on the water.

There's also my intense fear of dolphins.

I try not to think about that.

The sun is moving higher into the sky and the effects of the coffee are starting to wear off. I check my watch and note that it's around the time I'd normally be reaching in my drawer for a midmorning snack.

"Since you're forcing me to play hooky, are you at least going to feed me?"

I'm slowly progressing to the hangry zone and once I reach it, my attitude problem gets a free pass.

And also, you know, Ella did basically kidnap me.

Still not totally over that.

"Of course. Who do you even think I am?" She lifts her sunglasses, letting me see the truth in her eyes, before dropping them back in place. "Remember when I told you I had a friend who works on boats? He's a chef. He planned a whole menu for us."

If there's one thing Ella and I have in common besides genetics, it's a serious love of food. We can thank our parents for hiring a nanny who also went to culinary school for that. None of us are cooks, but we still know exactly what we like—which is pretty much everything when Ella isn't saving the environment by cutting out meat—and we can order in like nobody's business.

Food is also the fastest way to my heart and all lingering anger I felt at my sister vanishes as we inch deeper into the Atlantic.

"A chef? I thought he cleaned the boats or something."

While I'm fully aware that there is an entire yacht-based industry, it's almost impossible for me to think of anything other than Keanu Reeves's character in *The Replacements*. I can't help it. I love Keanu more than life itself and that movie is my favorite guilty pleasure.

"Yes, a *chef.*" The way she stresses the word lets me know I've annoyed her again . . . even if she's the one who forced me to come. "I don't know why you assume you're the only one with cool friends."

"To be fair, I don't think I have cool friends. Just steady, reliable ones I can count on." Which isn't something I think is all that big an accomplishment. We're adults, account-ability seems like the bare minimum to expect from some-one.

The majority of her face is hidden behind her sunglasses, but I can still tell she's rolling her eyes at me.

"Just because I'm choosing to live a life I actually like doesn't mean I'm less responsible than you. It means I have different priorities and goals."

"First, I caught the little jab you threw in there."

"I didn't try to hide it."

I ignore her and keep talking. "Second, I never said there was anything wrong with your priorities. But since you brought it up, what are your goals?"

This might make me a terrible big sister, but I have no clue what Ella wants to do with her life. She's always bouncing from one thing to another, and keeping track got exhausting quickly. But now that we're stuck out at sea to-gether, there's no better time to ask.

"I just want to be happy and free," she says.

I wait for her to elaborate, but after a few moments of silence, I realize she's done.

Happy and free are her plans.

What kind of seventies hippie bullshit is that?

It feels like we're having some kind of a moment here, so I try my very, very best to fight back the expression threatening to take over my face. I keep my mouth shut a little longer, trying to gather my thoughts and measure my words.

"I know you're trying not to sound like an asshole right now, but it looks like you're sucking on a lemon. Just say what you want and get it over with."

Apparently my efforts are all for naught.

"Okay, well, happy and free are great goals. I think—"

I stop, still not wanting this to go bad or to offend her. "I think I'm more curious about how you plan to obtain both of those."

She doesn't miss a beat before she answers. "I already have them." She pushes up onto her elbow and gestures to the blue sky and water in front of us. "I'm on a boat in Miami with my sister. Before I came here, I was instructing dance classes in a little neighborhood studio in Harlem. I go where I want, when I want, and I do the things I love along the way."

This sums up my frustration with her so well.

Ella's just out there teaching dance classes in Harlem, traveling, and apparently living her dream life without even trying, without even making a plan! Then there's me—trying to get the dream career. Trying to get the perfect relationship. Trying to live free and happy.

Trying *all the time* and not getting the same outcome.

"But you can't just float around forever. Don't you want to put roots down someday? And not to sound like Dad, but how are you saving money? What if something happens, will you be okay? I've already got enough saved to put my future kids through college, and I just don't want you to find yourself in a jam down the line because you didn't think about saving sooner. I mean, do you even have insurance? What if you get sick?" I don't know if I'm asking for me or for her.

"I'm fine." She waves me off in a way that brings me more anxiety than peace. It also makes me wonder how I'm going to force her to take my money at the end of her stay. Otherwise I'm going to worry that her next venture into freedom will lead her to homelessness. "I can see you overthinking this. Just because I don't have a million financial spreadsheets doesn't mean I'm destitute. And I know you think Mom and Dad are perfect, but they aren't. I can take care of myself, without their—or your—permission."

I scrunch my face up tight and stick my tongue out at her. "I don't have a million spreadsheets."

Seven maybe, but definitely not a million. It's called being financially responsible! From the way she was acting you'd think I was a terrible sister for wanting to make sure she's okay.

"Anyways." I change the subject when I realize this line of conversation isn't going to go anywhere good. "You were supposed to tell me about this chef friend of yours and feed me?"

"Oh yeah!" She pops up and snatches the sunglasses off her face. "He's so cute! I met him when I was backpacking in Europe. He was in Spain learning about their cuisine. We hit it off over gazpacho and wine."

Okay, maybe there really is something to this happy and free thing. That sounds amazing.

"Wow." I'm genuinely impressed and—impossibly—more hungry. "Culinary school in Spain is pretty cool."

Something in her expression shifts a little bit, but before I can figure out why, she glances over her shoulder and screeches.

"You remembered!" She jumps onto her feet and is running before I can even process what's happening. "Oh my god! I haven't had this in forever."

My shift dress sticks to my sweaty back as I turn around. Ella's gulping down an orange drink next to the most attractive man I've ever seen in my life. This is her chef friend?

"My, you have to try this," she says when she finally unwraps her lips from the metal straw in the glass. "Obviously not this one, because I'm not sharing. This was my favorite drink in Spain and I haven't been able to find it anywhere since I left."

"A chef *and* a bartender? Impressive." I rise from my spot on the towel and meander toward the stupidly beautiful duo.

There aren't many people who can stand next to Ella without fading into the background. This man is the exception. He stands out in a way that isn't fair to the rest of the population.

And by population, I mean me.

Stuck in the middle of the ocean with two of the most gorgeous people I've ever seen while I'm a sweaty, gross mess? *Of course* this is how I would spend the only day I've taken off in years. I don't know if God or the universe or both are conspiring against me, but this is starting to feel personal.

Before I loved Vaughn, I lusted after him. He's big in a way that makes me feel delicate and soft in his strong arms. His style is always put together and he owns more suits than anyone I've ever known. His hair is always low and well maintained from the haircut or two he gets every week.

This guy though? He's the polar opposite of Vaughn and everything I never thought I'd be attracted to.

Until this very moment.

His overgrown shaggy brown hair is scattered with blond highlights that would normally cost a fortune, but for him probably come naturally from the sun. Instead of the football player's girth that I'm used to, his body is long and slim like a skater. Each muscle looks just as relaxed as his smile. A surfer boy through and through, he even has blue eyes that rival the beauty of the ocean. His gold-tinted skin looks like the sand and I've never wanted to roll around on a beach more.

He's paradise in human form and I'd like to book my ticket right now, please.

The more I look at him, the more thoughts of Vaughn drift away with the waves.

". . . not really a chef." He snaps me out of my very inappropriate train of thought.

"Sorry, I'm so hot. I was distracted by the drink." The lie falls effortlessly off my lips and I avoid Ella's knowing smirk. "What were you saying?"

A fan of the Iowa winters I grew up with, I don't love being hot. Right now though? I could not be more grateful that you can't discern the flush of heat from the flush of embarrassment on my face.

"Sorry!" he says instead of repeating himself. "I would've brought you one too, but Ella didn't know if you'd like it. I can go whip you up something really fast though, just let me know what sounds good to you."

I know it's his job and all, but I'm still thrown a little off balance by his eagerness to make a drink for me. Since we started dating, I was always the one to make a plate for Vaughn or bring us refills for our drinks. I think the only times Vaughn has ever done something like that for me were maybe the first few Valentine's Days we spent together.

"Umm, yeah . . . sure. Thanks." I stumble over my words, not sounding at all like the confident woman on the verge of a historic promotion that I am. I know I should say no; drinking this early is not usually for me, but this man has fried my brain. "A Crown and Coke would be amazing actually."

"Nice." He nods, his mouth forming a lazy smile as his gaze drops and he gives me an approving once-over. "Nothing better than a woman who enjoys her whiskey."

"Oh!" Ella chimes in, and even though she hasn't said anything, I already want to punch her because I can only imagine what's coming. "You should see her when she gets her hands on tequila. That's way, *way* better. This one time in high school—"

I slap my hand over her mouth, not needing her to tell Mr. Gorgeous about the time I got drunk after homecoming, yelled at Veronica Grey for always buying the same Abercrombie outfits as me, kissed Tyler Clark, and then immediately threw up all over his shoes.

Not my finest night.

"And I'm so sorry, but I don't think I got your name," I say over the sound of Ella's mumbles beneath my palm.

"Kai." He smiles and reaches out his hand to shake mine.

I let go of Ella and extend my hand to his. As soon as his skin touches mine, nerves that I thought died years ago race back to life and leave me feeling as if I'm vibrating. My heart rate accelerates and my breathing grows heavier. I didn't know it was possible to feel like this with a simple touch of the hand.

"Kai," I repeat, loving the short and simple name almost as much as I love the strong, confident grip of his handshake.

"Now let me go make that drink for you."

He pulls his hand away from mine, and I thought losing his touch would be the worst thing to happen to me.

Wrong.

Because his lazy smile turns megawatt and dimples as deep as the water we're on appear on his face, making him simultaneously hotter and sweeter.

I assumed the only harm I might encounter today was lurking beneath us in the ocean, but I'm starting to realize the real danger might be on board . . . and providing me with alcohol.

10

THE GOOD NEWS is there's no such thing as perfection.

While at first glance Kai didn't seem to have a single flaw, it didn't take long to realize he's the male equivalent of my sister.

Like Ella, he values freedom and happiness above all. This, for some reason, means resenting the constraints on creativity that traditional education imposes—his words, not mine. I learned that he did cook in Spain, but rather than attending the "soulless, moneygrubbing culinary institutes," he took the college fund his parents had saved up for him and spent it traveling and learning to cook from locals all across the world. Which apparently is enough to land a job cooking on a yacht.

But to be fair, he's a damn good cook, and who am I to knock how he landed here?

"So, Maya." He levels me with a stare that does very rude things to my insides. "What do you do?"

Normally, this is a question I love. I'm proud of my career and all that I have achieved. But sitting on a yacht with Mr. and Mrs. Antiestablishment causes an unfamiliar thread of discomfort to weave through my veins.

"Um . . . well . . . I work in finance." I bring the insulated cup filled with ice and whiskey to my mouth and ignore his grimace.

Long gone is the dimpled smile. Now he's looking at me as if I'm the enemy.

"Finance? Huh." He glances at Ella, who just shrugs her shoulders and pops another grape into her mouth. "I'm surprised."

"I love numbers and I'm really good at making people money." Though my usual confidence is missing, he must hear the truth behind my words. His smile returns and so does the warmth in the blue eyes I want to stare into forever.

Or for however long we're on the boat.

"As long as you're doing something you love, that's all that matters." He grabs one of the bacon-wrapped scallops that Ella won't eat because of her newly chosen vegetarian lifestyle. "Life's too short. I took a break from traveling when my grandma got sick. I spent two months with her, and even on the bad days she would tell me at least one story from when she was young. It really stuck with me. She loved her life and, in the end, isn't that all that matters?"

His words knock my breath away. I already know he's a great cook and easy on the eyes, but this newest piece of information is like the icing on the most decadent cake. Good guys aren't easy to find and Kai seems like he could be one of the very best.

"She *doesn't* love it. She loves our mom's approval. She likes the feeling of security even though it's a total myth." Ella states her opinion like it's a fact, bypassing the tender information her friend just shared with us. "But don't even try to wake her up from her delusions. She's in total denial."

I try to gather enough energy from the sun to shoot lasers at her, but alas, it doesn't work.

"I'm not in denial. Just because my life"—my stable,

safe life—"is different from yours doesn't mean it's wrong or bad. Isn't that what you said to me the other night?"

"Oh, so now you want to admit I'm right?" She gulps down the remains of her fourth (but who's counting) drink.

"I just worry about you." I try to defend myself, but I know she's right. She flipped the table on me and I didn't like it one bit.

Sometimes I think I'm so hard on her because I feel like she's been excused for things I was always lectured about. I hate to admit it—and I probably never will out loud—but I don't think I actually judge Ella as much as I resent her.

God.

I really am a bitch.

"Whatever, I didn't come out on a yacht to talk about this." Ella stands up and tosses her sunglasses next to the tray of appetizers Kai made for us. "I'm going swimming."

Like the anchor I'm sure the boat is about to drop, my stomach plummets.

"What do you mean you're going to go swimming? You can't just go swimming." Panic rises like the tide with every step Ella takes toward the side of the boat.

"It's the ocean, of course I can go swimming." She toes off her sandals one by one, leveling me with her most irritated glare, but it doesn't faze me.

I naturally run on the anxious side, but usually I'm good at getting a handle on it.

Not right now though.

I'm not even trying to handle it.

I'm letting all of my fears run wild and free because I'm too freaked out by the images of my sister getting attacked by a shark, swallowed whole by a whale, or worse, or assaulted by those nefarious dolphins.

"You don't even know what's out there!" I clamp my

hand around her wrist, yanking her back to the safety of the middle of the yacht. I try to slow my racing pulse, looking to Kai for some kind of backup. "Isn't there a shark-tracking system or something? Some kind of radar to check the water before she literally dives headfirst into the great unknown?"

Disney brainwashed us with *The Little Mermaid.* People are out here thinking there's a kingdom of sweet and caring merpeople hiding in the depths of the ocean when it's really sea monsters, shipwrecks, and dead bodies.

"I'm not sure our boat is equipped with shark sonar capabilities," Kai says with a straight face.

I don't realize until I hear Ella's laughter that the backup I was hoping he would provide me with isn't coming. His dimples make a quick and unwelcome return and the "free and happy" assholes surrounding me break into hysterics.

"Fine. Go get eaten by sharks for all I care." I stomp away, the onslaught of indignation temporarily squelching my fear. "I'll just be right here, enjoying all the food you'll never again taste."

Ella stops laughing and her deep sigh echoes off the water like I'm the one out of line here. I mean, I'm not the one jumping willy-nilly into a gigantic body of water, the full depths of which are still a mystery to mankind. I read an article once that said more than 80 percent of the ocean still remains unexplored. *Eighty percent!* What the hell is hiding in 80 percent of the ocean? Oh that's right, *we still don't freaking know*! And don't even get me started on Steve Irwin.

But yeah, I'm the irrational, dramatic Johnson sister here.

Cool.

Whatever.

"If you're acting like this just because you're feeling left out, I did bring a bathing suit for you to wear." She slides next to me on the bench and wiggles her eyebrows at me in the way that always made me laugh as a kid.

"Do you have a bathing suit for me or a leftover scrap of fabric like you're wearing?" I ask. "Also, did you really not think to offer it to me earlier? I've been sweating my boobs off in this dress for the last hour and a half!"

"I got it out of your drawer, so I'm assuming you'll like it. And I was going to give it to you, but you had a bad attitude."

"So you went through my drawers and then withheld my own stuff from me as punishment for not being happy about the fact that you kidnapped me?" Does she hear herself speak sometimes?

"Yup." She leans across me and nabs one of the prosciutto-wrapped melon balls and tosses it into her mouth like she wasn't lecturing us an hour ago about the evils of eating meat. "One doesn't count."

And if that isn't Ella in a nutshell, then I don't know what is.

"Sometimes I wish I could live in your brain for a day." I tilt my head to the side, trying to figure out what in the actual fuck is going on inside that beautiful head of hers. "I feel like it's wild in there."

"It is. You'd love it." She takes my insult as a compliment. "So are you going to get your bathing suit on and swim with me or not? I know you have that weird dolphin thing, but I'm pretty sure that's completely irrational."

"A dolphin thing?" the previously silent Kai asks.

"She's afraid of them," Ella says at the same time I say, "They're fucking evil."

Kai's mouth falls open and I can tell he doesn't know

whether or not to laugh. "Dolphins?" he asks again. "The sweet fishies people pay money to swim with? The lovable topics of countless children's tales?"

"They're actually mammals," I correct him thanks to the knowledge I've acquired from nights of endless dolphin doom scrolling. "And yes, those very dolphins are in fact evil, murderous monsters. They're the Ted Bundy of the sea. You're so charmed by them you don't even realize their true motives until it's too late."

"Oh god," Ella mumbles beneath her breath before sliding away from me. "You've gotten her started."

"Wow." Kai still looks like he wants to laugh, but at least has the common decency not to. "I never knew."

"I'm happy to impart my hard-earned wisdom where I can." I look at my glass and realize the only thing left in it are some sad, melted dredges of an ice cube. More alarming is the fact that it was already my second drink.

No wonder I'm turning into a total aquatic lady. I'm tipsy! In the ocean! With a hot guy who can cook, make cocktails, and is the polar opposite of my now ex-boyfriend.

I don't know.

I'm drunk.

Ella's a terrible influence.

"So do you want your bathing suit or not?" Ella is trying to sound annoyed, but I know her too well to believe it. She's proud she's got me out of work, on the water, and ranting about dolphins. This was probably her plan all along. She's an evil genius.

I contemplate sweating for the next few hours just to prove a point—my dress is already ruined so it doesn't really matter if I keep it on. And compared to Ella's bikini, mine is going to look like I bought it off the set of *The Golden Girls*. But the sun isn't setting anytime soon and my deodorant can only take so much.

"Fine, but if you make one joke about my suit . . ." I want to threaten to throw her overboard again, but knowing she wants to go in the ocean ruins it. "I don't know what I'll do, but please don't."

"What are you talking about? All of your suits were really cute. Why would I joke about them?"

I'm used to us giving each other such a hard time that Ella being nice to me about my bathing suit after I was rude about hers really throws me off . . . and fills me with guilt.

"Oh, um . . . no reason. Thanks." All of a sudden, the floors on deck are the most interesting thing I've ever seen.

"You're being weird," she says. "Kai, I'm gonna show her where her suit is, but do you want to be my favorite person in the world and make a couple more cocktails? She's gonna need one if we're going to get her in the water with us."

"Yeah, because being drunk in the water with a slowed reaction time is way less scary." I feel bad about being a bitch, but not enough to be peer-pressured into the ocean. "But it will help me not have a total heart attack as I watch you two frolic."

"Frolic?" Kai repeats after me, his white teeth shining bright against his gold skin and his dimples popping. Holy hell. He is so hot. "I don't think I've ever frolicked before."

"Oh, sir, I can tell—you most definitely have frolicked." I regret the words as soon as they're out of my mouth.

I haven't even touched the tequila yet!

But as I lock eyes with Kai, the regret fades and nerves set in. I don't know what he's thinking, but I have the distinct feeling it has something to do with frolicking . . . with me . . . and in a bed.

Or maybe the water.

I don't know what he's into.

Or at least I hope that's what he's thinking, because it's most definitely what I'm thinking.

*   *   *

After I've had four cocktails, three shots, and more food than I've maybe ever eaten, the Miami shoreline finally comes back into view. As my reckless sister swam all day long, I sat on the deck with Kai, trying all of his food, listening to stories of his travels, and even filling him in on the not-nearly-as-entertaining details of my life. I'm normally a person who takes a while to get to know, but I couldn't help but let my guard down around Kai. And while I'd like to blame it on his amazing bartending skills, the truth is that there was just something about him that I couldn't ignore.

Even though the water should seem more ominous in the nighttime, the dark, inky sheet surrounding us has turned into a mirror. The moon and stars sparkle and sway all around us and it's like I'm floating inside of a magical storybook. All thoughts of sea monsters drifted away with the fading pinks and oranges of the sunset, replaced by diamonds dancing on the water, and all I can imagine are the secrets, the romances lost beneath the surface.

I finally see the appeal of a midnight swim. What wouldn't I risk just for a glimpse of the promises lurking beneath us . . .

My thigh grazes against Kai. It's as if just the thought of dipping into forbidden waters pulls me toward him.

"So did you have fun?" Kai asks.

As the day went on and my reservations slipped away, our proximity grew nearer and nearer . . . something that excited me as much as it scared me.

I pull my bottom lip between my teeth. The nervous habit I've worked so hard to rid myself of is reappearing all because of a cute guy who's twisted my insides into knots in just a few short hours. "I probably shouldn't admit this, but I don't think I've ever had this much fun." My voice is barely a whisper, my confession washing away with the sound of the waves. "I go out with my friends, and I have the occasional big night out, but nothing like this. Never disconnecting and letting myself . . . just be. I don't think I've ever felt like this."

"Ella told me you're very . . . focused." The pause as he searched for a kind word to describe me makes me laugh.

"She told you I was uptight and snooty." I give him the adjectives more along the lines of what I know Ella used, even though they might be too generous. "Don't worry, we're sisters. We've said worse about each other, and we've said it to each other."

Ella went inside the cabin after taking a final tequila shot and declaring her desire for a nap. I'm not positive, but I'm pretty sure I saw her wink at me before walking through the door. Until that moment, I thought she brought me out here to spend time with her. But now, sidled up next to Kai as we accidentally touch every few seconds? I'm not so sure.

He raises both of his hands in front of him. "I didn't want to be the reason for a family rift."

"Not possible." I tell him the God's honest truth. "We might fight like crazy, but I don't think anything could keep us apart forever."

"That's good to hear. Sometimes family can be difficult."

That feels like maybe the most massive understatement in the history of understatements. Difficult is choosing between two different movies you really want to see or learning how to knit. Dealing with family feels more like conducting a mission to Mars . . . but somehow still harder.

"She's the most frustrating person I've ever known, but she would do anything for me and I'd do the same for her."

The evening breeze is picking up. I rub my arms in a weak attempt to chase away the goosebumps.

"Are you cold?" Kai asks, not waiting for an answer.

He's out of his seat—my body instantly mourning the loss of his warm body—and hustling across the deck. When he turns around with a giant blanket, his smile is as bright as the moon.

Instead of handing me the folded-up blanket, he takes his time unfolding it and tucking it around one side of my body before taking his seat next to me and pulling the other side around him.

"There," he says. "Is that better?"

"Um." He lifts one arm around me, mindlessly moving his hands up and down my arms to keep me warm, the sweet and simple gesture causing me to forget what words are and how to speak. It's such a small gesture, but I can't remember the last time someone has done something like this for me. I feel like I'm always the person taking care of everyone, never on the receiving end of kindness. "Yeah, thank you."

"My pleasure." He doesn't seem to notice his effect on me and I'm not sure if I'm grateful or furious. "Now, what were we talking about?"

I search my mind trying to remember something other than the way he's making me feel.

"Just Ella and how she knows how to push all of my buttons." *High five, brain!* "But even so, I love her. It's the Ella charm. I swear, she could punch someone in the face and they'd just be grateful to get some of her attention. The earth regularly shifts for her. Unyielding rules are happy to bend to her will."

"Maybe you should call it the Johnson charm." His hands slow down, but he never pulls them away. "I see it in you too."

"You do?"

I don't think I've ever been called charming before . . . I'm much more used to being described as uptight—and yes, I've been called uptight multiple times, thank you very much. But never *charming*.

"That spark." He leans in, and his smooth voice that always sounds like he's on the verge of laughter changes. A seriousness creeps into his tone and—even though I've known him for less than a day—it feels big. Huge. Important. "That thing that makes people want to be around Ella? It's in you too. It's just quiet. Ella's a shot of tequila. Loud and in your face, the party you always want to be invited to. You're not that—you're like a glass of brandy. It's powerful and something to savor. You're the kind of person people want to be around forever." He pauses for a moment and looks at me with a mischievous—and very sexy—glint in his eye before he finishes his thought. "Even when you're ranting about dolphins."

I feel like I could melt in his arms and leave a big ol' puddle of Maya on the deck of this yacht right now.

But I have a plan, and becoming a puddle doesn't fit into that plan.

I wrote my plan down when I was twenty and I've lived by it ever since.

Every decision I make gets filtered through the lens of that plan. Will this help me reach my goals? Will this set me back? What will the consequences be and are they worth it? The inner dialogue running through my brain never shuts up about The Plan.

But right now, drifting back toward Miami with nothing but the sound of the breeze and the waves around me, peace envelops me, and for the first time, I don't think.

I just do.

I lean in, my mouth finding his before my mind has the opportunity to catch up. The full lips that I've been staring at all day are hesitant. Nerves and embarrassment begin to rise in my stomach and I move to pull away, but before I can, his strong arms pull me in closer and his lips push back against mine.

The breeze stops.

The water comes to a standstill.

Time ceases to exist.

It's been ten years since my last first kiss, but surely this isn't what they're usually like. I would have remembered this.

His soft lips are gentle at first, mirroring my movements, learning and adjusting to what I want. Then something happens and he takes over—the softness falls away as his teeth nip at my lip, his tongue tracing away the sting.

I'm suddenly aware of every place our bodies are touching and how much of my skin is exposed to his. Electricity crackles down my arms and into my belly, moving lower and lower until . . .

"Are we almost in?"

Ella's distant voice is a hammer smashing the thinly veiled fantasy I allowed myself to believe in for a few moments.

As reality sets back in, so does the panic.

And shame.

"Oh my god. I'm so sorry." I jerk away from him, not registering the loss lingering on his face.

I throw the blanket off me, rushing toward Ella's voice without so much as a backward glance and counting down the seconds until we're back on solid ground.

The ground where I have a job I abandoned even though I'm trying to get a promotion. The ground where, according to my mom, I should be trying to formulate a plan to carry on the Johnson family college sweetheart tradition and piece my relationship back together, not totally blow it apart for good.

Yes, Kai is a dream, but I live in the real world.

UNREALISTICALLY UNCHECKED

Do you feel that? The churning and unease beneath your feet? Well that, Lovers, is the rumbling of change.

Since episode one, we've been drooling over Drew. We've been cheering for the dentist from the moment he stepped out of the limo with those emerald eyes, big heart, and bigger biceps. When the superhot pair of Miami residents bonded right away over their shared love of Hurricane football and obscure horror movies, it seemed as if the rest of Delilah's suitors should've called it a day. Insiders of the show placed bets early on that he would be the winner.

However, it still might be too early to start ordering your #Drelilah shirts.

According to my sources, while the producers have been hard at work to get viewers falling in love with Drew, things are about to shift. Anthony, the lovable lawyer from Chicago, seems to have taken everyone—Delilah included—by surprise and swept her off her feet. Drew might have frontrunner status, but it sounds like he shouldn't get too comfortable there—after all, he hasn't put a ring on Delilah's finger just yet. Apparently, Anthony thinks that while Drew may be the safe choice, Delilah didn't sign up for *Real Love* to be safe. She signed up to find love and excitement, and he thinks he's the man for the job. But can a man as good-looking as Anthony ever be trusted?

And the gossip mills out here in the real world have been going just as wild lately. Rumors are swirling that Delilah is abandoning responsibilities to spend time with her new beau and is ready to keep exploring the vast possibilities life has to offer instead of settling back into her old life. I'm not sure what to believe, but one thing is for sure, I'll be tuning in every week to watch it all go down.

XOXO,
Stacy

11

IT'S EASY TO work through the weekend when you're trying to avoid going home.

Besides a killer glow from hours in the sun, the only thing my day playing hooky with Ella gave me was a hangover . . . with a side of regret and sexual frustration.

After catching an Uber home from the marina, I had to return to the scene of the crime the next morning to retrieve my car. Talk about mortifying.

But while my overarching feeling about my actions is shame, there is still a part of me that wishes Ella hadn't interrupted my kiss with Kai. And that part of me is why I'm avoiding Ella. I'm not sure I can trust myself not to beg her for Kai's number and track him down to finish what we started.

There was a time in my life when maybe I wouldn't have thought this was such a big deal. There was a time when I started to think I could do it all, where I could live wild and free like Ella but still hold everything together and make my mom proud at the same time.

Vaughn had just finished his second season in the NFL and I was laying the foundation at an investment banking firm in Iowa with my sights already set on Wright, Ghoram, and Degrate. Simply put, we were thriving—a power couple in the making.

Things had never been better and I missed him like crazy while we were apart.

Even though it was the off-season, Vaughn decided to stay in Miami to attend team workouts and stay in shape while getting face time with his coaches. Sometimes I think the true love of Vaughn's life was football. He dedicated himself so fully to the sport that I don't believe it was ever possible for him to commit to anything or anyone—including me—in that way again.

My birthday was coming up and I had time off that I'd been saving since I started working, so on a whim, I decided to take Friday off and surprise Vaughn with a long weekend visit.

It was going to be perfect.

And from the very first moment, it seemed like it was.

I was upgraded to first class on my flight, my suitcase was the first on the carousel, my driver was fast, efficient, and the perfect amount of chatty. When I arrived at Vaughn's apartment, the butterflies in my stomach and the ache between my legs had reached a fever pitch. I knocked on his door fully prepared to jump his bones the second he opened the door.

And I would've, except Vaughn didn't open the door. Instead, it was a woman with smudged lipstick and no bra who answered the door. Now, as I've mentioned before, once my temper hits a certain level, I lose all ability to think rationally. When that woman answered the door with her bed head and perfect body, I saw red. And the misty rage didn't clear from my vision until I answered Vaughn's millionth call while I was back in Iowa in bed next to another man.

Vaughn flew to me the next day.

We didn't mention what either of us had done, and when we kissed each other before he left for the airport, an unspoken agreement passed between us. We never talked about that weekend again.

Now, all these years later, on the verge of another birthday, I'm not sure if I'm so intrigued by Kai because I want to punish Vaughn for breaking up with me, or if it's because I really do like him. My emotions are all over the place, and no matter how many hours I work, I can't get a handle on them. It's almost as if my tried-and-true technique of bottling up my feelings and burying my problems deep down and never addressing them doesn't actually work.

And that's why it's late when I push open the door to my apartment.

Ella had texted me earlier that she was going to check out an art museum and maybe hit a show. Part of me feels bad for ignoring her while she's here and making her explore on her own, but the other part is excited to have my place to myself for the night to try to sort out my thoughts.

"Told you she'd come home earlier if she thought I was gone." Ella's voice cuts through the shadows before I flip on the overhead lights, revealing her lounging on my couch next to Delilah and Bailey.

"What the hell?" I put my hand over my chest. My heart feels like it's about to jump out of my body. "You scared me!"

I hate being scared, something Ella both knows and weaponizes against me. I can't tell you how many times she got us in trouble as kids because she'd hide in my closet—for hours even—just to hear me scream.

Total. Sociopath.

"We wouldn't have had to resort to ambushing you if you weren't avoiding us all," Delilah says.

Bailey nods in agreement. "Yeah, you even bailed on lunch when we went to Cipriani. You love that place."

I do love that place. I *love* Italian food. I hope in my next life I'm reborn into a small Italian village where I spend all my days dedicated to nothing but wine and pasta.

"I've been slammed, and with Suzanne leaving, I really have to put my best foot forward if I want the promotion." It's only a half lie. I am slammed, but I am also avoiding them. "Anyways, wasn't *Real Love* on tonight? Shouldn't you be watching?"

I thought I had successfully dodged having to watch Delilah prance on the beach, making out with one hot guy after another this week. I love her to death, but watching her carefree and ultimately successful quest for love is the last thing I need when I'm in this headspace. I'm going to be seriously pissed if that's why they're here. Plus, on my lunch hour, I may or may not have pulled up a private browser on my phone and read some of the blogs because I wanted to know what was going to happen without having to face a whole two hours of someone else's happiness. I'm not proud of my behavior. But I have to step away from this shit for a minute before it consumes me.

"It was." Bailey leans back into my couch cushions, and even though she's across the room, I can still see the ex-aggerated roll of her eyes. "We watched it before you got here. Delilah still likes Ben, which is the wrong choice. Dentist Drew got all possessive, which was kind of hot. And dark horse Anthony came riding in like a knight in shining armor, but they're obviously not a good match. Then she got rid of Justin and Darren R.—the redheaded Darren from Ohio." She clarifies when it's clear I have no idea who the fuck Darren R. is.

"How long did it take you to remember all of their names? I feel like they should all have to wear name tags for the first week." Ella asks the question we all really want to know. "Also, I'm totally Team Anthony, Bailey's a fucking hater."

"Am not!" Bailey shouts, and Delilah's deep, throaty, and sexy-as-hell laughs fills the room.

"I like Anthony too," I say. "He's super handsome and I think he has a good heart."

Like Kai.

I try to shut down that line of thought, but no matter what I'm doing or thinking about, Kai is never far away from my mind. Not his eyes or sinewy body or soft lips . . .

"If you're so sure, then why don't we make a bet?" Bailey shoots off the couch and runs to her purse. "I bet two hundred dollars that once the season is finished airing, Anthony suddenly has a change of heart because he doesn't want the commitment and steps away from being a lawyer to try to do movies. And I'll bet an extra hundred that he does a big tell-all interview about the show to get his name out there."

She slams three hundred dollars on my counter and turns with her hands on her slim hips.

"Who carries around that much cash?" Ella comes through again with the important questions. "But I'll take that bet."

I don't do bets, they seem like a waste of money. I went to Vegas when I turned twenty-one and only went to the casino once. It was too much. If I was going to waste my money, it was going to be wasted on Chanel, thank you very much. I mean, what's the point of the big high-powered moneymaking job if I don't splurge on myself every now and again? Ella, on the other hand, has proven time and again that she never turns down a bet or competition. Even when . . . no, scratch that . . . *especially* when the odds are stacked against her.

She once challenged Vaughn to a race when he came

to our house for Thanksgiving. She very nearly won. I've never told Vaughn this, but I think if she hadn't been four glasses of wine in, she might've beaten him. I'm not sure his ego ever would have recovered from it if she had.

"And I'll raise you all another five hundred to say you have no idea what's actually happening, and if you did, you wouldn't be making any of these bets." Although Delilah is still smiling, her tone is off. It doesn't take a genius to figure out that she's not pleased with the direction the conversation has taken. And even though this was Ella's misguided attempt to stand up for her, she looks properly chastised.

Bailey, on the other hand, is smiling like a Cheshire cat. She opens her mouth to respond, but I speak first, hoping to avoid the fight that's beginning to feel inevitable.

"So now that the bet is covered, do you want to tell me what you're all really doing here?" I say without thinking. My mom always warned me not to ask questions I don't really want the answer to, and after seeing the fresh wave of guilt that crosses Ella's face, I realize this is one of those moments.

Too bad it's too late to call take-backs.

"I just thought you could use a night with your girls." Ella's gentle tone causes every alarm in my head to go off. "I talked to Mom today and she told me about you and Ralph."

"You . . . Mom called you? And she told you?"

Oh. My. God.

I've never had a tire screech moment in my life. I've had embarrassing shit happen—more than the average person probably—but I've never experienced something like this, when a spotlight appears out of nowhere to focus on me and everyone around me slow blinks as they comprehend what just happened. This is *exactly* why I told Ella it was just a fight, not that we'd broken up.

"Wait." Delilah stands up, understanding dawning in her whiskey eyes. "What happened with Vaughn?"

I want to glare at my bigmouth sister and hit her with another pillow, but unfortunately, I'm the only person to blame for all of this.

And Vaughn.

He's definitely to blame.

"Okay, so . . ." I pause to contemplate my next words—and also to see if I could make it down to my car without being caught. "Remember when I told you that our special date night went great?" Bailey and Delilah both nod while Ella chews at her nails, the habit my mom has been trying to break her of since I can remember. "Well, what actually happened is that he broke up with me."

"WHAT?" Delilah, who can cut a person to the quick with a look or a whispered threat, screams at the top of her lungs. If I had anything hanging on my walls, I'm sure it would have caused my frames to rattle.

"Oh my God." Bailey sits on a stool at my island. "What are you going to do?"

I open my mouth to tell them about the text I sent to him and my mom's advice, but before I can get there, Ella speaks over me.

"She's not going to do shit. She's been in a relationship with this man for a goddamn decade and he's still playing these stupid games." She must sense I'm about to interject with excuses for Vaughn. She faces me and points her long finger in my face. "No. I don't want to hear it. He sucks, he's always sucked, and he always will. This is maybe the only kind thing he's ever done for you."

Bailey, who always has an opinion, is watching Ella with her jaw hanging open and a look of admiration—or fear—on her face.

"Fucking preach!" Delilah high-fives Ella. "If he could break up with you while you were wearing that lingerie, then he doesn't deserve you and he absolutely never will."

I was hoping to go the rest of my life pretending that I didn't get dumped while wearing the sexiest lingerie I've ever seen, so although I don't necessarily appreciate the reminder, she's not wrong. If that happened to one of my friends, I would be livid and tell them to never speak to the jerk again. Why am I not giving myself the same advice?

Why is it so hard to love and respect myself as much as I do the people around me?

Def calling my therapist this week.

"Wait." Ella's face turns fire engine red with fury at this new piece of information that my mom—thankfully—was unaware of. "He dumped you while you were wearing lingerie?"

"To make a long story short"—because no way in hell am I recounting the entire night—"I was noticing that our relationship was lacking some spark and excitement. I asked Bailey and Delilah to help me plan a special night and it included some Agent Provocateur. We went to dinner, came back here, I changed, he fell asleep on the couch, and then broke up with me after I woke him. I was just too embarrassed to tell you guys because, you know, it was beyond mortifying."

Yup.

Even condensed, it's still making my whole body cringe with the memory.

"Just when I thought I couldn't hate him anymore," Ella says to herself more than anyone else. "Okay. Listen, I know you aren't going to want to hear this, but I'm going to say it anyways." Considering she tells me a lot of things I don't want to hear without them warranting a warning, I brace for the deadly impact this will probably have. "Ralph was never good enough for you and I wish you knew that, but you don't see yourself the way I do. You've settled in your life because you don't think you deserve more. You don't think you deserve a relationship where you are truly cherished. You don't think you deserve a job that lights you up because you love it, not just because you're good at it." She glances at Bailey and Delilah. "No offense, but I don't think being an investment banker is anyone's dream job."

"Facts," Bailey chimes in. "I just do it because my dad wanted me to go into finance and I like expensive clothes. If I could make this money doing something else, I'd quit yesterday."

I know Bailey has never loved the job, but I expect Delilah will back me up. She's struggled getting back into the swing of things since *Real Love,* but I know she's as passionate about her career as I am.

"You're not wrong," the backstabber says instead. "I thought I loved the job until I went on *Real Love* and realized that it didn't make me happy, it just kept me busy. I've actually been considering putting in my resignation since I got back. I don't think I can do it anymore."

Now I'm the one standing there, staring at everyone, completely speechless.

Have I been wrong about everything and everyone in my life? Am I the one who's been doing things wrong all these years?

"You know I love you, My." Ella threads her fingers with mine and holds on tight. "I just want to see you be truly happy. You deserve that."

"Ella . . ." I come this close to arguing and telling them all they're wrong, but I can't. "Please tell me you brought booze."

"Obviously." Ella squeezes my hand one more time before letting go and walking to my fridge to reveal bottles of wine and tequila chilling right beside take-out bags from Delilah's favorite Cuban restaurant. "Like I'd allow my sister to face this sober and hungry? I don't think so."

Maybe my carefree little sister who I've spent too much time judging knows more than I ever have.

Sure, I've been fine my entire adult life. But at what point is fine not okay? *Fine* isn't a standard of living. *Fine* isn't what anybody should strive for.

Joy. Happiness. Freedom. Love.

Those are goals. Those are what make life worth living.

I've been breathing, I've been going through the motions, but now it's time for me to *live*.

"Then what are we waiting for?" I ask my friends who dropped everything to come support me. "This definitely calls for shots."

Shots were a terrible idea.

"Ugh, Ella!" Delilah says through a tequila-contorted face as she tries to fix her features after downing the clear liquid. "I can't do another. I really think I'll die."

"Same." I stumble to my fridge and grab everyone a bottle of water. "We all need to hydrate."

I can't help it. Even when I'm letting loose, I still have to be somewhat responsible.

Bailey cracks open her water bottle and takes a deep gulp before directing her attention back at Ella. "So you live in New York? How long have you been there?"

"I've been there for about a year, but I'm thinking of leaving. Being around soft beaches and clear water this week has reminded me how much I missed it."

"Really?" I ask. She hasn't said anything to me . . . but to be fair, I have been avoiding her. "You might move to Miami?"

I would've hated this before, but now it actually excites me a little bit. I'm grateful for my friends, but even though I've denied it before, nobody has my back like Ella.

"I'm not sure about Miami. I don't think I could handle Florida long-term." She winces slightly and looks around the room apologetically. "Sorry. No offense to all you Floridians."

"None taken," Delilah, a Florida native, says. "I used to think I'd never leave, but I'm not so sure anymore. It might be nice to get out there and travel. See what else there is."

"Exactly! Life is short. Why stay in one place?" Ella kicks her feet up on my coffee table and I don't even say anything. Look at me, being all easy, breezy. "I'm considering South America. I did the Europe route already and I've taken a few trips down south, but I feel like I need to immerse myself in it. I've heard Argentina and Brazil are fun. Maybe I'll do both."

"I want to marry you." Delilah leans into Ella. "Will you marry me?"

"I think out of all of us, you have enough options for marriage. Plus, I'm not really sure how I feel about the whole institution of marriage. I just don't know if I can commit to being with anyone forever. That's a long time, you know?" Ella shrugs and then looks at Delilah. "But you are stunning, and if you weren't dating twenty men and I wanted to get married, I would totally marry you."

"Are you a lesbian?" Bailey has no qualms whatsoever about asking something so personal to someone who is practically a stranger.

My irritation spikes at her for asking such an intrusive question. I'm about to say something snarky when Ella answers and surprises the shit out of me.

"I think putting myself in a box for sexuality is ridiculous. If I've learned anything over the years, it's that gender is a social construct and things are much more fluid than we've been forced to believe for so long. I've dated women and men and nonbinary people. Gender has no factor in who I'm attracted to."

It takes more effort than I knew possible to keep my jaw from falling to the floor. I don't care at all who my sister loves, but part of me is embarrassed that I'm just now learning this about her.

"I think I love you even more now?" Delilah half states, half asks. "I didn't think it was possible, but I do. I love you more."

I can see the unasked questions lingering behind my friends' eyes. *How is this your sister? How is she so free and fun and you're . . . you?*

The same questions always linger when I share space with Ella. Usually it's something I resent, but today it's different. I'm so proud to be her sister even if she is way freaking cooler than me.

"Well, thank you." Ella hops up and goes to grab a second helping of flan. "Now that Maya sees I'm not going to totally embarrass her in front of her friends, hopefully she'll allow me around more often."

Delilah turns to me with comically large puppy dog eyes. "Please let her come back!" She clasps her hands in front of her chest, a pose that probably looks adorable coming from a five-year-old, but not as appealing from a thirty-something. "Let me lust over your sister in person again!"

"You're ridiculous." I roll my eyes and toss a wadded-up napkin at her, my accuracy surprising both of us when I hit her right between the eyes. "But Ella's welcome whenever she wants to be here."

Which, knowing Ella, could be for an entire year or never again.

"Well . . . not to change the subject or anything," Ella says, and the way she draws out her words and looks at me makes me immediately regret my open invitation. "But my big sister's birthday *is* coming up soon and I'm thinking we need to plan a banger of a party."

Oh no.

Definitely extended the invitation too soon.

"No, no." I wave her and, by proxy, everyone else off. "I don't really do birthdays. A banger is definitely not necessary."

"You don't *do* birthdays?" Ella repeats, her incredulous tone loud and clear. "I'm sorry, but aren't you the same person who used to call all the local radios and TV stations to get birthday shout-outs? Aren't you the same person who forced Mom and Dad to take us on a road trip to middle-of-nowhere Middle America to stay at an authentic farmhouse where I ended up getting a tick but wasn't allowed to complain because it was your birthday? Because I really wish this 'not a birthday person' was around before I had to get a tick head burned out of my leg."

"Whoa, whoa, whoa." I hold my hands up in front of my chest, feeling extremely attacked right now. "This feels very unnecessary. That barn house was adorable and I warned you not to lay in the hay. The tick was totally your fault. And also, we're allowed to evolve. Birthday parties are so ten years ago."

"Cough-bullshit-cough." Bailey doesn't even make the effort to do a fake cough sound, which is both lazy and rude.

"Ooooh!" Delilah giggles in the corner, taking way too much joy in what is now feeling like a targeted and planned attack. "Looks like Bailey has now entered the arena."

"You're all very annoying and I don't think I like any of you." I aim a very pointed glare at Ella, the traitor. "A Midwestern road trip is a far cry from a South Beach banger. Also, I'm turning thirty, and I don't know if I want to shout that to the world."

Don't get me wrong. I'm very happy to be getting older.

If I wasn't getting older I'd be dead, and I definitely don't want to be dead.

It's just that I had a plan for what my life would look like when I turned thirty and living alone, freshly dumped was not exactly the dream.

Shocking, I know.

"I'm just saying." Bailey tosses her long blond hair over her shoulder and takes a sip of the margarita she made herself. "Vaughn is a club promoter. This is the perfect opportunity to rub it in his face that you're thriving without him."

"Yes! Fuck Ralph, this makes it even better!" Ella grabs her phone and starts to frantically scroll and tap away at the screen. "Where does he work? How can we force your hotness onto his feed?"

You could say this is the moment I regretted not staying at work and just sleeping there, or you know, fleeing the country. Live and learn, I guess.

"I really think something small could be better? Like tonight. The four of us ordering in and having cocktails sounds perfect."

I may as well have not spoken at all because all three of these bitches ignore me.

"He's definitely worked with Cliffhanger and Victory," Bailey tells Ella. I watch in horror as the two of them lean together to—I assume—plot my demise.

I turn to Delilah. I know it's a long shot considering she already proposed marriage to Ella, but I have to try. "What about going to The Standard again? That was fun."

Delilah, my most levelheaded friend, has always been there for me. She might be the lead on a reality show who now wants to quit her job and travel the world, but my old friend is surely still in there somewhere. However, I quickly realize that might be wishful thinking when she turns to me and my last bits of hope die as my veins turn to ice. Her eyes are wide and her smile is three times larger than I've ever seen it before. She looks truly deranged.

"Oh no." I scoot away from her. "What did you do?"

"I don't know if you remember Paul, the host from *Real Love*? Well, he's the producer too, and even though you left them high and dry, he still really loves you," she explains, and it's somehow worse than I ever could've imagined. "They are casting the new season and he told me to let him know if I thought we could get you to commit this time around. And now that Vaughn's out of the picture, it couldn't be a better time."

The loud conversation Bailey and Ella were having comes to a sudden halt and silence fills my living room for the first time all night.

"I'm sorry," Bailey finally manages to say. "What?"

Delilah opens her mouth, but before she can repeat the terrible thing she's just told me, her phone rings.

"Holy shit!" she screeches, and shows us her phone with Paul's name lighting up the screen before putting it to her ear and leaping off the couch. "Hello? Yes! Paul, we were *just* talking about you . . ."

I try to go after her, because I am 1,000 percent not ready. Not at all. But she's in my room with the door locked before I even have a chance.

Okay then.

So I know I agreed to some change, but this is just getting ridiculous.

12

AFTER A NIGHT of drinking too much and unexpectedly announcing my breakup, all I wanted to do was sit around my apartment, drink more, and wallow in self-pity. Unfortunately, having my sister occupying my favorite spot on my couch put a major kink in that plan. So instead of sulking, I decided extra motivation would have to be the cure.

I woke up early, took some Advil with my coffee, and was the first to arrive at the office. This felt simultaneously like a huge win and a massive loss. Add Delilah already stopping by my desk twice to bring up *Real Love* and Ella texting me every five minutes to ask where something is, and I feel like I'm dangerously close to losing my mind.

I finish up the spreadsheet I've been working on and am beginning to text Ella after ignoring her for the last hour when a tap on my shoulder scares the crap out of me.

"Bailey! Fuck! Stop sneaking . . ." I spin around in my chair and promptly want to die when I don't see Bailey standing there, but Greg and Marcus, *my freaking bosses.*

Of course.

"Oh my goodness! I am so, so sorry!" I stand up and then sit down again and then start to stand, like the mortification has caused my brain to misfire and my body doesn't know how to function anymore. I stay standing this time because my knees are locked and I don't think I could sit again if I wanted to. "I didn't mean to say that or scream or . . . I'm so sorry, I was just startled."

Kill me now.

My face is so hot that I'm convinced if I were to touch my cheek I'd burn myself. A feeling that only grows when the quiet chuckles of my coworkers nearby penetrate my bubble of embarrassment.

"It's okay," Marcus says, amusement clear in his voice. "We're grown-ups, we've heard the word 'fuck' before. Plus, Bailey's running late today."

I'm sure he said this to make me feel better, but hearing the word out of his mouth just makes this so much worse.

But for real. Somebody please freaking kill me.

My inability to look them in the eye and stop fidgeting must clue Greg in to my total mortification, because he offers much less cringeworthy words of encouragement.

"You're fine, we're sorry for startling you." His apology begins to quiet my nerves. "But would you mind coming to Marcus's office with us?"

It's not a lesson I necessarily wanted to learn firsthand, but I now know for a fact that the fastest remedy for embarrassment is fear.

An invitation to the boss's office can't be good. I would say this reminds me of being called to the principal's office when I was a kid, but I was never called to the principal's office. I'm a rule follower. Remember? This is new, terrifying territory for me.

I nod and follow them through the maze of cubicles and bodies, racking my brain, every worst-case scenario running through my head. They're probably going to fire me for skipping work to play on a boat with my sister. Maybe I accidentally started daydreaming about lying in the sun, looking at eyes bluer than the ocean and I messed up an account or made a bad investment?

That totally could've happened.

It's inevitable in this profession to lose a shit ton (yes, that's the technical term) of money at one point or another. It comes with the territory. However, I'm really good at what I do and it's been a good while since I really blew it. Leave it to me to wait to mess things up right as the position I've been dreaming of is finally available.

Can anyone say self-sabotage?

Marcus holds the door to Greg's office open and gestures for me to enter first after what felt like the longest walk of my life. Since I'm an expert on passive-aggressive behavior, I obviously overanalyze whether they're being gentlemen or showing dominance. Then I realize that I'm not sure there's actually a difference between the two. Yay patriarchy.

I take a seat in the chair across from Greg's desk and barely manage to conceal my wince when the door snaps closed behind me. I'm definitely in trouble. You don't close the door unless it's something you don't want other people to hear . . . like a stern talking to. Or a firing.

My anxiety is so high I'm starting to feel light-headed.

I tuck my foot behind my ankle to stop it from incessantly tapping and clasp my hands on my lap, wincing when I realize my palms are already sweating profusely. I really need to get it together. Five minutes of stress shouldn't completely unravel me.

"So." Marcus sits back in his chair, his hazel eyes shining with kindness and probably sympathy. "How have things been for you lately?"

God.

Small talk.

Are they trying to torture me? Just get to the point already!

"Things have been good. My sister is visiting from out of

town, so that's been . . . interesting. We are adults, but she's still my little sister and sometimes I think it's her mission to piss me off." I hear the words coming out of my mouth and I know that I don't want more of them to come, but this is what happens when I'm stressed. It's word vomit in its truest form and I. Just. Can't. Stop. Talking. "But you probably don't want to know about that. Work is going well too, or at least I thought it was, but now I'm here, so maybe it's not? Delilah and I have been working on the accounts I took over for her while she was gone and I thought that was going well. And then you know about—"

My mouth keeps moving, but thankfully, Greg interrupts me.

"That all sounds . . . wonderful." Laughter is thick in his deep voice. "I'm sure it's nice to spend time with family and you and Delilah are doing a fantastic job. Have you been watching the show with her? This has been the only time my wife's been even the tiniest bit interested in my work. She says it's a great season."

"Your wife is right, it is really good this season."

If I had to take bets on the last conversation I would ever think to have with my boss, I think it would be this. At least he's not mentioning the fact that I was offered the lead.

And might be offered it again . . .

The thought that I've actively been trying to ignore barrels its way to the front of my mind at the most inconvenient time ever. I don't want to think about it. I should say no again. But since Delilah came back, she's been a different person . . . a *happier* person. Now, seeing how content she is, I can't stop thinking about the offer. If it worked for her, why couldn't it work for me too?

"There was a guy with chaps who was pretty funny," Marcus says, pulling me from my thoughts and shocking the living daylights out of me. He does *not* seem like a person who would watch *Real Love*. I'm learning the show has a much larger fan base than I originally assumed.

Greg looks at Marcus, shaking his head and finally letting his laughter free.

"Okay then," Greg says after he's composed himself. "Now that we got that out of our system, we wanted to talk to you about something . . ."

Like a well-polished song and dance team, Marcus picks up where Greg trails off. They're the finance equivalent of Broadway, and their conversation is so well rehearsed that I'm nearly expecting them to break out into a tap dancing number next. "We want you to know that we've noticed how hard you've worked since you started here. You're quiet, yet you efficiently and consistently bring in the highest numbers each month. Every client you've worked with has given you rave reviews, and you stepped in for Delilah when she left." He takes a long pause and looks to Greg for a beat. My anxiety skyrockets, knowing the but is coming, waiting for them to drop the bomb. "I'm sure you know that Suzanne's last day here is quickly approaching and we've been looking for her replacement."

My skin turns electric, every nerve ending buzzing like it's lined with bees. All thoughts of *Real Love*, Kai, Ella, and every other distraction that's plagued me recently fade into oblivion. I lost focus for a bit, but right now my life plan snaps back into my mind's eye sharper than ever. This is the moment I've been waiting for.

"We wanted to tell you that we've narrowed down our contenders to fill Suzanne's position to three people: Jackson, Leon, and—" He stops talking, channeling his best Ryan Seacrest impersonation and taking way too much joy in stringing me along. "You."

"Oh my god!" I jump out of the plush seat and run around the desk to hug them both, something I would normally never do . . . but who cares? I'm going to get my promotion! "Thank you so much! I promise, you will not regret this!"

"You know we haven't made the final decision yet, right?" Marcus says as he hugs me back.

"I know." I take a couple of steps back, moving out of their personal space. "But I'm confident I will prove I'm the right person for this job."

They look at each other again, and this time, without the fear present to distract me from the truth, I see it's not humor in their eyes, but a knowing. And that just lights the fire under me even more.

They know the job is mine too—and I can't wait to prove them right.

As soon as I step foot out of Marcus's office, the foggy haze I've been working under lately lifts. When I sit back down at my desk, I do so with an energy I haven't felt in years. The next few hours fly by and I'm opening a new browser on my computer when Delilah slides into my cubicle and hops onto my desk.

"So a little birdie told me something exciting," she whispers even though I'm pretty sure nobody is paying attention to us. "Should we head to lunch so we can discuss?"

I should say no. I should work straight through lunch and only get up to nod to Marcus and Greg, but I need to scream about this somewhere. Ella will lecture me about not loving what I do, Mom will tell me not to count my chickens before they hatch, and Bailey only wants to gossip about who knows what, so I decide to celebrate this moment with my friend.

Instead of answering, I close down my computer and grab my purse out of my drawer. "This calls for Cipriani, correct?"

"You read my mind."

*   *   *

"Can you even believe it?" She taps her glass of champagne against mine. "Out of everyone at the office, you're poised to edge out all of those men for this promotion."

She's right. This is a big deal for me as a woman, but it's an even bigger deal for me as a *Black* woman. There are so many unseen battles that Black women face every single day. Reaching this point feels like a miracle. I know I deserve it. I know I'm the best person for the job, but to have that acknowledged by two white men? It doesn't always happen.

"There's no way Jackson is going to get this over me." It's not that Jackson isn't good at his job, he is. I'm just better. Same goes for Leon. It's nothing personal, just the truth. "But I have to be honest, I always thought you'd be here with me."

"I know." Delilah's dark brown eyes soften, but not with remorse. "Who would've thought when we auditioned for *Real Love* it would lead us here?"

"Definitely not me." Talk about the understatement of the century.

It's almost impossible for my mind to drift back to the day I was offered the lead; it feels as surreal now as it did then. Speaking to Paul that day, I thought I knew exactly what I was saying no to, but sitting across from Delilah with my dream job within reach, I'm not so sure anymore. I thought once Delilah realized she was passed up for the position, regret would start to set in. Instead, she's sitting across from me, sipping on champagne like she doesn't have a care in the world.

"Me either." She sets her glass on the table and aims all of her attention at me. She always used to be so distracted, as if there was something more pressing on her mind. But now it's almost disconcerting how present she always is. "I thought I knew my path. I think it's the initial reason we connected so quickly; we both knew what we wanted and were determined to get it. But I'm so happy now that it makes me wonder if I ever really knew what I wanted."

"I guess that's the best part of life, you don't have to have it all figured out, and even when you think you do, you're allowed to change your mind."

Thank god Ella isn't around for this conversation. I can only imagine how she'd react to those words coming out of my mouth.

"Have you changed your mind? Because it seems like your fork in the road is repeating itself. I know I keep pestering you about the opportunity to do *Real Love* again, but I just really want you to genuinely think about it." She stops talking and aims a dazzling smile at our poor waiter as he sets her chicken salad in front of her. When he rounds the table to place my giant plate of gnocchi in front of me, I almost forget what we're talking about. I mean, gnocchi is like the pinnacle of carbs. Pasta made of potatoes? Yes, please.

"I haven't changed my mind." *Yet*, I think before shoveling a fork full of fluffy potato goodness into my mouth. "But I'd be lying if I said seeing you since you've gotten back hasn't forced me to open it."

"I guess that's all I can really hope for." She takes a sip of her champagne and looks at me over the rim of the glass. "I know that it seems like *Real Love* is very surface-level, dating-show crap, but I promise, it's so much more than that. I learned more about myself in those few months than I had in my entire life. It sounds cheesy, but disconnecting with the world allowed me to connect with myself."

That does sound cheesy, but I keep that to myself because it also sounds amazing. And I'm genuinely happy for my friend.

"Well, between my sister invading my house and breaking up with Vaughn, disconnecting does sound ideal. But no matter what happens, you have to promise not to ambush me on live TV ever again. That might've scarred me for life."

"I knew it!" she shouts, and slams her fist on the table. Her cheeks turn bright red when everyone at surrounding tables turns to look at us. "I told Bailey that I thought we should warn you at least a little bit. I kept trying to convince her to tell you as you were driving, but then I got pulled away by production and couldn't call you."

"I must have heard that wrong, but now that I know, thank you for attempting to give me a warning call."

I could've sworn Bailey told me that it was Delilah's idea to keep everything a secret, but the night was such a blur. Maybe I'm remembering wrong.

"Well, you don't need a warning for this." Delilah lifts her glass into the air before I can think back on my TV debut any longer. "To new beginnings and bold moves on whatever paths we may choose."

"Cheers to us." I tap my glass against hers, taking a small sip of the bubbly beverage.

As happy as I am for my friend for taking the leap into the unknown, I just don't know if I could do the same. I've worked so hard to follow The Plan, and with my promotion right around the corner, this isn't the time to deviate from it.

And I don't think anything or anyone could change my mind.

13

BETWEEN ELLA CANCELING her ticket back home to New York, Delilah constantly bringing up *Real Love*, and the pressure mounting at work to turn in a perfect performance, both my work life and my home life are total disasters. It's like the closer to thirty I get, the messier my life is. I've never ended a week feeling more exhausted. All I wanted to do was lock myself in my bedroom and sleep straight through the weekend.

Unfortunately for me, this was not a plan Ella agreed with.

When I got home from work last night, she informed me that she had made plans for us this weekend and I had no choice but to tag along or she would call Mom and convince her to come visit.

As far as threats go, that is the most terrifying one she could have come up with.

And since Ella is a notoriously late sleeper, I assumed that I'd still get to sleep in before this little adventure.

I was wrong.

"Where are you taking me? And can we please get coffee?"

The early morning sky dances with oranges and yellows as the sun rises. Even though I want to be in my bed admiring the three-hundred-dollar pillow I splurged on, I can't help but appreciate the beauty of a calm Miami morning.

"I tried to tell you to leave work early last night." Ella doesn't take her eyes off the road in front of her. Even though she hasn't had a car since she lived with our parents, she looks at ease behind the wheel. "You have no one to blame but yourself."

Because I still haven't been caffeinated, I don't attempt to hide the dramatic roll of my eyes.

"Cool, but can I blame myself while I'm holding a cup of coffee?"

She turns her head to level me with a glare. "For a person who wakes up early every day, you're very annoying in the mornings."

I reach over the center console and pinch her as hard as I can on the back of her arm. I don't know why. I guess I woke up today and chose violence.

"Ouch! What the hell? Do you want me to crash your precious car?" She rubs furiously at the underside of her arm. The only thing better than instant gratification is delayed revenge, and I take not-so-secret pleasure as I remember the way she pinched me when she first got here. "You can't pinch me when I'm driving!"

This is actually the brilliance in attacking her right now. She's so concerned about not crashing and killing us—thank god—that she's not going to fight back. This might be my only opportunity to beat her in a fight.

"I'm hangry for coffee. Cangry? Angfee? I don't know. Whatever the term would be, I'm that. I need caffeine."

She lets out a groan and sounds just like our mother. But while the pinch might've stung a bit, comparing her to Mom might be something she'd never forgive me for.

"Fine." She finally gives in and I can already feel my mood changing for the better. "But no chain coffee shops. Their unsafe coffee practices are destroying the world."

I can't tell if she's kidding or not, but I have a feeling she's serious, and I can't deal with an environmental lecture from the sometime vegetarian this early in the day.

"Fine by me. I try to shop local whenever I can." I want to tell her about my butcher, Joey, but again . . . sometimes vegetarian. I swipe open my phone and will technology to lead me to the closest small-business coffee shop. One that hopefully has breakfast burritos or pastelitos or better yet, both.

It's amazing what quality coffee and sugary breakfast treats can do for one's attitude. Even Ella pepped up by about a million percent when she bit into a cream-filled puff pastry that tasted like it came from the heavens.

Ella takes us down Highway 1, something I'd never heard of until she pulled onto the road. As we're driving, I see why she insisted on being behind the wheel. In the Midwest, our road trip scenery consisted of cornfields, cows, and the occasional hill. This? It's almost hard to put into words. It's like we're driving on water. The narrow road hovers just above the clear ocean. The sun that has now fully greeted us glistens brightly off the water like gems just out of reach. By the time the two-hour drive is over, I'm ready to turn around just to enjoy the view all over again . . . or at least I was until we drove down Main Street in Islamorada.

"How did you find out about this place?" I ask as I throw my purse across my body and put my sunglasses on.

"I don't know why you bother asking anymore." She unfolds out of the car and smooths some of the wrinkles from the long sundress she's wearing. "You know I'm not going to share my sources. But also, how have you lived in Miami this long and not explored anywhere?"

"I have explored," I straight-out lie to her face. "Delilah has taken me to some great little places only locals know about and Bailey is all about exploring." *We just happen to be on the hunt for the perfect happy hour and not cute coastal towns . . .*

Even though Ella has shown several bouts of wisdom during this trip, I'll probably always have a hard time admitting when she's right. The most exploring I've done since moving here is trying the restaurants on the way home from work and testing all the spas within a ten-mile radius. Work has consumed so much of my life I've forgotten that I need to actually live it.

"I spent one night with your friends and I already know you're completely full of shit."

"Whatever." I choose to ignore her so I don't add another lie to the long list of things that will be held against me when I die. "What's the plan today?"

"Do you not listen to anything I say?" She shakes her head and does the Mom sigh again. "The plan is that there is no plan. We're going to vibe. Do what feels right. I heard there are some good restaurants and lots of little shops. We're just going to walk around and live in the moment."

I look around to make sure nobody is close enough to hear her.

We're already two Black women in a small Florida town, Ella can't make her liberal, hippie nature even more well known. This town might look adorable, but if *Lovecraft Country* and Jordan Peele taught me anything, it's to stay alert.

"Okay," I say when I see we're alone. "Then why don't we start with the shops and then head to a little place for lunch when we get hungry?"

Her perfect smile—thanks completely to modern dentistry—shines a little brighter under the morning sun. "I love this for you."

"Love what for me?" I ask, confused by her nonanswer.

"This." She opens her arms wide and gestures around us. "You away from work, you going with the flow. We just got here and I swear, your energy is already so much different."

"You're such a weirdo, and please don't talk like that in front of people, you'll scare them."

"Somebody's deflecting!" she says in a singsongy voice behind me as I pick up my pace.

It's getting way too frequent, her being right.

I don't check my horoscope. I don't know what my enneagram number is. I have no idea where in the hell Mercury is or what it has to do with my electronics going wonky. But I do know that since Ella pulled onto that highway and I lost the signal on my phone (thanks a lot overpriced cell service), I've just felt . . . lighter. Like this load of bricks I didn't even know was resting on my shoulders has finally lifted. My breathing feels deeper. The ocean looks more vivid. Time seems to linger instead of rushing by in a flurry of anxiety and fear. I can exhale and breathe in this moment instead of rushing ahead to the next one.

My therapist once told me that anxiety was the antithesis of spontaneity, and the truth in those words has never been more apparent than it is right now.

It doesn't take long before Ella's long strides have caught up to mine. We chat about nothing and everything as we wander aimlessly, flowing in and out of stores, buying things we don't need but absolutely must have. And when we stumble into a bohemian courtyard, it's like my peak happiness is reached.

The sidewalks are made of wooden planks, and even though the ocean is still a few blocks away, sand fills the space between the abundance of greenery. Wooden benches and oversized dream catchers line the little shops of Islamorada that look more like cozy bungalows than retail spaces. It's so far from what I've come to know as Florida, and I can't believe all this was only a short drive away.

"Oh!" I grab Ella's arm and pull her when I see a cute little art gallery among the boutiques. "Let's go see what's in there. I've been thinking about adding more stuff to my apartment."

When I first moved in, I thought I wouldn't be there for too long. Just a pit stop before Vaughn and I were engaged and creating our life together. Aside from my furniture and some rugs I couldn't say no to, it's lacking any personality whatsoever. I say it's modern, but it's really just boring.

"Oh . . . this place? Yeah, let's go explore."

There's weird laughter in her voice that I don't understand, but I rarely understand Ella, so I brush it off.

When we walk in, the acoustic version of a popular rap song sets the tone of the space. Immediately I know this isn't your average art gallery that you'd find in any small Florida town. Paintings of Black women sitting in fields of flowers and laughing with friends that would just seem pretty if they were of white women feel inherently political. Black joy showcased on canvas instead of trauma. Bold prints with bright colors and powerful designs cover the walls, and they each catch my eye. But it's the blown glass scattered around the modest space that really calls to me.

I've seen the little glass flower tchotchkes in gift shops in hospitals and airports, and honestly, when I think of glasswork, it reminds me of the vases my grandma used to have in her house. But these pieces? These are whimsical and *fun*. They seem indestructible yet infinitely delicate. As ridiculous as it should be, my favorite one is a beautiful cake stand with a glass apple pie on top of it. Maybe it's a stretch and I'm being one of those ridiculous people making something out of nothing, but it feels like a joke. Like the artist is poking fun at the perception of what perfect Americana is supposed to be. A beautiful pie that not only can't be eaten, but will shatter if you even try. Just like the lives of people trying to portray perfection. Apply pressure and it will crack.

I look around the glass for something telling me how much my new favorite piece of art costs, but there are no prices anywhere. Which, if experience has taught me anything, doesn't mean good things for my bank account.

"Excuse me," I call to the saleswoman who earlier introduced herself as Ruby and then—to my complete pleasure—left us alone to browse. "How much is this?"

"The pie?" Ella laughs. "You want to bring the pie into your ultramodern apartment?"

"Shut up," I hiss as Ruby walks toward us with her supercute nose ring and bright pink pixie cut.

Thankfully, if she hears our bickering, she pretends she doesn't. She looks at the pie I'm interested in and a smile makes her already kind face even kinder. "Oh my god, I love this one!" She practically claps, and I get an unexpected burst of pleasure knowing my taste has impressed someone who surely must know art. "We have local artists display their pieces in the gallery on weekends, so I'm not exactly sure what the price is." She must see the disappointment on my face, because she rushes on. "But this artist just stepped out and should be back soon, so you can ask them then."

"Great, then I'll just keep looking around if that's okay."

"Knock yourself out," Ruby says. "But if you like this one, we have a space upstairs with some more pieces I think you'll really enjoy if you want to check them out."

I didn't realize there was more space to explore when we walked in. As she guides me to what feels like a hidden corridor, I feel even more special. This place feels like a magical art wonderland.

"Ella," I call from the back corner when I realize she isn't following us. "Are you coming?"

"I'll be up in a second, I'm just going to step out and make a quick phone call."

I give her a thumbs-up—which I regret immediately—and trek up the narrow and creaky staircase to the top floor.

Unlike the main room that smells like an essential oil diffuser that hasn't ever been turned off, this space has the distinct musty smell of an old book. The sconces lighting the staircase illuminate the particles of dust floating around me as I disrupt them from where they're lying on the wooden steps beneath me. The door at the top of the stairs seems old and in need of a good sanding and paint job. As I approach it, I lose faith that I'll find anything good up here—it's not exactly a customer-ready space. When I push through the door, I'm prepared for a continuation of this space—old and dark, where the art must go to die.

But instead I'm hit with sunlight as bright as if I stepped outside. Unlike the typical modern art gallery downstairs, this matches the free spirit vibe of the bohemian courtyard outside. Patterned rugs overlap one another, only letting glimpses of the tattered wooden floors beneath them peek through. Plants hang from the ceiling along with lanterns providing even more lighting than the window-lined wall at the back of the room. What I assume are oil paintings hang on the walls behind colorful dressers with their drawers pulled out and filled with handcrafted jewelry. Low tables are surrounded by poufs and pillows in different jewel tones. Some tables are topped with glass lanterns, while others are covered with glass vases that at first seem to be separate, but at second glance are so dependent on the others they could never stand alone.

It's the complete opposite of any place I've ever lived or even imagined myself living, but—and maybe I've just been around Ella too much lately—it feels like the first space I've ever been *meant* to be in. The rich tones and deep, earthy scents of cedarwood and spice call to a part of my soul that I never even knew existed.

And it scares the absolute shit out of me.

I can't let myself start to slip into this fantasy world Ella lives in, not now that my dream is closer than ever. Despite what Ella thinks, I know what I'm meant for. I'm meant for a high-powered job in finance in a big urban city, not some little hippie hideaway like this. I fight back against my desire to linger, to break the rules I so vigorously follow, and to touch all of the art here that speaks to me. I ignore the velvet pillows I want to settle on and resist the urge to breathe in this space a little longer, and instead pull open the door and quickly rush down the stairs.

But as soon as I enter the modern gallery, I realize that upstairs in my secret fantasy world was a much safer space than this.

Because right next to the pie, the saleswoman is having a very animated conversation with Ella and the person I'm assuming is the artist.

And it's Kai.

Of fucking course it is.

14

I'M GOING TO kill Ella.

You know I'm not going to share my sources.

The conniving little sneak.

It just really sucks that I'm going to have to murder her just as I was beginning to enjoy her company.

I'm not sure if the floors creak or if I gasp, but three sets of eyes spin to face me at the same time. Ella looks amused, Ruby looks thrilled, and Kai . . . well, I can't look at Kai for long enough to decipher the soft look in his eyes or the crooked smile tugging at his lips.

Just seeing him again causes my body to react. My lips begin to tingle and it's as if every single piece of me is begging for more.

Freaking Ella.

"Did you find anything you liked upstairs?" Ruby asks, the sweet, unsuspecting woman having no idea that tensions are rapidly rising inside the gallery.

"It was all beautiful." I tell her the truth and her eyes light up. Part of me wants to skip back up those stairs, fall into my bohemian fantasy, and buy every single piece that makes my heart sing. And not just to escape from being around Ella and Kai either. "It just wasn't really for me."

I soften my voice as I tell this lie and I don't know if I'm saying it for her or for me.

Ever since Ella got here, I've been lying all the damn time. Whether it's a lie of omission or just straight-out false, I haven't felt any real guilt over it. But for some reason, this feels different. This feels like I'm intentionally shutting down a part of me that I just discovered has been yearning to be freed. This feels like I'm betraying myself more than anyone else.

"That's too bad." She sounds as sad as I do before her entire face brightens as she remembers something. "Oh! And the artist for the glass pie you loved is back, but I think you already knew that."

She winks at me, and on anyone else it would've looked totally dorky, but with her pink hair and nose ring, it was supremely cool. And also mortifying, because now I know without a doubt that Ella said something embarrassing before I came back.

I try to give her my best smile as a response, but I'm about 99 percent sure it just looks like a grimace.

"Kai." I nod my head and try to beat back the traitorous fucking butterflies that infiltrate my stomach when I mention his name. My palms itch to touch his hair that looks like it's grown since I last saw him. "Nice to see you again."

"It's been too long," he says, and I couldn't agree more. "I've been harassing Ella to give me your number, but she refused. Said it broke sister code and that I'd have to get you to give it to me yourself."

Ella sticks out her tongue at me like this somehow negates the fact that she drove me two hours away from home to ambush me with his presence.

"It's nice to hear that she at least has *some* boundaries." I want to stay where I'm standing . . . or better yet, be a couple of blocks away in my car. Being around Kai is dangerous, because there's a disconnect that happens between my body and my brain when I'm near him. It's like I'm incapable of thinking, I can only feel. I slowly close the space between us until my shoulder is nearly grazing his arm and we're both looking at the glass pie I still viscerally need. "You left out that you were an artist when we were on the boat."

"It's a yacht, not a boat," Ella cuts in, because God forbid she ever stays quiet. "There's a difference."

Ruby must see my face and realize that Ella is putting her commission in jeopardy because she moves lightning fast.

"Why don't I show you the upstairs space?" She loops her arm through Ella's, quickly and effectively removing her from me and Kai.

Hmmmm . . . Maybe I should've asked Mom and Dad to have a third kid so they could've run interference on Ella and I our entire lives.

Kai's raspy chuckle pulls me back into the moment. "She's a nut."

I glance away from the corner Ella disappeared into and look up at Kai, laughing with him. "Understatement of the century."

The relief I felt at Ella's temporary removal disappears as soon as I realize that not only am I alone with Kai, but that I was also too distracted to remember to keep my guard up. And now that I've made the mistake, it's too late to do anything about it.

Seeing him across the room was one thing.

As long as I didn't look into his eyes, I'd be fine. I could close the space between us and savor the closeness as his T-shirt brushed across my bare arm. It'd be like pulling from an unlit cigarette. I'd get the fix without the damage.

But now that I'm inches away from the lips I've been craving and staring into the blue eyes that have undressed me in my dreams almost every night since I met him, I can't look away. I can't separate what was a dream from what was reality or why they can't be one and the same.

I should've run.

I should've just said no like the D.A.R.E. officers taught me in school. I just wasn't prepared for this. They didn't know anything was as addictive as the man standing beside me.

"So . . ." I squeeze my eyes shut to try to clear my head. "Why didn't you mention you were an artist?"

"You didn't really ask." He shrugs.

"Do people normally ask if you have a glassblowing hobby?" I know I'm not the most skilled person at small talk, but even I know that's not a common question.

"It doesn't always come up in everyday conversation." His dimpled smile pulls at the corner of his lips. "I was so busy learning about the many dolphin atrocities that it must have slipped my mind."

The teasing tone in his voice makes me laugh, and as seems to be the norm when I'm around him, my body reacts before I can think about it. My hand reaches up and lightly shoves his—very firm—bicep. "Shut up!"

I want to hate being around Kai. I want to feel awkward and uncomfortable. I don't want to love the way it feels to laugh and joke with him. I don't want my laughter to come so easily and naturally. I don't want to remember how much I've missed this feeling. It's a wonderful, terrible distraction from the steps I know I *should* be taking to get The Plan for my life back on track.

The playful dynamic Vaughn and I had when we first started dating faded away years ago. The fun and easy relationship that drew us together lessened with every bump we hit until we were just fighting to stay on the road.

And I've worked so hard to course correct and make him happy that I forgot what something truly easy and natural felt like.

I thought I just wanted the spark back when in reality, I wanted *this*.

So I let myself indulge in this moment. I let my hand rest on his arm for seconds longer than I should. I savor the fuzzy giddiness that I feel when I'm around him. I don't question the way my heart races when he reaches up and our fingers interlock.

Hand holding seems so innocent, something you do with your elementary school crush. Between social media, apps, and television shows, everything feels like it needs to be overtly sexual, and small moments like this seem obsolete. I mean, I couldn't even tell you the last time Vaughn only wanted to hold my hand. Maybe that's why this small thing feels so big. The pureness of this moment. It's quiet and tender. And it's like his touch has awoken every nerve in my entire body.

Kai's hands feel so different than what I'm used to. His fingers are long and his skin is soft. Vaughn's grip always felt tight and demanding, but somehow, Kai's gentle embrace feels more secure . . . solid.

There's a rightness between us that I can't deny.

That I *won't* deny.

So instead of holding back and talking myself out of what I really want, I don't stop myself from rolling on my tiptoes and touching my mouth to his when I look into his ocean-blue eyes.

Vaughn who?

"I really like you," he whispers against my mouth, his fingers flexing with mine.

No games. No chasing. No bullshit.

"I really like you too," I whisper back. "And I like your pie."

"The pie?" He smiles, and for the first time, I think we both remember where we are.

I pull away and regret it instantly, but even though Ella would be beyond delighted to catch us kissing, I can't give her the satisfaction. Not yet, at least.

"It's really beautiful and my apartment is woefully underdecorated." I try to focus on my breathing . . . and on remembering what words are and how to use them. "I've spent the last two years telling Ella it was an intentional design choice, but now I'm obsessed with a glassblown cake stand and pie. I'm pretty sure she thinks I'm having a midlife crisis."

"You're not old enough to have a midlife crisis. Maybe you're having a quarter-life awakening," he says with not one ounce of irony in his voice.

If Ella told me I was experiencing an awakening, I would mock her endlessly. But for some reason I let the idea sink in when Kai says it. Maybe it's because his thumb is drawing circles across the back of my hand as he says it . . .

"An awakening?" I test the word, seeing how it feels. "I kind of like the idea of that."

The incoming sound of high heels clicking against the floor alerts us to incoming company. I step away from him, but even though I probably should, I can't let go of his hand just yet.

"Hi!" Ruby barges back into the gallery with a frazzled look on her face. She doesn't even notice our interlocked fingers. "So I just got off the phone with Melissa and I have good news—she told me four of your pieces have sold through the online listing she sent out over the week."

"Oh my god! That's amazing, Kai!" I didn't know I could

be this excited about art, but here we are and I'm into it. "Congratulations!"

"Thanks, Maya." He looks down at me, and even though it's not his dimple-popping smile, I get the distinct feeling that it's not a look he gives many people . . . and for that reason I think I like this one a whole lot more.

Like . . . loads more.

I wonder if this is how he'd look at me if we woke up next to each other.

"There's just one thing . . ." Ruby reminds me that she's still in the room with us. "One of the things that sold is the pie."

"Oh." I look away from Kai, trying not to let the disappointment over a material object I never even owned show, but failing miserably.

"I'm so sorry." Ruby sounds more upset than me, and I have a sneaking suspicion Melissa just got a huge commission. "Maybe a painting or something else has also called to you?"

I look around, and even though everything in here is cool and would look great pretty much anywhere, I really had my heart set on that damn pie . . .

And even more so on its creator.

Maybe I should go back upstairs and look around?

I shut that thought down just as fast as it comes. If I go up there right now, after the way Kai has made me feel, I'll be buying the place out.

"No, not today." I can see the disappointment on her face, and even though I know I don't owe her anything, I still feel really guilty. "But can I give you my number so if anything good comes in, I can get on whatever list the people who bought my pie were on? I could really use an art curator. All of my walls are bare and it's starting to get depressing."

I'm pretty sure Ruby thinks I'm joking and I'm too embarrassed to tell her I'm not, so I laugh along with her. Her eyes light up and her bright smile covers her face again. Thank freaking god. Because if it didn't, there's a good chance I would've just spent five hundred dollars on art I didn't truly love just to make her feel better.

"I would love that!" She claps and bounces on her toes. "You'll be my first personal client! Let me go grab the client book and get your information."

"Really? I feel so special!" I know I might sound sarcastic, but I'm being dead-ass serious. Plus, because this will be my first time buying art, it makes me feel like we're on more even ground knowing this will be a first for her as well.

She doesn't respond before she runs out of the gallery space, the click of her heels overpowering the acoustic hip-hop still floating around us.

"Soooo . . ." I turn to Kai, happy to be alone with him again. "How much money did I just save?"

"I mean, I would've given you a friends-and-family deal." I love the feel of his hand tightening on mine as he avoids answering my question.

"I wouldn't have taken it, so stop avoiding the question." I don't feel my feet moving, but before I know it, my chest is brushing against the abs I know are lurking beneath his shirt. "How much?"

Color rises in his face, and it's such a stark contrast to Vaughn that it almost takes my breath away. Vaughn is so confident—bordering on cocky—with everything he does. I can't give him a compliment he hasn't already given himself and I can never do anything as good as him—ever. It's not that I want to have to validate the people around me, but for some reason, Kai's bashfulness makes him impossibly more attractive.

"Eight." His voice is so quiet, I almost don't hear him. But I do.

"Eight hundred dollars!" I do *not* whisper. "Good for you! Why do you sound embarrassed about that?"

"Fuck capitalism," Ella says as she enters the room. "That's why."

The lusty little love bubble I've been floating in with Kai, holding hands and innocently brushing against him, bursts as soon as I hear Ella. I let go of his hand and put more space than I want between the two of us.

"Down with the man!" Kai says to Ella, but never looks away from me.

I try to shake the feeling that I'm a teenager who just got caught sneaking a boy into my room. Thankfully, since Ella is actually incapable of not saying whatever's on her mind, I can assume that means she didn't notice the hand holding. Or maybe she did notice but didn't think anything of it because we aren't seven and running around on the playground.

"Aren't you the man in this case?" I struggle to keep my tone nonchalant as I look between the hot pair.

"He's the man, but he's not *the man*," Ella says, trying to clarify while failing to clarify anything.

"That made zero sense and now I'm more confused." I roll my eyes and now I'm the person sighing like our mom.

"Kai's a small artist," Ella explains in terms I can follow. "A small artist can't be the man. He just has to stick it to him. Which Kai does by selling them art that mocks them and doing it for exorbitant prices."

I hate that I understood that. But I also hate that I think she might've just insulted me. I might have to pack her up and send her home if this continues. "So am I the man in this conversation?"

"You're a Black woman." Ella rolls her eyes, but doesn't expand further.

"So I'm not the man?" I ask one more time, needing confirmation.

"It's fucking impossible for you to be the man in this country," she says. "And you know I still think you should leave that soul-sucking job you pretend to love——"

"It's not——" I try to object because I do not want to have this conversation again. But in true Ella fashion, she ignores me and continues speaking.

"But you being so good at a job that has been reserved for cis white men is also sticking it to the man. In a country built on white supremacy, Black excellence is inherently political."

I open my mouth to respond but no words come out.

I've never thought about it that way. I know I've had to work harder to succeed. I know there are fights I've had to battle in private that my coworkers have never even considered. But I've never thought of my success and happiness as a radical statement on anything other than myself. Hearing Ella put it that way, I can't decide if her words have alleviated some of the pressure I've put on myself or added to it.

Thankfully, before I have to admit any of that to Ella, Ruby's chaotic energy bounds back into the room, the now-familiar *click-clack* sound of her heels gives her away.

"I'm back!" she needlessly shouts, the echo of her voice bouncing off every hard surface in the small gallery space. She's hugging a notebook tight in her toned arms as she barrels toward us.

"Are you getting the pie?" Ella asks the innocent question, not knowing what a sore spot it is for me.

"No," I grumble, not bothering to mask my disappointment anymore. "Someone else bought it already."

"Damn, that sucks," Ella says, stating the obvious. "But maybe, since you have an in with the artist, he can figure something out for you."

I want to do a lot with the artist, and as much as I loved the pie, talking about this is not the first thing on my list.

"Yeah," says Kai. Poor guy, being around Ella and me isn't a relaxing day at the beach by any stretch of the imagination, and now he's done it twice. "The artist thinks he could figure something out."

"Ummm . . ." I purse my lips and tilt my head to the side. "Does the artist talk about himself in third person often? Because if so, that might change my mind about some things . . ."

And hopefully cut back on the naughty dream appearances . . .

"No, he . . . I mean, I don't." The color rises in his cheeks again.

"I know Kai tends to take a lot of time and care with his pieces, so I'll make sure I keep you up-to-date on what we have coming in," Ruby cuts in, probably worried about getting axed from this deal too. Poor lady. She hands me what I thought was a notebook but instead is a very thick art catalog branded with the store's name and colors. "I brought you this. If you want to go home and flip through it, let me know what stands out to you so I'll be able to have a more accurate idea of your taste."

"Oh, thank you." I try to keep my tone even and measured because I'm not sure what it says about the sad status of my life to be this excited over a catalog. I do know that Ella would take the opportunity to tell me it's a sign of how much I hate my life though. And I've had enough of that in these last few weeks to last for a lifetime.

"You're so welcome." Ruby's white teeth beam against her lips, which are painted the same color pink as her hair. "I put my card inside so you'll have my email address, but if it gets misplaced, my email is listed on our website."

"Wonderful." I take the catalog from her and tuck it beneath my arm. "Thank you so much for all of your help today. I can't even tell you how much I'm looking forward to working with you."

"The feeling is mutual." She turns to Ella and Kai. "It was nice meeting you as well, Ella. And, Kai, call me later so I can confirm your payment information for the pieces that sold."

"Got you." He nods and I notice for the first time the way her skin blushes when he looks at her.

Good to know I'm not the only one who can't seem to control herself when they're in his general proximity. I feel like there should be a law that people as good-looking as he is shouldn't be allowed to just wander around publicly. There should be a hot-person tornado warning or something. We deserve a chance to seek shelter before being hit with their hot storm.

"Okay!" Ella positions herself between Kai and me, looping her arms through ours so we look as if we're about to skip down a yellow brick road. "Who's hungry?"

"I could eat." Kai leans forward, answering Ella's question but only looking at me.

It's a gesture she couldn't—and doesn't—miss if she tried. But in the most un-Ella way ever, she just smiles, but says nothing. And instead of relief, pure panic coils down my spine. Because if Ella is on board, I don't stand a freaking chance.

And worst of all, I think I'm okay with that.

UNREALISTICALLY UNCHECKED

I know they say every season of *Real Love* is the best season, but Lovers, this time they might be right. I don't think we've ever had a lead like Delilah before. She knows what she wants and she's unapologetic in going after it. She is exploring all of her options, and even though my sources are telling me the producers weren't thrilled with her approach at first, they now see that she's changing the show for the better.

So far, Delilah has eliminated fifteen suitors. Some were surprising—we miss you Silas, please never stop posting shirtless pictures on the gram!—and some were expected. I mean, did we really expect chaps guy to be there until the end? Absolutely not. While a few underdogs are really trying to fight for Delilah's heart, it's clear that the contest is between Drew and Anthony.

My inside source says that Delilah is being tight-lipped about the winner. Not even close friends know who wins her heart. They also told us that even though Drew does seem like the safer, smarter pick, Delilah is thinking about some major life moves, so it could be anybody's game—and Drew does seem to be fading into the back of Delilah's mind lately, despite being an early front-runner. Next week, Delilah will be bringing the men to Miami to show them around her city. I've heard rumors that one of the contestants doesn't even last until the elimination. The competition is starting to get real for everyone involved and we just hope that Delilah follows her heart and picks the right person for her.

In other news, casting for the new season has started and some of the rumors are verging on unbelievable. I'll report once I've confirmed!

XOXO,
Stacy

15

UNBEKNOWNST TO MY beautiful, meddling sister, Kai and I exchanged phone numbers when she excused herself from the table that day after the art gallery and we've been texting and talking on the phone every day since.

Though I was initially worried that my attraction to him had more to do with getting back at Vaughn, all of my doubts have since vanished. I honestly haven't thought about Vaughn in ages and I don't know if it's related, but I haven't felt this happy in years. I don't think I realized how genuinely stressful our relationship was. Not having to worry about if he's with another woman or if I'm enough for him has lifted a weight I didn't know I was carrying.

Now I'm light and breezy and I can't stop checking my phone. It's the only thing keeping me from freaking out about the completely over-the-top party that Delilah, Bailey, and Ella are planning for my birthday.

I've forced Kai to send me approximately five thousand pictures of the glass he's blown, the food he's cooked, and the travels he's been on. He's asked me to send pictures in return, but the killer spreadsheets I create and Iowa selfies just aren't nearly as exciting.

I've always known I wasn't leading the most thrilling life, but it's become abundantly clear that I'm just flat-out boring. As far as self-realizations go, it's a pretty sad one. I'm almost thirty and I need something in my life other than work. And now, thanks to the magic of the internet, I found a local art studio that offers classes for adults.

Usually I spend a solid week overanalyzing everything I'm considering to make the best, most informed decision possible before I commit to anything. But I guess Ella really is rubbing off on me because I signed up for the class right away. She would be proud of me if she knew, but I haven't told her because I know she'd want to come with me. And where Ella is all creativity and feelings, I am . . . not. I kind of want this class to be just for me.

At one point my mom thought I might be colorblind because the art I brought home from school was so bad. That was embarrassing when I was ten, and at twenty-nine I don't need my loud-ass sister to witness this embarrassment.

I walk into the building ten minutes before my class is scheduled to start. Some people are standing around, chatting enthusiastically about the pieces they're creating, while others head to the door, quietly nodding their goodbyes to one another. Little kids sprint down the hallway, shouting at their parents to keep up. The mix of different ages, ethnicities, and genders reassures me that talent also must be diversified. I might not be good, but I doubt I'll be alone.

I check in at the front desk and the older woman with a sharp gray bob and a kind smile points me toward the room my sculpting class is located in. She tells me where I can find aprons and to sit wherever calls to me. Obviously, the only place "calling" to me is the far back corner. The fewer witnesses to this clay massacre, the better.

I pull my phone out of my purse and take a picture of my workspace to send to Kai.

Finally going to have something art adjacent to send to you. It will probably be closer to trash adjacent, but I'm trying! Will need generous applause and encouragement. Thank you in advance. 😋

I wait for him to respond, but when no bubbles pop up immediately, I open Instagram and scroll mindlessly until class begins. I don't go on the app often, so when I do, it's like a gold mine of ridiculousness, free entertainment, and food videos that almost convince me to cook instead of ordering out. As time ticks by, I don't know why I do it, but I search Delilah's name.

Even though I still have (almost) no interest in joining *Real Love*, I can't help but be curious about what it could be like if I did decide to say yes. Delilah's out of town again and it seems like she's gone more than she's home. I don't love airports or airplanes, so this adds to my reasons *Real Love* is not for me. But then I look at her pictures of her out and about in LA and New York and I waver.

I watch her stories. Little clips of this new glamorous life of hers flash by in fifteen-second intervals. There are videos of her getting her hair and makeup done, still photos of her with entertainment reporters that even I recognize. Her feed is covered in boomerangs of her sipping martinis and photos of her smiling huge at someone just off camera. I was right, she's never looked happier. I didn't think I wanted it, but now I'm not so sure. What would it feel like to live as if I had no worries? Could I have a version of myself where my mom's approval wasn't even a blip on my radar? Where my skin glowed and smile gleamed?

Thankfully for me though, before I'm able to tumble too far down that rabbit hole, an older woman wearing mustard-yellow gaucho pants with a rainbow-patterned sweater walks in and grabs the attention of everyone in the room. She has bright red lipstick on lips that—if the lines surrounding her mouth are anything to go by—are always curved up. Her long blond and gray-streaked hair is pulled into pigtails with blunt bangs covering part of her forehead. She's every art teacher stereotype rolled into one, and it's glorious!

"Hello, I'm Sue." She stops next to my desk area and extends her hand. Her fingers are devoid of any jewelry and her nails are caked in clay, but when I put my hand in hers, I'm pleasantly surprised by how soft her skin is.

"Hi, Sue, I'm Maya." I smile wide as I return her handshake. All of the nervous energy I've felt since signing up transforms into pure excitement.

"Beautiful name." She releases my hand and takes a step back, returning some of the personal space I didn't notice she'd entered. "I saw you on the list of students; it's lovely to place a face to the name. Is this your first time sculpting?"

"Very first. I do have to warn you though . . ." I pause, cringing a little as I think to past "art" projects of mine. "I'm not the most artistically gifted person in the world. So please be patient with me."

She narrows her eyes and her hands go straight to her hips. "Nonsense! There is no such thing as good and bad art. There's just art that we've put our hearts into and art that we haven't. I'm going to teach you how to create with your heart."

"I think I love you." My eyes bug out of my head and I slap my hand over my mouth, mortified that I just spoke those words out loud.

I really need to get away from Ella.

But instead of kicking me out of the class and immediately inquiring about a restraining order, Sue throws her head back and begins to laugh.

"I think I love you too," she says when she's managed to stop laughing. "This is going to be a fun session."

She winks at me before walking away and calling out to a person sitting across the room.

I tuck my phone back into my purse and instead focus my attention on the supplies set out in front of me.

Sure, no matter what Sue thinks, I will probably still suck at this. But at least I'm branching out and trying something new. And how badly could that really go?

I think I might be the first student to convince Sue that leading with the heart is not enough.

The "face" in front of me looks more like an abstract rendition of Mount Rushmore . . . before we stole Native land and eventually desecrated it in the name of patriotism. I know what I want to create, but there must be some serious misfiring between my brain and my hands because, woof, it's bad.

The door opens behind me and a group of children wearing plastic-coated aprons covered in paint begin to file into the room.

"Little Picassos!" Sue shouts in a way that even though it's my first time hearing the phrase, I know she uses it frequently.

"Hi, Ms. Sue!" tiny voices call back warmly. Giggles and the sound of small feet running on the tiled floor fill the room.

I ignore the hopeless slop of clay in front of me and watch as they pile onto Sue, wrapping their dirty little fingers around her legs. Sue, who has smiled the entire class, even while lying straight to my face about my "art," smiles impossibly brighter.

"Excuse me," a child says. "Did you make that?"

The young girl has a bow roughly the size of her head clipped to the top of her curly ponytail. Her brown cheeks are flushed pink, the glow that only comes with youth sparkling along in her eyes as she aims her huge grin showcasing a missing front tooth at my blob of clay.

Geeez.

Even she can tell I missed the mark here.

"I did." My voice goes up a few decibels, the way one does when talking to a small child. "It's my first class and I don't know if I'm very good at this."

She looks up from my disaster piece, her brow furrowed and confusion written all over her face. "Why not? I think it looks like a superhero."

I tilt my head and squint, trying to see what this little motivator next to me sees.

"See, there's the cape." She points her tiny finger at what she sees. "And there's her hair, and that's the smile, so I know she saved the world."

I follow along, viewing my work through her sweet, innocent eyes and letting her excitement change my perspective.

"Come on." She grabs my hand when I don't respond fast enough. Her grip is surprisingly strong for such a small human as she pulls me out of the room. "Mr. K has glitter that will make it even more better!"

I resist the urge to correct her grammar because even I'm not that big of an asshole and instead trail behind her as she pulls me through the hallway. She tells me all about her favorite colors and the "super special" glitter that will be perfect for my unintentional superhero.

"Ms. Sue taught me this summer and she said that glitter makes everything better." I'm not sure if she's taken a breath since she started talking. "And she's right because my mommy said that glitter is forever and ever and will never leave our house no matter what."

The pride in her voice makes me think she didn't quite understand what her mom was really saying about the glitter, but I don't burst her adorable little bubble.

"So now I put glitter on all my art. Mr. K taught me how to make a necklace with a heart made of glitter. I can show you." She pushes into the room, never easing her grip on my hand. I only vaguely wonder if I should warn her mom that she might need to work on the stranger danger talk. "Mr. K! Can my new friend have glitter for Ms. Sue's class? She made a superhero that needs sparkle."

I don't know if I should be entertained or slightly embarrassed by my new little friend's investment in my sculpture . . . and I never find out.

"Maya?" The same voice I've been unable to avoid in my dreams—and apparently reality—pulls my attention away from the curly haired girl guiding me farther into the room.

"Kai? Wh-what are you doing here?"

Okay, so I can't lie. When I looked up art classes, I searched for glassblowing classes first. I only decided against them because I thought the chances of running into him would be too high and there would be no way to deny that I was being a total stalker. I assumed sculpting would be safe territory.

"I work here," he says, stating the obvious.

I guess I thought wrong.

My new friend is watching us closely, her eyes following our sparse conversation like a Ping-Pong ball.

"But you do glassblowing . . . this isn't glassblowing." I also state the obvious and it's not lost on me that in moments like this, it's a small miracle I've been able to achieve any levels of success at all with my conversational skills.

"You're right." He glances down at the little girl standing very quietly by my side. I'm sure he thinks this is a very elaborate setup. "But I do seem to recall telling you that since I sell my art, I had to find other creative outlets." He says it with a tease in his voice and looks down at her with the most beautiful smile I've ever seen, and I'm pretty sure my ovaries shimmy. "Working with kiddos like Sofia here makes it even more rewarding."

When he says her name, I realize I hadn't asked her that yet. Even my social skills with children could use work. That's not saying much for me.

Sofia's already round eyes double in size and her mouth falls open. "You get a reward for teaching us? Like treasure? Stickers?"

I bite back my laughter, loving that she sounds equally excited for both treasure and stickers.

"Not that kind of reward." Kai's bright blue eyes wrinkle in the corner and his dimples pop out. "Seeing all the art you make and getting to help is the reward."

"That's not a reward." Sofia's shoulders slump and her bottom lip sticks out. "A lollipop could be a reward."

"She's not wrong," I tell him, suddenly thinking I need to stop at the gas station on the way home for a blow pop. And then my cheeks must flush scarlet because my mind— *very rudely*—drifts off to other things I could suck on . . .

"So where's this magic glitter?" I shout, and even though sweet Sofia probably thinks I'm just very excited about sparkle, I'm worried Kai can read the dirty thoughts floating around in my brain. If I would've known I'd be seeing him so soon, I would've rethought sending him a few more-than-flirty texts last night.

Go to art class, I said. It will be fun, I told myself.
Lies.

"Oh! It's back here!" Sofia has lost all interest in whatever was happening between Kai and me. She takes hold of my wrist and yanks me to the side wall covered with cabinets and very organized shelves.

Kai follows us over, not saying a word as Sofia grabs a little stool and climbs up until she's eye level with more glitter than I have ever seen. Even as an adult with a slight aversion to glitter, I'm excited. I mean, is it possible to be in the vicinity of this much sparkle and not be happy? Don't think so.

"Mr. K." She glances over her shoulder and my stomach drops to my shoes with images of my young friend tumbling backward off the stool. "Where is the special mix that I like to use?"

"Let me see." Kai moves to the shelves and his hand lightly brushes the small of my back as he squeezes past me.

I'm sure I've been touched more by strangers trying to get past me in the produce section of the grocery store. But right now, from that almost nonexistent touch, my arms are covered in goosebumps and chills waltz up and down my spine. I lean into the cabinet behind me, worried that my legs might actually give out from how tightly clenched my thighs are.

This is why I shouldn't be allowed in public . . . or around hot people. My body doesn't know how to act.

Kai moves around a few bottles of glitter and rhinestones until he unearths a silver tin labeled Sofia's Mix in the far back corner. "Here we go."

I know she's only a small child, but part of me wonders the power she wields to have her own can of glitter here. My respect for this little firecracker skyrockets. It's not lost on me that she will rule the world one day.

"Thank you!" Her already high-pitched voice rises more than a few decibels as she hops off the stool and runs to what I assume is her work space. She sits in her tiny seat that maybe half of my ass could fit on and pulls off the lid, staring at the glitter like it is actual gold shavings.

"I wish anything made me as excited as glitter makes her," I whisper to Kai, not wanting to disturb Sofia's moment.

"This is the reward," he says. "Spending time around kids forces you to enjoy the little moments."

"I can totally see that."

"Plus, you know——" His voice drops to a whisper and he leans close enough that his perfect mouth grazes my ear. "Texting you makes me more excited than glitter ever could."

I'm in a dusty room covered in glitter and paint with a small child only feet away; I should not have the urge to throw someone on the table and rip their clothes off. But thanks to the magic of Kai, that's exactly how I feel. My knees are wobbly and I can't get my breathing under control. I know if I turned my head just enough, his lips would be back on mine.

And I've never wanted anything more in my entire life.

But of course, I don't do it. I don't do anything but stand in silence, watching Sofia get lost in her treasure.

I wonder when I stopped finding joy everywhere I looked. Was there one definitive moment that snapped me out of childlike, blissful joy at the small things in life? I don't know when I decided to be more Warren Buffett than Oprah Winfrey or why I decided to stay in Iowa and study finance instead of going to the school in New York City with the amazing broadcast journalism program.

I wish I could say it was one thing. But the truth is, I think occasions I don't even remember might've shaped me the most. All of those instances where I ignored what brought me joy and placed everyone else's happiness over mine turned me into who I am today. A person staring in awe—and maybe with a little jealousy—at a little girl I don't even know, as she dives wholly and unapologetically into what makes her happy. Even if it's just a canister of freaking glitter.

All while ignoring the overwhelming urge to kiss the man beside me breathless.

"Hey." Kai's warm hand squeezes mine. "Are you okay?"

I nod and hold tight to his hand. I don't think I was okay before, but now, next to him, realizing that I still have my entire life to live the way I want to live it?

"Yeah." I smile up at him, feeling happier and lighter than I've felt in ages. "I think I actually am."

And even though I know it might not be the most appropriate timing in the world, I tip my chin up and touch my mouth to his. It's quick, but efficient as hell.

He tugs on my hand and tucks me securely into his side. I'm acutely aware of every place our bodies touch. I'm convinced my favorite J. Crew dress will start smoking from the heat and electricity sparking along the entire right side of my body. "I really love it when you do that."

Before I can respond, he drops his full, soft lips to my forehead and makes my world go Technicolor.

I hold my breath. Everything is so pure and perfect I want to live in this moment forever. I don't want something silly like breathing to ruin it.

Being with Kai makes me feel different, special. I don't think anything he does is meaningless. He makes even the smallest moments feel monumental. There's reverence in every glance and every touch. Like I am somehow the most important person who has ever walked this earth and it's his privilege to be with me.

And I've never felt that before.

With anyone.

The little voice cuts into my fantasy. "Is Mr. K your boy-friend?"

"Oh! Ummm . . ." I jump back, putting the appropriate amount of distance between Kai and me and instantly re-gretting it. "So is the glitter ready for me?"

I ignore Kai's quiet laughter and the disapproving, more-than-a-little-disgusted look on Sofia's sweet face.

"Yeah." She points to the canister tucked beneath her arm. "Lets go show Ms. Sue before my mom gets here."

This time, she doesn't use her brute strength to yank me out of the room. She just starts marching, assuming (cor-rectly) that I'll follow. I look back at Kai and the memory of his touch causes my cheeks to heat.

"So I'll see you later?" It's more of a hopeful declaration than a question.

He nods, his dimple-popping smile lighting up his face. "Definitely."

Go to art class, I told myself. It will be fun, I said.

Damn straight.

Good for me.

16

"I MIGHT START to think you're stalking me." I readjust the strap of my purse as I cross the almost empty parking lot.

"Me?" Kai straightens his long body leaning against the passenger side of my car. His smile somehow manages to be as bright in the dimly lit parking lot as it was beneath the fluorescent lights inside. "You're the one who keeps showing up where I work. I think I'm the one who might need to worry."

Welp. He's not wrong.

"The first two times were all Ella, I was merely an innocent bystander." It's a weak defense, but it's all I have.

"Then what was tonight?" His voice is thicker than the wet Miami air.

"A coincidence?" I struggle to keep my steps and my voice even and calm as I approach him and the space between us closes. "Or maybe another setup? You didn't tell me you taught here."

I'm a fairly confident person. I've held meetings with men who questioned whether I deserved to be in the room with them. I'm friends with some of the smartest, most beautiful humans in the world and I don't feel small around them. Even when Vaughn played in the NFL, I was able to hold my head high at his side. So the way my voice wavers and tension wraps its claws around my throat is a new feeling for me.

It's terrifying.

And it's also really exciting.

Because for the first time in maybe forever, I feel like I'm doing something just for me. Forget what anybody else has to say about it.

Kai peels away from my car and walks around to meet me on the driver's side, and he doesn't slow down when he reaches me. He slams into me, wrapping his arms around my waist and spins me around. I clasp my hands behind his neck and burrow my head into his chest, letting the laughter escape from my lips.

"I didn't set you up and it's definitely not coincidence." He stops spinning and tightens his grip on my hips as he steadies me on my feet. "It's fate."

"Fate?" I repeat. "Are you serious?"

"Dead serious." His dimples deepen and he doesn't seem the least bit offended by my reaction. It's so refreshing to be around someone who is happy and carefree and doesn't need me to agree with him all the time and isn't looking for a reason to argue. "And now I think fate is calling for us to go on a real date."

"A real date? Like to the movies?" I haven't been asked on a date in so long that I'm not sure I even know what this means anymore.

"Dinner, a movie, an art class," he says, amusement written all over his face. "We can do whatever we want."

The first thought that crosses my mind is no.

I really like Kai, but what are the chances this will lead to anything other than more distractions, more deviations from The Plan? Maybe I should just keep my head down and focus on work.

The old me would have said no. But you know what? The

old me wouldn't even be here right now. I might not have joined a dating show, but Delilah isn't the only person making changes to her life.

Not anymore.

"Yeah, that could be nice." I try my hardest to sound as cool and nonchalant as possible, but I think the way I'm gnawing on my bottom lip and clinging on to his neck so hard I'm sure my fingerprints are indented onto his skin might give me away.

"Yes? Really?" He sounds surprised that I agreed and it takes every ounce of restraint in my body not to kiss the excited expression off his hot freaking face.

I nod, not trusting myself to speak without blabbing about how much I like him. He doesn't push for more. He releases my hips and links our hands. The quiet hum of music and energy that seems ever present in Miami fills the comfortable silence between us. The stars that always seem muted by the bright city lights sparkle above us almost as vividly as the glitter Sofia shared with me, like they too are invested in the universe's plan for the two of us.

I try to tamp down the ridiculous thrill I get when Kai opens my car door for me.

"What day works best for you?" His body fills my doorway as I try to buckle my seatbelt with trembling fingers. He's not a big man by any means, but something about him is huge, all encompassing . . . and I can't see past him.

"I'm free most nights, what about you?" I don't want to admit that my plans pretty much only consist of hanging out with my little sister and work. I have to give the impression that I'm at least semicool.

He reaches into my car, and almost as if he doesn't realize he's doing it, tucks a stray piece of hair behind my ear. My hearts stutters at the simple gesture.

"I know you're busy. Why don't you check your schedule

and let me know what works best for you? I can rearrange my stuff and make it work."

And if I didn't think I could handle any more, my heart explodes at his words.

At a certain point in my relationship with Vaughn, he not only stopped putting me first, but he stopped prioritizing us at all. There were days where I felt like he expected me to be his secretary, penciling in time for us because he couldn't be bothered to make the effort to look at his schedule. I did it without complaint because I was trying to make the relationship work and thought that he would eventually return the effort. He just never did. I forgot that this is the way it is supposed to be.

"I really like you," I blurt out, not able or wanting to hold it in. "I really didn't want to, especially because I'm pretty sure getting us together was Ella's plan all along and she will never let me live this down. But you're so hot that it's bordering on offensive and it's so nice that it *is* offensive. I'm not sure I understand why or how you're still single, and part of me is waiting for the other shoe to drop because there has to be something wrong with you. You can't just be this hot, kind, glassblowing chef who works with kids in his free time, right? Are you a secret serial killer? Not that you would tell me if you were . . . but are you?"

Okay.

So.

It could be said that I didn't mean to tell him all of that.

I feel the heat rise in my face as the silence between us stretches on . . . and on . . . and on. I'm about to take it all back and blame it on paint fumes or something when, without warning, Kai's mouth collides with mine.

All thoughts dissipate and I'm only left with feeling.

I twist in my seat, ignoring the pain that shoots up my

arm when my elbow slams into my steering wheel as I dig my fingers into Kai's hair. Instead, I focus on the electricity flowing through my veins as it gathers between my legs and the heaviness of my breasts under the weight of Kai as he leans into me.

His touch is urgent and I know I'm not the only person who's been dreaming about this. His mouth is frantic against mine, tasting and exploring in the darkness of the parking lot. One of his hands clutches the back of my head as he holds my face to his and tugs on my bottom lip with his teeth while the other fumbles with my seatbelt buckle until I'm free.

I haven't kissed many people in my life, but I don't need experience to tell me that this kiss is freaking amazing. Extraordinary. There's no sloppiness as my mouth opens and he takes full advantage. His tongue finds mine, twisting and taking charge, finding the perfect rhythm as our bodies connect. It's like we've been doing this forever.

He's in control of the moment, but there's no pressure. His free hand slips beneath the hem of my modest work dress, the pads of his fingertips digging into the back of my thighs enough to make them clench, but he doesn't try to go any further . . . even though I might actually want him to. We may be making out in my car like teenagers, but that doesn't mean he's not kissing me like a grown-ass man.

I'm not in control of myself as I writhe under his hard body, wanting more of this. But when my legs are pretty much pinned beneath my steering wheel, it becomes very obvious why people stop kissing in cars as soon as they are old enough to find better locations.

"Jesus," he says when we finally manage to break apart. "How do you do that?"

"Do what?" I can just hear him over my pounding heart and rapid breath.

"How do you make me more into you every single time you open that gorgeous mouth of yours?"

Ho. Ly. Shit.

My mouth, which has never been referred to as gorgeous before, falls open and stays that way until I come up with my very eloquent response. "What?"

Kai scans my face and his expression changes from one of amusement to one of pure determination.

"I really like you too." The admission is so quiet I'm almost about to convince myself that I made it up . . . that this is some sort of break in reality and I'm going to wake up at any moment. "You're smart and beyond beautiful. You seem almost unattainable and you go off on wild tangents about dolphins. You let a little girl you've never met before drag you around an art studio and listened intently as she talked your ear off about glitter. You pretend your sister is constantly annoying you, but it's clear to everyone around you how much you love her. You're too good for me, but fuck if that doesn't stop me from wanting you more."

My breath hitches as I try to process everything he just said to me.

Nobody . . . *nobody* . . . has ever spoken to me like that before. Not even Vaughn, in the height of our relationship, saw me the way I think Kai sees me. There's no pressure to be anyone except who I want to be when I'm with him. I don't need to prove I deserve a promotion or that I'm a responsible daughter. When I'm with him, I'm free of expectations.

I'm free to be me.

He's the first person, in maybe forever, who sees me for the person I want to be. I lean forward, eager to resume the kissing we ended much too soon, when my phone begins to ring.

Ella's name flashes bright on the screen in my car.

"What was that you said about me loving Ella?" My voice is almost unrecognizable to my own ears in the best way ever. "Living with her can be a serious buzzkill."

I think about ignoring her call, but decide against it when I remember that she will just keep calling until I finally answer.

"Hello, Ella," I say. "How can I help you tonight?"

"What the hell, My?" Ella, my sweet sister, doesn't even bother with pleasantries. "I know you're excited about the promotion or whatever, but this is insanity! Are you ever coming home? Are you just going to forgo your mortgage and move into work? You're giving me a complex. I know we have different interests, but I know I'm more exciting than a damn financial report!"

Kai, bless his heart, is trying his hardest to stay quiet, but I can feel his body vibrating with laughter. "Do you see now that rambling is a family trait?" I ask.

"What? Wait . . ." Ella says, her loud voice echoing in my car. "Am I on speakerphone? Who are you talking to? Are you not at work? Why—"

"That's a lot of questions, let me answer those first." I cut her off because again, I know how the rambling thing plays out. "Yes, you are on speakerphone, I'm talking to Kai, and no, I'm not at work."

I answer her questions in order, watching as Kai stops laughing and something much different settles over his face.

When Kai and I first exchanged numbers, I made it very clear I didn't want Ella to know. I didn't know what was going to happen between us, but I knew Ella being involved and adding pressure—however well intended—wouldn't be helpful. Being secretive was fun—and kind of sexy— but I don't want to hide anymore. I want to enjoy this man anytime I can and I don't care if the whole world knows it.

"Wait . . . Wait!" Ella repeats, only about twenty times louder. "Did you just say you're with Kai? My Kai?"

"I don't think he's anyone's Kai, but after the way he just kissed me, I'm pretty sure he's more mine than yours." I know what I'm doing when I say the words, so I'm prepared when her high-pitched scream explodes through my speakers.

"Oh my god! I knew it! After the gallery, you looked all kinds of smitten and blushy! I knew it!" she keeps screaming. "Kai, you're supposed to be my friend. How could you not tell me?"

"Sorry." Kai pulls away from me and I miss the feel of him immediately. "You know I love you, but I had to do as asked."

"Fine." Ella groans, but I can tell her heart's not in it. "I guess this is good for Maya so she can finally see what a decent man who isn't a giant—"

"Okay, that's enough," I say, cutting her off again. "Thanks for calling. I'll see you when I get home."

"Maya, no! I'm sorry, bring fo—" I hang up before she can finish her sentence. Kai looks at me as I drop the phone back down onto the seat.

"Don't worry, I know she wants more Cuban food anyway." I wrap my arms around his neck and pull him back to me. "Now, where were we before we were so rudely interrupted?"

He doesn't need to be prompted any further, and outside of my art class, in the front seat of my car, I prove to myself that growth and change can be a lot of fun.

Are you ready, Lovers? Because the season's end is nearing and things are starting to get real for our girl Delilah right about now. The final four are set in stone and we can't wait to see who she picks.

Producers seem to have really pushed the new narrative that Anthony is the current frontrunner of this season, and it has never been more clear than last night. After the men met Delilah's family, she was able to choose three men to go on one-on-one dates with. We all knew she'd pick Drew and Anthony, but the third was a toss-up. She ended up going with Noah, who seems like a nice guy, but it's clear he's not in her top two.

Delilah and Noah explored Little Havana. She told him stories of her childhood over delicious food, and they ended the date at the Tower Theater with a private viewing of Humberto Solás's *Lucía* and a kiss. It was sweet, and although viewers like Noah, it's clear he's not winning. For Drew, they set out on a helicopter—which sounds like torture to me, but others find romantic?—to a private island in the Bahamas. There was an abundance of food, twinkle lights, and sand to roll in . . . and boy did they roll. It was magical, and I don't think I would've left. I know I've said he was falling behind Anthony as a favorite, but I think he might make a resurgence at just the right time.

Now Anthony? They truly could not have chosen a less romantic setting if they tried. The producers packed them up and sent them on a boat for some afternoon deep-sea fishing. While it didn't take long for our lawyer with a heart of gold to take off his shirt and show off his impressive abs of steel, it didn't take much longer to realize that his stomach wasn't quite as tough. Thanks to the magic of television we can't be sure of the exact timing, but our dear Anthony spent the majority of his date throwing up over the side of the boat.

He was so sick that his color still didn't look great at the elimination ceremony. But despite all the obstacles, the connection between him and Delilah was still palpable on our screens.

Drew, Anthony, and Noah have moved on to hometown dates, and from the preview, Drew decides to throw down, while Anthony is made to look like he might be having second thoughts as a result. I'm not sure what to believe, but I can't wait to discuss!

XOXO,
Stacy

17

MAYBE I MADE a mistake when I decided to go public with Kai.

And by public, I mean telling Ella, who promptly told Delilah, who told Bailey, who then created a group text where they sent me an abundance of eggplant, fire, and peach emojis for an hour straight. Because apparently, we're twelve.

"So . . ." Ella is sitting on my couch, a huge smile on her face. "Where are you two going on your date?"

"I don't know, he wouldn't tell me. He only told me to dress cool and wear closed-toe shoes, which seems oddly specific." I sit down next to her and point at the sneakers I had to dig out of the back of my closet. "Also, are you ever going to stop grinning about this? You can't be smug forever. It's impractical."

"It's obvious you've never had to deal with an older sister who always thinks she knows better. This will never get old and I will hold this over your head until I'm on my deathbed." She gives me the answer I expected but am still not thrilled to hear.

"I don't think I always know better," I say, ignoring her snort of laughter. "Just because you're reckless and I worry about your safety and well-being doesn't mean I think I always know better."

"Okay, so when you told me to ignore Megan Yoder and start hanging out with Isabelle instead, that was because you were worried about my well-being?"

This is why little sisters are the worst! She has no idea what she had for breakfast yesterday, but she can remember every single personal affront and remark I've ever made. If my fault is being a know-it-all, hers is being a giant pain in my ass.

"Megan was mean and I saw her teasing the dog next door one day when Mr. and Mrs. Rickner were out of town. I was just trying to keep you from falling in with the wrong crowd."

Ella has always picked troublemakers, and for some reason, our mom always punished *me* when Ella got in trouble. I was just covering my own ass.

"I know you don't spend much time on social media, and when you do, you probably only watch science and baking videos." She's teasing me and I force myself to roll my eyes because she's pretty dead-on with my viewing preferences. "But I'm friends with Megan on Facebook and she runs an animal sanctuary now. So I'm not sure what you thought you saw, but it wasn't that, because Megan is practically a saint."

"It's called redemption and guilt," I fire back, refusing to admit that I could be wrong. "Google it."

"Whatever." She rolls her eyes, and even though I know she's semijoking, she's still semipissed. "And not like you can talk much when Bailey is one of your besties."

"Hey! What's wrong with Bailey? I thought you liked her." This is the first time she's said anything about her, and Ella never holds back her feelings about people for longer than a nanosecond.

"I can't really point to one thing, it's just a vibe I get from her." She shrugs and points my remote at the TV. "She has a funky energy to her that puts me on edge."

Only Ella would think that saying "vibe" and a "funky energy" explains everything.

"Okay, well, I don't really know what to say about that. At least I thought I had something to stand on with Megan." Sure, that might be considered defamation now, but I had good intentions as a kid.

"You're a disaster." She rolls her eyes, but her voice is thick with laughter. "Anyways, for tonight. I realize a sister in your one-bedroom apartment might possibly be a mood killer, even with a sister as awesome as I am, so I'm going to hang with Delilah just in case you're planning on bringing Kai back for some evening activities."

I want to tell her it's not necessary and she can stay with me, but I can't force myself to say it. Not when I really, really, *really* want evening activities with Kai. Lots of them. Maybe until they turn into morning and early afternoon activities. It feels like all the time I spent around him not ripping his clothes off was the equivalent of twenty hours of foreplay. Your girl is primed and ready to go.

"Thank you," I say with zero sarcasm whatsoever. "I appreciate your willingness to give us space and for not telling Mom that I'm planning on having sex with someone who isn't Vaughn."

As far as my mom knows, I'm still trying to work things out with Vaughn. And while Ella and I have almost nothing in common, we both fear our mother. No way is Ella getting involved in anything that could place her in the line of fire of Deborah Johnson's wrath.

"I would ask you to expand on the Vaughn statement, but Kai should be here to pick you up soon, so you're just going to have to explain later."

I glance at the clock on my stove and my stomach does flips when I see that she's right. "Oh my god." I wipe my now-sweaty palms across my denim shorts. "Why am I so nervous? Are you sure I look okay?"

"You're nervous because Kai is great and this is the first date you've been on with someone who isn't the world's biggest d-bag in ages." She narrows her eyes, daring me to say otherwise, and I keep my mouth shut. Vaughn hasn't reached out to me since he walked out of my apartment, so I've decided it's no longer my job to defend him. "And also, you look fantastic. But I promise, no matter what you wore, Kai would be thrilled because he's just that into you. As he should be! You're a catch, don't you ever forget that again."

I know I wasn't thrilled when Ella showed up here unannounced, but as time goes on, I don't want her to leave. She really knows how to make me mad, but she's my number one hype woman and I love the crap out of her.

"I am a catch." I repeat the words I think I'm finally beginning to believe. "Thank you."

"No problem." She hits play and Delilah's face pops up on my TV screen. "Now go knock him dead, tiger."

As far as surprises and dates go, Kai is top-tier at both.

"Are you serious?" I ask him as I look around the cavernous space. It's dark, dingy, and industrial as hell, and if anyone else brought me here, I'm pretty sure I'd be convinced I was moments away from my death.

He rocks back onto his heels with his hands in his pockets. "I figured since you didn't get your pie, the least I could do was help you make something else you'd like. But we can go somewhere else if you're not into this."

When I climbed into his car in front of my building,

I figured we'd being going to dinner and maybe a movie. But of course, Kai being Kai, he had other ideas. I'm sure that taking your date to an empty warehouse full of giant kilns and torches might not be a traditional first date, but in my opinion that just makes it even better. Plus, if I play my cards right, there might be a chance I won't have to wait until we make it back to my apartment for other . . . activities.

"Are you kidding me? I'm pretty sure this is the coolest date in the history of dates."

"I'm so glad." His shoulders relax and his left dimple pops out. "I've never brought anyone here before. I was nervous."

My toes curl in my sneakers and my chest feels so heavy it becomes hard to breathe.

Vaughn sucked at dates. He was terrible at anything that required thought and not just money being thrown at it.

With Kai, it feels like the opposite is true. His joy and thoughtfulness radiate from the inside out, and just being near him makes me feel as if the skies have opened up and the heavens are shining down on me.

It also doesn't hurt that he is perhaps the most attractive human to ever walk this earth.

I've seen him four times now, and each time he's impossibly more attractive than the time before. I really thought he reached peak hotness with his skin glistening beneath the sun while he lounged on a yacht. But somehow his ocean eyes and sun-kissed skin glow even brighter in the dim lighting of the warehouse.

"So is it just the two of us in here or are more people coming?" Besides our romp in my car, we haven't spent any time alone. However, considering the number of potentially life-threatening tools lingering about, I wouldn't doubt his need for backup. I'm great with numbers, but I don't know if I'd trust me with liquid glass.

"Just the two of us," he says, and though I can't be certain, I think his eyes darken. "I'm friends with the owner and he told me we could have the space for the night."

"Wow, that's really nice." I try to keep my mind from drifting to how large the work surfaces are or how many ways we can get hot and sweaty in here.

And I fail.

Massively.

"So where do we start?" My voice is way too high and my cheeks feel like they've touched the kilns that are burning bright. There's no way he doesn't know where my filthy mind was drifting.

Of course, because Kai is a gentleman, he doesn't call me out and instead takes my hand in his.

"So first we decide what we want to make. I was thinking either a set of glasses or a vase or two. Which would you prefer?"

"Oh. Ummm." I'm so focused on the feel of his hand in mine that I almost miss the question. "Let's go with glasses."

Most of my glasses are from Target, and most of them are plastic. It might be nice to have glasses actually made of glass.

"Perfect." He gives my hand a gentle tug and pulls me into his chest. "I just want to warn you that glassblowing is fun and beautiful, but part of the reason is the dichotomy of glass. It's solid, but it's liquid. It's sturdy, but it's fragile. We have to treat this process with respect. I will guide you, but you have to promise to listen. I can't let you burn your hand off or Ella will kill me."

I don't know how he does it, but he makes glassblowing

sound like poetry. It makes sense why he loves it so much; it sounded as if he could've been describing himself. The softness of Kai, the way he speaks to me, the way he touches me, makes me feel more secure than I have in a really long time. His strength is his softness.

"I promise to listen to you." I hold up my hand in scout's honor. "As fun as this looks, it also looks terrifying and I don't want to cause you to get hurt either."

"Appreciated." His smile broadens and he drops a much-too-quick kiss onto my mouth. "First you'll need a pair of glasses to protect those beautiful eyes of yours."

He guides me over to the side of the room and opens a drawer full of goggles. Knowing there's not a pair in there that will look good on me, I don't overthink it and just grab the first pair I see.

"Okay, that was easy." I slip them onto my face and wink. "What next?"

"Next we get started." He walks us toward the furnace burning bright and hands me a long metal rod. "That is a blowpipe; you're going to stick it into the furnace and gather glass on the end."

"Wait, I'm sorry." I don't know why, but I thought I'd be his assistant. And by assistant, I mean like when I was in third grade and my mom "helped" me with my science project by doing the entire thing with me watching. I was fully prepared to sit my behind on a stool to watch and listen as Kai crafted a new set of glasses for my kitchen cabinets. "I'm actually going to do this?"

He looks like he wants to laugh at me, a look he has quite often if I'm being honest, but again because he's Kai and is a sweet, angel gentleman, he holds it in. "Yeah? I thought you wanted to learn."

"I mean, I do. I just thought I'd be learning like I would

with a PBS documentary or something? With my eyes and not my hands? Should I get gloves?" I'm trying not to panic, but as a person who has a tendency to think of worst-case scenarios everywhere I go, being surrounded by fire and glass is like the beginning of a horror movie for me. "Will these glasses even protect me if something touches them? How hot is that thing anyway?"

Numbers usually relax me. Maybe if I get the numbers and facts I can chill out.

"We keep the furnace at 2,150 degrees Fahrenheit." He's so calm when he says this that for a moment I'm almost convinced it's not that hot.

"So the sun, you've harnessed the power of the sun." Have I mentioned that I can be a tad bit dramatic when I'm anxious?

The laughter he was doing so well at concealing slips out. "I'm not positive, but I think the sun is a little hotter than that."

"You know what I mean." I try to glare, but my heart's not in it. He's very fucking cute and it's distracting me. "This is just already the best date I've ever been on and I will be highly upset if I die during it."

"You dying would definitely ruin my plans, so I was planning on keeping you alive." He takes the blowpipe from my hand. "How about I start the first glass so you can get a better idea of what you'll be doing and then you can do the second one?"

"That would be wonderful, actually." This feels much more doable. I like to study before I do something, and if my attempt at pottery is anything to go by, I should not dive headfirst into molten glass.

He takes me by the hand and guides me to stand beside him at the furnace. His carefree smile is gone and replaced by a look of quiet confidence. His food was great and he was a fantastic teacher, but seeing the way he settles into his body, I know this is where he is most comfortable.

"Okay," he says, pulling my attention away from his arms. "To start, you dip the blowpipe into the furnace, rotating it slowly, to gather the molten glass."

The blast of heat escapes the furnace when he opens it and I watch, fascinated by the simple yet graceful movement as he gathers the glass. The long, lean muscles in his arms flex beneath the warm amber light from the glowing orange liquid glass. It's probably not an appropriate time to lust after him, but I can't stop the way heat flows through my body . . . and not from the open furnace door.

"Now that we have some glass, we're going to take it over to our workbench and block it. That basically means we're going to spin it around on a big, wet wooden spoon." He pulls the blowpipe out of the furnace and nods for me to follow him across the room filled with large worktables and other equipment. With every step he takes, I can't help but think about how these big tables would be the perfect surface for blowing on more things than glass.

"What do you need me to do?" I ask when we reach the workbench. I know what I want to do, but I'm hoping I can keep my thoughts hidden for at least a little while longer.

"Come grab the end of the blowpipe and rotate it, slow and steady." He stops talking and I think there must be a catch. No way it's that easy. "I'll be on the other end, keeping the glass in the block, which cools and shapes the glass so we can gather more to have enough for your glass."

I have no idea what it is, but something happens when I'm around Kai. The wild and loud parts of my brain quiet down. It's like his calming presence gives my body the permission it needs to relax and finally go with the flow of things. Seeing Kai handle this with such ease and mastery has proven that I have nothing to be afraid of.

"Like this?" I follow his directions closely all while trying to ignore the innately sexual nature of glassblowing.

"That's perfect," Kai says in encouragement, but I don't miss the rasp in his voice that wasn't there moments ago. Maybe I'm not the only one affected right now. "Next you're going to blow on the pipe and we'll put it in the glory hole to reheat."

"I'm sorry." I stop rotating the pipe, probably destroying the piece. "But did you just tell me to blow on the pipe and then go to a glory hole?"

That's it.

Glassblowing is officially the horniest art form ever.

"Yeah." Red rises up Kai's cheeks. I'm not the only one with my mind in the gutter. "You blow into the pipe to put a bubble in the glass to shape it, and then stick it in the glory hole to keep the glass soft and moldable."

"I knew you wanted things to progress tonight, but glory holes maybe seem a tad too adventurous for a first date." What I forgot to add when discussing my friends being super immature with the eggplant and peach emojis is that I'm also very immature.

"I swear, I've been doing this for so long that I didn't even think about the terms and details of what we'd be doing until I started saying it out loud just now."

I can't tell if there's laughter, embarrassment, or lust in his voice. Maybe it's all three.

Either way, I know what I feel and I'm tired of always holding back.

"Well then, teacher." I put the blowpipe up to my lips. "I think if I'm going to blow this pipe, you should come a little closer to make sure I'm doing it right."

He doesn't hesitate. He walks from the end of the table, taking his place right behind me. Between his body pressed against my back and the heat of the furnace, the temperature keeps rising. Beads of sweat gather on the nape of my neck and I struggle to keep my hands steady as I bring the blowpipe to my mouth.

As soon as my lips touch the metal, Kai's fingers dig into my hips and the only sound louder than my pounding heart is his rapid breathing.

"Yes," he says into my ear. "That's perfect."

As much as I want a new set of glasses, right now I want Kai's mouth more. Carefully, I set the blowpipe on the table in front of us and turn to face the man who makes me feel things I didn't think were possible.

"This is perfect," I say before rolling onto my toes and pressing my mouth to his.

Kissing him is just as good as I remember it.

Better, actually.

Our bodies are already primed and glistening, my hands gliding up his arms as his move lower. My stomach tightens with need as goosebumps that shouldn't be possible in this hot room race down my spine.

I wrap my arms around his neck, then pull him closer to me, not wanting any space between us, and I am unable to hold back my gasp as his bulge pushes into my stomach.

Everything about him feels perfect. Everything about this moment feels perfect. And it's exactly then, when I give in to the idea of spreading him across the table, that a loud crash breaks us apart.

We spin around, staring breathlessly at the shards of glass that were on the end of the blowpipe only moments ago glitter across the floor.

"Oh." I tighten my hand in his. "I guess we should probably take care of that."

"I think you're right," he says. "And I promise, after we finish these glasses, I'll take care of you."

My legs spasm and his eyes darken. This date has only just begun, and it's the best night I've ever had. And thanks to Kai, I know things will only get better—and hotter—from this point on.

18

I PUSH OPEN my front door, hoping Ella didn't pull an Ella and end up staying home instead of going out.

Thankfully, I think she's just as invested in me getting lucky tonight as I am. To say I've been wound a bit tight lately is perhaps the understatement of the century.

"Welcome." I gesture to the open living space that is still barren of wall art, color, and—one could argue—warmth. "Make yourself at home."

What I lack in interest and personal touches I make up for in cleanliness and tidiness. Plus, I did make sure to buy the most comfortable couch I could find. It was my first piece of furniture that I didn't get as a hand-me-down and I'm very proud of it.

"This place is great." Kai smiles and links his fingers with mine. It's such an innocent gesture, but he does it every time we're standing near each other. It's like he can't help but touch me, as if holding my hand satisfies a need deep within him . . . and it makes me feel so special.

There's just a different feeling that comes with desire when you know someone wants you for your entire essence. As much as I loved Vaughn, being around Kai has made me question if Vaughn ever really loved me in return—and also if I was capable of receiving it. Not that Kai loves me or that I love him . . .

"Um, can I get you something to drink?" I pull my hand away from his and shake my mind free of the wild and slightly unhinged thoughts. I don't wait for him to answer before walking toward the fridge. "I don't know what I have, but I know there's a wide variety thanks to Ella."

How Ella has survived as an adult human is more of a mystery now than it ever was before. Her eating habits make no sense at all, and neither does the inordinate amount of money she spends on beverages. Alcoholic, non-alcoholic, sparkling, flat, you name it and it's been in my house. I went to the grocery store with her and she bought a bag of almonds, a few avocados, a mango, two boxes of sparkling water, four different brands of kombucha tea (that, in my opinion, all tasted like vinegar), one case of Diet Coke, and a liter of limeade "just in case we need an emergency mixer" for the tequila she bought the day before. Because apparently she has had multiple experiences where her biggest emergency was not having a mixer.

I love her, but I still have no idea how we're related.

"A water would be great actually, thanks."

After our first glassblowing faux pas—we got serious and managed to keep our hands to ourselves long enough to successfully make four glasses—Kai took me to his favorite taco truck around the corner from the warehouse. I wouldn't call myself a food snob, but part of me was concerned when we pulled into the parking lot. I shouldn't have had any doubts though—they were the best tacos I've ever eaten and I was able to order a Coke in a glass bottle, which is obviously the superior Coke. I saved the location in my phone and plan on adding them to my rotation of takeout.

I grab a plastic cup out of my cabinet, thrilled to soon replace them with the masterpieces we made.

"You have to sip out of plastic for now," I say. "I never thought I'd be so excited for glasses made out of glass."

"You'll have to come back with me one day to make some more, but with color next time."

When he asked what color I wanted, I froze on the spot. My apartment is so bland—I mean neutral—that choosing a color was overwhelming. I convinced Kai to go with regular clear glass, much to his disappointment.

"I was thinking red, but I don't know. Is that too bold after years of white, beige, and gray?" This indecision is why I still haven't placed my art order. Maybe I should just hire a designer and tell them to surprise me.

"Any color would be great," Kai says. "But if you don't like color, there's nothing wrong with clear. The best part of glassblowing is that it's all up to you. The rhythm, the piece, the color—it's all what you're feeling in the moment. You do what you love, not what you think I would like or Ella would like. It's about you."

I mean . . .

Fuck.

How am I supposed to develop normal feelings at a normal rate for him when he's constantly saying the most wonderful things?

"I like that. It's hard for me not to have a solid plan in place, but I guess I'll try to wait until we go again." I hand him the cup I overfilled with ice and point to my sofa. "Do you want to sit and maybe watch a show or something?"

Alone and in my apartment with Kai, it could be said that the last thing I want to do is sit on my sofa and watch television like we're in a freaking PG-13 sitcom. What I really want to do is point him directly to my bedroom, rip his clothes off, and engage in activities that would require a minimum XXX rating.

While we managed to control ourselves after we got carried away the first time, we spent the next three hours sneaking in extra touches whenever we got the chance. And

I wasn't wrong about glassblowing being sexy AF. It may not be sexual as in Patrick Swayze and Demi Moore doing pottery in *Ghost*; it's too hot and dangerous for that. However, between the glory holes and blowpipes and everything taking on a phallic shape at one point or another, I've been able to think of nothing but sex for the better part of the past three hours.

"Sure." Kai follows me across the room and sinks into the deep cushions beside me. "What do you want to watch?"

Since Ella has been in town, she's taken control of my television. I've watched more rom-coms and murder mystery shows in the last three weeks than I have in my entire life. There have been a few documentaries that I've wanted to watch, but the sad truth is I won't be able to focus on anything other than Kai sitting next to me.

"Doesn't matter," I tell him honestly, and pass him the remote. "You can pick, I'm not choosy. Just please no horror movies, I can't deal with those."

I went to a horror movie with a guy I liked while I was in high school. My best friend at the time convinced me that pretending to be scared was the best way to get a guy to put his arm around you in the theater. And while she wasn't wrong about the arm thing, we forgot to factor in that I'm genuinely terrified of those movies. I definitely screamed, I might have cried, and the boy never called me again. It was the last horror movie I ever watched.

"I don't love scary movies either. I'd much rather laugh when I'm watching TV." Kai takes the remote, and when he pushes a button, the screen lights up and reveals Delilah's gorgeous face. "Do you watch this?"

There's definitely surprise and maybe even a thread of judgment in his tone. I go on the defensive immediately.

"I didn't before, but that's my best friend." I point to

Delilah and watch his reaction. It would be such a shame if after thinking he was damn near perfect, *Real Love* was what ruined the illusion for me. "So I guess you could call me a super fan now."

"No way!" He drops the remote and then breaks into a dimple-popping smile. "They asked me to be on this season."

"Stop! Did Ella tell you to mess with me about this?" I roll my eyes and shake my head. Freaking Ella.

"Why would she tell me to do that?" His eyebrows scrunch together and he's definitely being genuine, because he's looking at me like I might be losing it.

"She's still mad I turned down being the lead on *Real Love*." Ella loves to mess with me, but I'm not biting this time. "Right?"

"Wait, what? You were supposed to be on the show too? Ella doesn't even know I was chosen, and she definitely didn't tell me any of this," he says, and I slowly realize that he's not messing with me. "They found me through my art page on Instagram. They interviewed me a couple of times and offered me a spot. I was going to do it, but pulled out at the last minute because it didn't feel like something that aligned with who I am."

Everything around me feels as if it's moving in slow motion, like time has stopped so that I can imprint this moment in my memory.

When I was thirteen, I was obsessed with amusement parks. I asked my parents for season tickets and went almost every single day that summer. My mom was worried; she thought I was developing an adrenaline addiction. There was one roller coaster I was particularly obsessed with. The climb to the top was so long and slow you'd wonder if it might be broken, and when you finally reached the top, it would come to a complete stop. You'd sit there for a moment, taking in the view from the top, enjoying the total stillness and almost forgetting why you're there. Then, just as you managed to relax, the brakes would release and you were plummeting toward the ground. In those seconds, I wouldn't be in control of anything. My stomach would leave my body as I laughed and screamed and felt whatever I was feeling to the fullest as we raced down and up and then down again. And long after the ride ended, even as I was lying in bed, if I closed my eyes tight enough, it was like I was back on the roller coaster.

Sitting here with Kai, hearing that he was asked to be on *Real Love*, just like me, and also turned it down, just like me? I'm right back on that roller coaster, free-falling through the air. I can only feel the rush of adrenaline as my stomach flips and I lose control.

"So we were both supposed to be on, but we both said no and ended up meeting anyway?" My hands start to tingle as I let all rational thought disappear. I've never put much stock in signs from the universe before, but this almost feels too big to ignore.

Maybe Kai was right. Maybe this thing between us is fate? I've only ever trusted myself before, but it would be wonderful to trust some great unknown. To be able to let loose and not always do what sounds right, but what feels right.

Fate or not, I decide to kiss Kai.

Unlike our other kisses, there's no sister or art students lingering, no glass nearby, no seatbelt buckles digging into my back. There's nothing to stop us, but from the frantic movement of our hands and mouths, our bodies haven't gotten the message.

Kai flips me over, my back slamming into my couch as

his body weight settles over me. His hands are everywhere. They move from my side, to his fingertips grazing the curve of my breasts, then to the dip of my waist.

"I've wanted to do this since I first saw you standing in that black dress with your arms crossed on the yacht." His voice has a delicious rasp and his eyes turn midnight blue. "You're so goddamn beautiful and I'm going to take my time indulging in every single inch you deem me worthy of."

Goosebumps cover my arms and sparks shoot down my spine. Nobody has ever looked at me or touched me like Kai is right now.

"Every inch?" I manage to ask through my heavy breathing. "Promise?"

His lips tip up at the corners, but I can't see if there are dimples or not because his mouth is back on mine before I can register anything other than the feel of his hands as they slip beneath the thin material of my shirt.

Even though everything about him seems so soft, his touch isn't. His calloused palms trail across my skin, reminders of how skilled those hands are . . . a promise of what's to come. My skin tingles with anticipation as his hands move lower, electricity chasing their path. His tongue twists with mine and his hands keep moving lower . . .

And lower . . .

"Oh my god," I breathe against his mouth.

I tangle my fingers in his unruly hair, holding him to me as he unbuttons my shorts and removes any and all obstacles preventing him from reaching our goal.

I'm afraid to move, afraid to open my eyes, afraid of anything that could break the moment. But as his fingers drift between my legs, I can't stop my body from reacting. I can't remember the last time I felt like this, like I could burst at the seams, as if his touch alone could push me over the edge. I'm trying to keep some modicum of composure, but I don't know how much longer I can hold on.

"You're so fucking beautiful." He lifts his head, staring down at me with those gorgeous eyes of his. "Always so in control, let me see you let go. Let me take care of you for once."

I try not to let thoughts of Vaughn cloud my mind, I don't want to compare because there's no comparison. This is new to me—having a man care more about me and what I need than himself. I've never had this.

I didn't know what I was missing.

But now that I know, I'm never going back.

Not ever.

I bite my bottom lip, looking up at Kai's flushed skin and darkened eyes from beneath my heavy eyelids and nod. He doesn't hesitate before lowering his head back to mine and using his teeth to pull my lip and quickly tracing the sting away with his tongue. His nimble fingers quickly find the exact spot I need him. My back arches off my couch just as my eyes slam shut and color dances behind my eyelids.

We never make it to my bedroom, but between the glass-blowing and what happens on my couch, this is the hottest date of my entire life. Both figuratively and literally.

19

I LOVED HIGH school dances.

I was totally that girl who hoarded fashion magazines and went to the mall to try on homecoming dresses for months leading up to the dance. In my senior year, I was nominated for homecoming and prom queen. I lost both times, but I didn't care. Being a part of the court was just an added excuse to spend even more time putting together my look.

As Ella and Delilah crowd my bathroom sink, makeup and hair products spread all across my previously pristine countertop, I'm reminded of why I loved those dances so much. It wasn't the awkward slow dancing or worrying about who was going to ask me. It was this, getting together with my friends as we tried the newest makeup trend and gossiped about who was going with whom and how every girl in our class could do better. Like with most things in life, those small moments before the photos were taken were the most memorable.

And it's the only thing that could possibly take my mind off the night—and morning . . . and a few lunch hours— I spent with Kai.

"No, Ella." I swat my sister's eyeliner-toting hand away from my face. "This is enough, I think it's time to walk away."

"Please!" She sticks out her bottom lip, which is slightly

less effective now than it was when we were young. "Just let me tweak the line a little bit more!"

Where I was adventurous with my makeup in high school, nowadays blush, mascara, and nude lip gloss get me through my days. I am obsessed with watching drag queen makeup tutorials on YouTube, but it's definitely not an art form I see myself mastering in my lifetime.

Ella, however, is convinced she could moonlight as a makeup artist. She's loaded my face with winged eyeliner, two-toned red lipstick, and contour so precise it looks like I've had work done.

I can't lie, it's really good and I'm impressed, but it's also *a lot.*

"No." I already said yes the previous five times she asked, and enough is enough. "It looks fantastic, but if you start over again, I'm going to wash it all off. Neither of us wants that, do we?"

She knows I'm not bluffing, so she pouts but doesn't fight me on it. "Fine."

"Is it time to pick out her outfit yet?" Delilah asks Ella like I'm not in the room.

When they started planning this birthday party, I somehow signed over control of my life for the night without realizing it. I've been informed that nothing in my wardrobe will suffice for the party and that I will be given different options to choose from.

I could not be more terrified.

I'm pretty buttoned-down in and out of work clothes. My style is mostly J.Crew meets Ann Taylor, where Ella is Anthropologie meets Fashion Nova. Delilah is Miami through and through. I don't know how they make it work, but they do. I just don't think it will work for me.

Scratch that. I *know* it won't work for me.

"Are you sure nothing I have will work? I bought this really pretty blouse from—"

"Won't work." Delilah cuts me off before I can finish.

I try to narrow my eyes at her, but I'm afraid that even that little motion will somehow ruin the makeup Ella spent hours on. "How do you know? You haven't even seen it."

"Because you bought it," Ella very rudely says. "I love you, but this is a party, not a work conference."

Why have I been thinking I'm happy having her around again?

"Facts." Delilah nods in agreement. "You're turning thirty. This is a big birthday! You can't just be out here doing what you always do. You're entering a new decade. What you wear is going to indicate how you enter this new phase in your life. Are you just going to do the same shit, or are you going to branch out and explore the woman you're becoming?"

"And we're sure I can't explore that in my own blouse?" If they knew the woman I've become with Kai they wouldn't be saying any of this, that's for damn sure.

"You're ridiculous," Ella, my loving and adoring sister, tells me. "We ordered you six different outfits. They're all cute and you're going to try them all on and wear one happily to this party we've planned, and you're not going to argue with us about it anymore. Got it?"

"Geez. Fine." I take a step away from her, holding my hands up in surrender. "I'll wear one of your outfits, but just know, Miss I Love the Environment, that fast fashion comprises ten percent of total carbon emissions."

Ella loses some of her steam and visibly deflates an inch or two.

"Wait." She raises a skeptical eyebrow. "Are you being serious or are you just messing with me?"

I mirror her posture. "Are dolphins evil underwater lords?"

"Oh dear god. Not the dolphins again." Ella throws her head back with an exasperated sigh. "And that really doesn't make the answer any clearer."

"Yes I'm serious." I walk into my room and flop onto my bed. "You know random statistics are my jam. So if you care about the dolphins, you should really slow down your shopping because fast fashion is really messing up the water."

"Buying organic groceries is already expensive AF and now you're telling me I need to buy expensive clothes too?" Ella looks truly and utterly crestfallen because she hasn't single-handedly saved the world. "It would be so much easier to help the planet if it didn't cost a mint to do it."

I want to gloat so freaking hard right now, but I don't, because you could say that my time with Kai has mellowed me out in more ways than one. Also because I don't solely shop slow fashion and my apparel isn't the most earth friendly, and I know she'll be googling it soon. I can't have her throwing it in my face before the night's over. Picking and choosing my battles wisely is a skill I acquired very young.

"You're not wrong," I say. "It would be a lot easier if doing the right thing was more accessible to the greater public. But alas . . . capitalism."

Oh no.

I didn't not mean to say that out loud. This is why I should've said no to Delilah's Crown and Coke suggestion when she got here.

And I'm adding no more drinking to my future to-do list.

"Oh my god." Ella's forlorn expression is instantly replaced by a giant shit-eating grin. Because of course the only thing more important than saving the planet is messing with me. "Did you just admit that capitalism is the root of all evil?"

"I definitely did not say that."

Delilah moseys on out of the bathroom wearing a version of Ella's grin. "You did kind of say it."

"Excuse me, ma'am, we work for the same company!" I yell at my traitorous friend. "You aren't allowed to be on her side."

"Maya." Ella retrieves her best Mom impersonation by jutting out her slender hip and pointing a manicured nail in my direction. "You just said, and I quote, 'But alas . . . capitalism.' End quote. If you are not admitting that capitalism is the root of all evil, what did you mean?"

"If I promise to try on the outfits you picked out for me, can we not have this conversation?" This feels like a losing deal for me, but the last thing I want to do is debate the pros and cons of a capitalistic society with Ella.

"Deal!" Ella shakes my hand and a slow, evil grin spreads across her face.

Oh crap.

She totally played me.

"You know you really suck, right?" I say, and stick my tongue out at her.

"That's what Kai said!"

She barely has the words out before she and Delilah dissolve into a fit of laughter. I should really look into moving to Alaska. None of this would happen if I lived in a remote cabin there.

"Number one, weren't you both just talking about maturing and growth? And two, how dare you? I'm not one to kiss and tell, but Kai was saying a lot, and it wasn't that." I wink, but before I can roll off my bed, screams ricochet off my bedroom walls and Ella pounces on me.

"I knew it!" Ella is still screaming. "I knew your skin wasn't looking all glowy because of that damn serum!"

"And you totally have not been going to yoga for lunch, have you?" Delilah asks, and my cheeks begin to burn. "You've been sneaking off for some afternoon delight!"

"WHAT?" Ella somehow manages to scream even louder. "You, Maya 'Work Is the Most Important Thing' Johnson have been ditching work to get the D? Who even *are* you?"

If I knew it wouldn't bring my entire building down with me, I'd ask the earth to swallow me whole. I don't know what I was thinking trying to play this game with Delilah and Ella; they're so much better at it than me!

"Forget who is she, what about how has she been holding out on us this long?" Delilah says, and glares at me. "You've been watching my whole messy love life play out on national television and you can't throw your girl a sexy bone here? Are we even friends?"

I guess part of me got so used to hiding the not-so-great parts of my relationship with Vaughn that I forgot how to share at all. Which isn't fair to them, but also isn't fair to myself. I deserve to share my happiness with the people I love and who love me back. Especially since this wouldn't have happened without either one of them.

"Okay, so you know how we did the glassblowing on Saturday?" I nod to the glasses they're drinking their cocktails from. "Well, afterward we came back here—thanks again for letting Ella hang with you over the weekend."

"Anytime. You know I'm obsessed with both of you Johnson girls," Delilah says. "Now please continue."

Ella doesn't say anything, but her foot won't stop tapping and the nails she got done today are back in her mouth. I had no idea she was this invested in my love life.

"So we sit on the couch to watch TV, and when it turns on, the home screen for *Real Love* is on. He asks if I watch it, and when I tell him yes, I'm all up in his face, making sure he's not about to make some rude, jerky remark. And he doesn't, because he's the best. But what he does say"—I take a deep breath, enjoying stringing them along for once—"is that he was cast to be a contestant on this season but backed out last-minute because he didn't think it aligned with who he is."

Delilah's mouth opens and closes and then opens again, but not a single sound comes out. Ella, on the other hand, screeches so loud that I'm sure everyone in my building hears her.

"You're fucking lying to me!" Ella starts jumping on my bed like a maniac. The updo she pinned up falls all the way out and my pillows go flying to the floor. "This is fucking fate! I introduced you to your soulmate! You're going to have to name all of your kids after me now!"

Like I've said before, Ella can be a *tiny* bit dramatic.

Delilah, on the other hand, manages to keep her cool. "So you're saying that you, who were cast to be the lead on *Real Love* but said no, met and fell for someone else who was cast, but also said no to *Real Love*?"

"Yeah." I nod at her accurate summarization. "That's what I'm saying."

It is then that my beautiful, rational, and laid-back friend loses her ever-loving, freaking mind.

"Oh my god!" She hops up and starts jumping on the bed with Ella. "This *is* fate!"

They won't stop jumping and I look like a little kid getting tossed around on a trampoline.

"Can you two sit down?" I try to scold them, but between the bouncing and their over-the-top theatrics, I can't stop laughing, and just being with these two women I love so much already makes it feel like tonight is going to be one of the best birthdays I've had in a long time. "You're going to break my bed."

Ella and Delilah both stop jumping and stare at each other for a minute before shouting, "That's what she said!" in perfect synchronization.

I guess I had that one coming.

I roll my eyes, but my heart's not in it. I'm just as giddy and over-the-moon excited as they are. Well, actually . . . I'm more excited, because while Kai might be an incredibly talented chef and artist, I know that his biggest talent lies elsewhere.

"Okay, children. Story time is over. I don't know when you told Bailey we'd be there, but I don't think we have all night." I roll off my bed, resigning myself to the fact that Ella is going to have to touch up my makeup again. Even though Bailey is the one who is late on a consistent basis, she's also the person with the least amount of patience if we make her wait. "I'm going to try everything on, and for this one time and one time only, I will let you choose the outfit. As long as my butt's not showing."

"That might be easier said than done," Ella singsongs as I walk away.

If this happened a few weeks ago, I would have a list a mile long of regrets. But today, I'm not even fazed. Spending a few hours in a dress I might hate hardly seems like a steep price to pay to celebrate the night away with my sister and friends.

20

I WAS WRONG. A few hours in this dress might be the death of me.

"I can't believe I let you convince me to leave the house in this," I sneer at Ella and Delilah.

I try—again—to shimmy down the hot pink skirt that's so short I might as well be wearing nothing at all.

"You look so hot though!" Delilah—who's fully covered in her deep-cut, but still long and flowy dress—has the audacity to say.

I slump over to try and minimize the amount of midsection showing in this damn crop top. "I look like a troll."

"Stop it." Ella rolls her eyes like I forced her to leave the house in clothing that is considered illegal in certain countries. "You're acting like a troll, but you don't look like one."

Eww.

Rude.

"I didn't mean a troll that lives under a bridge and scares people, jerk. I'm talking about the movie *Trolls*. The main troll was pink, covered in glitter, and had hair out to here." I gesture the length of my pink, glittered, big-haired body. "You styled me like the skanky version of a children's movie character."

"I know this is way out of your comfort zone." Ella stops

on the sidewalk after making the understatement of the night. "But you look great. You need to own it. Confidence sells everything, got it?"

I nod, not because I get it, but because they also styled me in four-inch stilettos and I'm pretty sure my feet are bleeding. I need to get to wherever we're going so I can sit my ass down.

We turn a corner and Delilah points to the restaurant across the street. "There it is!"

She starts to skip and my steps falter . . . but not because of the heels adorning my freshly painted, possibly blood-soaked toes, but because above the door on the brick building she's prancing toward is a sign with the words "Lightning Rod."

When I said I didn't want a big party, I did that for a lot of reasons.

Admittedly, I haven't fully explored the nightlife scene in Miami. To be fair though, Vaughn worked at half of the clubs, which made it feel like eyes were always watching. Plus, the one time I did go, I almost got vertigo from the amount of Versace (and knockoff "Versace," because even though I'm not into brand names outside of handbags, even I could tell some of that crap was fake) wafting around me. I was quick to learn that South Beach was not my neighborhood, so I went to a bar downtown that had great reviews. The vibe was much calmer . . . and also much douchier. Between the fraternity banners, framed photos of "southern greats," and the way the bartender bro sneered when Delilah asked for a martini, I didn't last ten minutes.

Clubs have never been my scene, which is part of what made me so nervous about tonight.

And now, heading into a place where I'm assuming the walls are plastered with posters of cars and half naked women, cheap beer is served two-for-one at the bar, and the playlist only consists of country songs that talk about shooting whiskey and beers, all while wearing this neon mini monstrosity, my hesitancy has increased tenfold. Don't get me wrong, I love a good old-fashioned honky-tonk as much as anyone (I'm from the Midwest, after all) but this is definitely not where I thought the night would bring me.

"Ummm . . ." I stop walking, looking behind me to see how far away the car is and whether I could make it back without having to walk barefoot on the litter-lined street. "You know . . . I'm just not . . ."

I try to think of any words to get me out of this situation I most definitely did *not* ask to be placed in. Ella and Delilah must sense my desire to escape, because before I can turn and run, each grabs one of my wrists and begins to pull me toward the door.

"No way." Ella tightens her grip when I try to wiggle out. "You're coming and you're going to have a blast."

They drag me slowly across the street, less to give me time to think and more because if we moved any faster I would fall on my face in these damn shoes.

"Ready?" Delilah asks when she stops in front of the door, and I seriously consider filing for a friend divorce. She knows damn well I'm not ready! I nod anyway because there's no point in fighting the inevitable. I clench my eyes shut as though I can pretend it's not happening and they shuttle me inside.

Traces of the humid Miami air disappear with the gentle thud of the heavy door closing behind us, and when I open my eyes, I totally understand why this place is called Lightning Rod.

Because holy freaking crap . . . I definitely feel like I've been struck by lightning.

The warm pink from the overhead lighting is a stark contrast to the streetlights we just escaped. The exposed beams and ducts are draped with greenery that perfectly complements the emerald velvet couches lining the wall. Small gold tables are strategically placed throughout the bar, both close enough to converse with the new friends you're bound to make, but far enough for a semblance of privacy if you need it. Pink, green, and gold art deco wallpaper covers the walls, giving your eyes not a single place to rest. A pink neon sign shines brightly from the far back wall. Its inspirational message YES THE F*CK YOU CAN illuminates every patron, no doubt adding a little extra confidence to everyone's step.

But even with all of that, the bar is still the crowning glory. The gold bar top sparkles beneath modern glam diamond chandeliers. Glass shelves holding all of the best liquor—and some of the worst—go up to the ceiling. Gold martini shakers fill up one shelf, while cocktail glasses in all different shades of pink fill another. Women of all shapes, colors, and sizes stand behind the bar in some version of a white shirt and dark pants. Where in some places the diversity could be a fluke, something about this place screams intention. Like they don't want to just be about *looking* inclusive, but want to take the steps to actually *be* inclusive.

And that all happens before the hostess leads us to the private room and my little slice of heaven is revealed to me in all of its floral grandeur.

"Happy birthday!" my wonderful friends—whom I honestly don't know if I deserve—shout in perfect synchronization.

As a person who rarely cries and also wasn't really feeling this entire thing, I scoffed when Ella insisted I wear waterproof mascara tonight. But now, as my sinuses burn and my friends turn into a blur through my unshed tears, I know I owe her yet another apology.

It's honestly just getting ridiculous at this point.

"Wow!" I look around the small, intimate room, fanning my face and hoping these damn tears don't fall. The mascara might stay, but I can't imagine my foundation won't streak. "This is so amazing. I don't even know what to say."

"Don't say anything!" Bailey pulls me in for a hug before shoving a shot glass into my hand. "Just slam it!"

"Slam it! Slam it! Slam it!" Delilah and Ella start chanting.

And because I'm trash for peer pressure, I don't even ask what kind of shot it is before I throw it back, cringing as the familiar bitter heat of tequila burns the back of my throat.

"Aghhhh!" I groan, looking around for a lime or something to soften the blow but have to fight through it when I can't find anything.

"Woot! Cocktail time hath arrived!" Bailey punches the air above her. "I ordered everyone a My-Mai Tai that I had the bartender create just for our Maya here. It has grapefruit in it and it's phenomenal."

"Sounds delicious!" I would've drunk whatever Bailey handed me. But she knows me well, and that actually does sound delicious. Maybe I'll have two.

"Okay, okay, okay." Bailey stands and taps her glass with her fork.

Our table is dripping with flowers and covered with empty plates and glasses. My stomach hurts from not only how much I've eaten, but how much I've laughed.

I know I said I didn't want a party, but I'm learning that sometimes my friends know me far better than I know myself. This has been one of the best nights I've had in a long time, and the only thing flowing more than the alcohol tonight is my gratitude. I should've trusted my friends and beloved little sister not to force me into something I would hate. This is small, intimate, and absolutely stunning.

"I know our girl here hates being the center of attention, but I just had to say not only how much we all love and appreciate her, but also point out how fucking gorgeous she looks tonight!" Her voice rises a few octaves at the end, and Ella and Delilah start to cheer and whistle. "I never thought we'd see you in a miniskirt and crop top, but good lord do you look hot! In the words of the great poet and prophet Megan Thee Stallion, cheers to body-ody-ody!"

We raise our glasses and shout "Body-ody-ody" so loud I'm sure people across town can hear it.

The My-Mai Tais have well and truly gotten me drunk. Instead of being embarrassed by the attention, I stand up and take a bow.

"Thank you very much," I say to the round of applause. "But this was all Ella's idea, so don't get used to it."

Ella stands from her spot opposite me and curtsies.

"Well." Bailey, who might be the only other person as drunk as me, teeters on her heels. "She did a great job, and I think we need to let Vaughn know what a dumbass he was to let this go."

Vaughn would die if he saw me now. As he started working more seriously in the nightclub industry, I couldn't tell if my being so far removed was something he liked or hated. Either way, he would be shocked to see me out in Miami, drunk and in a crop top. I mean, who even am I right now and why do I love it so much?

Ella's influence truly knows no bounds.

"We should take a picture and post it on Delilah's IG." Ella reaches into her purse to grab her phone. "He'll definitely see it there. Let him see it and read all the comments talking about what a goddamn smoke show you are."

"Why use a middleman when we can show him now?" Bailey asks, and my drunken haze begins to lift.

You know in movies when the main character is just skipping about, living their best life, and all of a sudden, tires squeal and everything goes in slow motion just as all hell is about to break loose? That isn't just movie magic, because I swear that's what happens now.

All conversations stop and all focus is directed at me. I swear even the waitress who has started collecting the empty plates stops to stare.

"I'm sorry," says Ella, who's still standing. "What are you talking about?"

"You know how I told you I had a connection here?" Bailey says. Her smile hasn't dimmed and I think she's the only person in this entire restaurant who didn't feel the mood shift. "Well, I knew they had worked with Vaughn before, and when I brought it up, he told me they were friends! I invited them and he just texted me that they're in the parking lot."

"Bailey." Delilah looks as horrified as I feel. "You didn't."

If I wasn't frozen in panic, I would be relieved to know Ella and Delilah had nothing to do with whatever is about to happen, but I am too shocked to be able to process all of that right now. Of all the very worst-case scenarios I came up with for tonight, I can honestly say Bailey ambushing me with my ex was not featured anywhere on the list. Who would ever think that was a good idea? She knows full well I haven't even spoken to him in weeks!

"Why are you all looking at me like that?" Her southern lilt slips out when we don't react the way she anticipated. "This is going to be great! Vaughn is going to beg for her back after tonight."

In the days after we broke up, this is all I wanted. But

now? I don't know what I'm more afraid of, that he'll see me and want me back or that he won't. Both are equally terrifying.

Before I can decide whether to think on it or run like hell, Ella's eyes snap over my shoulder. The hairs on the back of my neck rise as the energy in the room becomes charged, and I've never sobered up so quickly in my entire life. Her lips flatten into a straight line and her gorgeous eyes narrow like they do every time she is in the presence of one particular person.

"Ralph," she says, calling him by the name he hates so much, and even though this shouldn't concern me, my anxiety spikes. "Would say it's nice to see you, but we both know that'd be a lie."

I turn around, and standing there, right in front of me for the first time in what feels like forever, is Vaughn.

He's just as handsome as ever. I'd hoped if I ever ran into him again, I wouldn't feel this. I hoped the butterflies in my stomach would be gone and I wouldn't notice the way his smile—the one that landed him on the cover of a magazine during the height of his football career—lights up every room he walks into. I wanted to be over him, done for good. I wanted to feel exactly nothing if I ever saw him again. But if the rapid beating of my heart tells me anything, it's that he still affects me, and the feelings I developed over ten years didn't disappear overnight.

"Ella." His deep voice is like butter, and my traitorous body can't help the way it responds to hearing him again. "I didn't know you'd be here. Nice to see that you haven't lost your spunk."

"You're such a condescending piece of—" Ella says, and I've been around this song and dance too many times before not to cut in. I know if I don't the tension in this room is going to be about a hundred times worse.

"Ella, don't," I say, and her eyes slice to me. "Please stop."

"Oh, you have got to be fucking kidding me." It's easy to see that she's pissed. But unlike all the other times we've fought over Vaughn in the past, I see straight to the pain. "Two seconds around him and you're already protecting him. After the way he treated you? Come ON!"

"I'm not! I just——" I try to explain that I don't want her to get worked up and mess with our night when it might still be salvageable. I want to tell her I'm not sure I want to even see him, let alone defend him. But Ella is passionate and she's running hot. The years of my ignoring her and taking Vaughn's side over hers are making it impossible for her to hear me. "There's no reason to get all worked up right now."

I'm so flustered that all my thoughts and words are jumbled, but even so, I regret the words as soon as I say them.

"You know what, Maya? Have him." She shakes her head, and her lips curl in disgust. She takes a step back, holding her hands up in surrender. "Have Ralph. Be miserable. I don't fucking care anymore. I really thought you were turning a corner for the better, but I guess not."

"Ella, ple——" I try to stop her. Explain or apologize. Anything. But she doesn't let me get another word out.

"Nope. I'm not interested." She grabs her purse and puts it over her shoulder. "I don't even know why I thought you were capable of living your life for anyone other than Mom. One second around him and you're right back in the same position. It's sad. No, *you're* sad. And I'm done with all of this."

All of the food I so happily indulged in just a short while ago threatens to make a reappearance as embarrassment and hurt twist my stomach into knots. I want to be pissed at her, but after the way I've behaved before, I can't exactly fault her for feeling this way. I just wish she could've not screamed it in public.

"Always a great time when you're around, Ella," Vaughn says, goading her as she storms out.

"How about you go fuck yourself? Or actually . . ." Ella says over her shoulder before stopping and turning to face him. Dread shoots through my veins because I've seen this look before, and I know she is about to choose violence. "Since I know you cheated on my sister, why don't you go fuck whoever? It's clear she'll take you back no matter what."

I know she's mad, but she couldn't have cut me deeper if she tried. The patience and understanding I was trying to hold on to flies out the window and anger sets in.

"Get your stuff out of my place." I can't even look at her as I talk. My hands are trembling and all I want to do is cry. "I don't want to see you when I get home."

I'm sure she can sense my rage, but she remains untouched. "My pleasure."

With one final roll of her eyes and a well-timed middle finger to Vaughn, she's out of the room without so much as a backward glance.

Bailey is about three shades paler than usual, and Delilah is staring at her lap, discreetly swiping the back of her hand across her cheeks. The laughter and joy that was filling this room only moments ago is long gone.

I try to think of anything to lighten the mood of the room, but I come up empty. Anything I say at this point is meaningless. We all know this party is over.

"I'm really sorry about that, everyone," Vaughn says after a few moments, acting like the host of this party and speaking for me despite being the reason my party was ruined. "But," he says to me in a stage whisper, "is now a bad time to tell you that you look incredible tonight?"

Like a petulant child who can't keep her mouth closed, even when she caused all of this, Bailey mutters beneath her breath, "I told them you'd say that."

"Ummm . . ." The poor waitress who's been laughing and joking with us all night comes in and takes in the mood. "Should I still bring the cake?"

And that's it. I don't know if it's the absurdity of the night or the almost overwhelming urge to break down in tears, but something snaps inside of me. I slap my hand over my mouth, but it does nothing to stifle the snort of bitter, ironic laughter that escapes. It's the only way to keep myself from crying in front of my friends. Before I know it, everyone, even Vaughn, is laughing along with me in an attempt to salvage what's left of the party. The sound is thin and a bit forced, but I appreciate the effort.

Even though I'm still attempting not to cry, there's really nothing else to do but go on with the show. As great as Delilah is on *Real Love*, she's no actress. She's trying to laugh, but I can still see a tear on her face, and Vaughn, ever the showman, is doing a thick, velvety stage chuckle, aiming to gloss over the lingering awkwardness. He moves toward me, and when I don't step out of his reach, he wraps his arms around me. In this moment, the familiar touch feels like home.

"I'm sorry about everything," he says into my hair. "I missed you so much."

I close my eyes, trying to take in his words and figure out how I really feel about him, when I hear another voice from across the room.

"Maya? Sorry, I'm late," he says. "What did I miss?"

I stiffen and push out of Vaughn's arms to see a confused Kai staring at me with an expression much like Ella was wearing only moments ago. The tension in the room still hasn't entirely dissipated, and I can see him figuring out what's happened—with my luck, he probably even crossed paths with Ella as she stormed out.

Because of course.

"I was just stopping by to wish you a happy birthday." His normally open, expressive face that I adore closes down before my eyes, and it breaks what's left of my heart. "But something actually came up. I've got to go, but have a great night."

"Kai," I say, but before I can say more, he turns and leaves the room.

"Who was that?" Vaughn's deep voice is way too close. The absurdity of the moment has passed and the reality is setting in. A reality where the two relationships I've cherished the most these past weeks are crumbling around me all because Vaughn is an entitled jerk, and the second I was around him again, I reverted back to the same person who never stood up to him.

And no.

Absolutely not.

I will not go back.

"You need to leave." I don't answer his question, not because I don't want to tell him who Kai is, but because it's none of his business and I owe him nothing.

"What? I just told you that I missed you. I apologized." His brow furrows and he looks truly confused. "Why would I leave?"

If I wasn't out-of-my-mind furious right now, I might feel bad for him. He's a grown man and still doesn't understand that his actions have consequences, that saying sorry doesn't magically erase all of the hurt he's caused.

"I appreciate the apology." I struggle to keep my voice even while my eyes are starting to burn with unshed tears. "But it's not enough. You hurt me and I'm not ready to be around you."

In fact, I don't think I want to be around anyone.

I spot my purse by my chair and shoulder past Vaughn, who looks like his brain might explode as he tries to process my rejection.

"I'm going to call an Uber," I inform Bailey and Delilah, who stopped laughing a long time ago. "But thanks for the party. This was . . . well, it was something."

And to think, all of this could've been avoided if my well-intentioned friends let me keep my ass at home like I wanted.

I'm never having another party.

Ever.

21

BY THE TIME I got home after my party, all traces of Ella had disappeared.

She didn't leave a note, didn't text, and hasn't returned a single one of my phone calls. I know she was hurt, but she said some messed-up things too. I don't know why I'm the only one trying to fix things. I've left her more voicemails in twenty-four hours than I've ever left anyone and she hasn't texted. If it weren't for Delilah telling me Ella was crashing with her, I would've sent out a search team by now.

I thought I'd be happy to have my space back and be able to spread out in front of my TV without her stupid long legs hogging half of the couch. But instead, for the first time ever, I feel uncomfortable in my own space. The quiet I used to revel in feels oppressive and I don't even know how to begin to change it.

And I'm so embarrassed by the way everything went down that I've been avoiding absolutely everyone. You know, like any thirty-year-old woman with solid communication skills who handles conflict well.

When Ella was here, she forced me to request my birthday off. I didn't really want to do it, but I gave in because she's very convincing and I was kind of hoping she had another secret road trip planned. But now that I'm sitting by myself in my stupid apartment eating slightly stale birth-day cake, I wish I hadn't given in.

I considered getting dressed and going to the office this morning, but when I thought of having to face Delilah and Bailey, I lay right back down. Plus, if I went in on a day I'd requested off, people would ask questions, and again, I'm avoiding everything and everyone. Because hiding from my problems instead of addressing them head-on continues to be so successful for me.

I don't know what I thought would happen when I turned thirty, but I hoped all of my problems would be fixed and I'd know the answer to everything. Instead, I have more questions than ever and nothing makes sense anymore.

There's a knock on my door and I thank the heavens for the abundance of food delivery services. Leaving my place for any reason today is completely off the docket. The only reason I put on pants was to greet the delivery person.

Thirty is starting really strong for me.

"Coming!" I yell as I run across the room. My fuzzy socks make slippery work out of the sparkling floors I cleaned all night to avoid my thoughts and I slide into the door.

I flip open my locks and pull open the door, fully ready to grab my Coke and birria tacos, but instead my mouth falls open as I stare at a more-gorgeous-than-ever Kai.

I swear he's gotten even more handsome since we've been apart. He's holding a big white box with a silver bow that only makes his hands—that I know are capable of magic—seem even bigger. His skin is sparkling, the gold flecks shimmering beneath the white lights in the hall-way. His hair that is usually falling in front of his face is pulled up into a little bun at the top of his head. I told him last time we were together that man buns were my guilty pleasure and I wonder if he chose this to entice me or torture me.

Or both.

After he saw me hugging Vaughn, Kai had lingered for a few minutes before quickly leaving. I didn't think I'd ever hear from him again. I've started about a thousand text messages to him and deleted just as many before I could hit send. I've been worried about Ella, but she can't avoid me forever. I was devastated about the thought of never seeing Kai again.

"Kai? Umm . . . hey." I try not to fidget with the hem of my oversized T-shirt that I've had since college or my hair I haven't brushed at all today.

Oh my god, my breath!

I pull my lips between my teeth, not wanting to breathe on him.

"Hey." His smile is hesitant, but to his credit, he doesn't outwardly react to my disaster of an appearance.

"Come in." I step to the side and gesture for him to come inside. I've been stress cleaning so it's spotless, except the glass sitting on my counter that I've been using since Kai dropped them off.

He notices it right away.

"Oh good." He points to the glass. "You've been using them."

"I love them. I feel very fancy every time I drink out of them." And then I feel sad, and then mad, and then back to fancy. They are very emotional items for me. I've been calling them my crying glasses.

He smiles, but it doesn't reach his eyes. "I'm glad you feel fancy, you did a great job."

"That's very generous of you to say, but we both know you did the majority of the work." And by majority, I mean

98 percent. I'm a terrible glassblower. I was hoping to get better, but I thought my chances were over when he walked out of Lightning Rod. So even though I'm not sure I want to know the answer, I have to ask. "I'm so happy to see you and I don't mean to sound rude, but what are you doing here?"

He sets the box in the middle of the counter, and when he looks up, I can't decide if I want to cry or jump over the counter and rip off his clothes.

"Today is your birthday, right?" he asks. "I had to bring you your present."

I don't know if his smile reaches his eyes this time because my vision blurs when my eyes flood with tears. "You didn't need to do that."

Especially after this weekend.

I'm not sure I would be able to do the same if I walked in on him hugging his ex. But I guess this is another reason Kai is a superior human.

"I know I didn't need to." His hand slides across the counter until his fingers find mine. "I wanted to."

Dammit.

The first day of my thirtieth year might also be my last, because Kai is going to destroy me.

"Well, then who am I to object? I'm glad I was here to accept this kind gesture." I flip my hand over and Kai's fingers interlace with mine. I never want to let go.

"Your sister told me you'd be here today," he says. "I was going to head to your job but she told me you took the day off."

"Oh, nice that she has time to talk to you." Snark that I don't usually possess colors my words. "She can't even tell me she's alive."

"From what I heard, it sounds like you both said a lot to each other."

God.

I pull away from him and bury my makeup-less face in my hands as mortification and regret heats my cheeks.

"She told you?" I mumble into my palms, and feel the heat of his body when he comes to stand next to me.

"Yeah, she said you both said some hurtful things." His hand finds my back and he rubs gentle circles across it. The kind gesture soothes the hurt this conversation is bringing to the surface.

"It was horrible. She said some terrible things, and even though I don't think I deserved them that night, I definitely deserved them before that," I say out loud for the first time. "I used to be terrible to her because she disliked my ex so much and it took hearing all of her hurt to understand how far we had drifted apart. I don't know if we'll ever be okay."

The tears that I've fought so hard not to let fall finally break free. A sob rips from the back of my throat as all of the anger, regret, and sadness from the last few days . . . maybe years, can't be held back any longer.

Kai's hand leaves my back for a moment before he's gathering me in his arms and pulling me into his chest. "Let it out," he says into my messy hair. "Let it all out."

I don't know how long we stay like that. He holds me tight, whispering sweet things that I barely hear while I sob uncontrollably. My tears turn his tee into a wet T-shirt contest, and when we pull apart, I'm drained.

"I feel like I just ran a freaking marathon." I lean all of my weight into him; I don't even have the energy to stand up straight.

"Have you run a marathon before?" He looks impressed with my athletic prowess.

"The farthest I've run is to the bathroom at work." I hate to disappoint him, but running for four to five hours straight is the last thing I would ever want to do. "Have you run one?"

He nods and his lips curl into the smile I first became infatuated with on the yacht. "I ran two and I'm thinking about training for another one."

"So now that's chef, glassblower, teacher, and runner. Is there any other talent you're hiding?" I mean really, he's great at everything. Share the wealth already! It feels like an attack at this point. "I considered trying to run a half marathon once, but decided against it after the first day of training."

My two miles on the treadmill is all I'm capable of. I'll take takeout and Bravo over marathon training any day of the week.

"Anyway . . ." I eye the box on my counter, unable to pretend like I don't love presents as much as I did when I was seven. "What's in the box?"

"Oh. It's nothing really." The teasing smile on his face falls and color tinges his cheeks. He sticks his hands into his pockets and rocks back onto his heels. I find this change in posture both intriguing and hot.

"It's a box that you brought for my birthday, so I don't think it's nothing." I finger the bow on the top of the box, the silver ribbon perfectly tucked and tied. "Can I open it?"

"It's for you, so sure." He avoids looking at me as he answers, and it piques my interest even more.

I can't pretend that seeing Vaughn wasn't a jolt to my system. It was the reminder I didn't want that no matter what we go through, I will always find a sense of comfort when I'm with him. Ten years of being with someone will do that to you. On the other hand, being around Kai is fun and exciting. I'm fascinated with almost every part of him, but it's the quiet confidence he carries through every thread of his life that really gets me. I've never seen him look nervous like this before.

I grab the box and carry it over to my coffee table, patting Ella's now-vacant spot for Kai to sit.

I slowly untie the bow, carefully folding the ribbon and putting it off to the side. The white box gives no hints of what it might be.

I remove the top of the box and am met with yet another obstacle.

"This feels like the nesting doll version of a present." I grab the Styrofoam inside the box and look at him. "Tell me the truth, is there going to be another box when I lift this up?"

He shakes his head and his dimples appear. "Why don't you look and see?"

He's appearing less anxious now, and I'm not sure that there actually won't be another box when I remove it. I narrow my eyes at him and it only makes his smile grow.

"Just open it," he says.

I roll my eyes for appearances' sake only—I'm much too curious to wait any longer.

The terrible feel of Styrofoam beneath my fingernails makes me shiver. I toss it to the side as fast as I can, and when I do, it feels like someone has sucked all of the oxygen out of the room.

"Kai." I whisper his name, my fingertips gently gliding across the top of the best present I have ever received.

"Do you like it?" The apprehension in his voice is back and I have to tear my gaze away from the glassblown pie in the box.

"I . . . I . . ." I shake my head, trying to get words to come out. "I love it."

Love doesn't feel big enough, to be honest.

I loved the first pie I saw in the gallery. It was beautiful and I could find meaning in it that was fun and ironic. It would've looked great in anybody's home.

But this one? This one wouldn't look great in just any-body's home. This one is only meant to be in mine. It's like Kai took all of the pieces of me that I've shown him and baked it into this absolute masterpiece.

It's missing the big, bold lifelike colors of the first one. This one is nearly all white, which somehow only showcases each and every detail of his precise glasswork. The only bit of color on the entire sculpture is a little golden brown coming from the lattice pattern crust directly beneath the bright red, sparkly cherry sitting on top.

"When did you even have the time to make this?" I strug-gle to take my eyes off of the most perfect gift in the entire world to look at the amazing man who somehow saw some-thing in me right away that I'm just now seeing in myself.

He shrugs. "I had an idea while we were making the glasses and you were talking about struggling to choose a color. I had a commissioned piece to work on, but when I got to the studio, I couldn't stop thinking of you."

He shifts his body so his long legs are tucked beneath him on the couch. All of his earlier hesitation has been re-placed with the excited energy I can only imagine comes from creating something so perfect for another person.

"I couldn't stop thinking of the way your eyes lit up when we finished the first glass and I remembered how you were with Sofia. That art class was the first time I think you really let me see you. Like when you were away from people who had expectations of you, you were free to be yourself. I could see you coming out of your shell. I mean, you listened to her tell you about glitter for at least ten min-utes and you were so into it. You sparkled. It was so cool."

I feel like I should participate in this conversation more than staring slack-jawed at him, but I can't. I'm too invested in what he's saying—it's like I'm hearing who I am for the first time.

"And then the parking lot." He leans back into the couch and my cheeks might go brighter than the cherry as I remember practically mauling him in my car. "And then this couch."

He wiggles his eyebrows and I couldn't stop myself from laughing if I tried. "Stop it!" I shove his shoulder, but my heart's not in it. Not when I'm thinking about the thing he did with his tongue and—

"I won't stop." He tightens his hand around mine. "The person I've been spending time with, that I've been loving getting to know, is not the person I saw Saturday night. Maya, you're so beautiful, and I don't just mean your face or your body or any of the physical stuff, I mean who you are. And when I walked in to your party, I wasn't upset that I saw you hugging that guy, I was upset because the shutters went back over your eyes and it was as if you were sucked right back into your shell. This gift, this is who you're becoming. You're already the cherry on top, you just need to let your color shine."

"Is that why only a little bit of the pie is in color?" I hold back the sexual innuendo I would like to make about my lit-up cherry, but it's not easy.

"Exactly." He nods so enthusiastically that pieces of his hair fall out of the bun his long locks are pulled into. "I know as much as you do that you're not the same person I met on that yacht. You might not want to admit it, but you can't go back and pretend all of this didn't happen. The color is going to keep spreading whether you want it to or not."

I guess he should add poetry to the list of things he's great at, because wow, this man really knows his way around a metaphor.

I close the lid to the box and move closer to him on the couch, needing to feel him close to me again.

"Thank you." I tuck his hair behind his ear before leaning in and touching my lips to his. "Thank you for the gift and for telling me how you see me."

Before things can go any further, he pulls away from me and stands. My veins turn to ice as anxiety floods my system. He's still mad, and rightfully so.

But before I can apologize again, he takes my hand in his and pulls me off the couch. "This time I want to make sure we make it to your bed."

Memories of all of the glorious things we did on the couch play in my mind like a movie, only chased away by possibilities of what's to come.

The short walk to my bedroom feels like a million miles, but when I push through my door, something in Kai snaps. Long gone is the gentle, patient artist I've fallen so hard for. He doesn't say a word as he picks me up and carries me the final steps to my bed.

He drops his mouth to mine, kissing me deep before throwing me—yes, throwing me—onto my bed. I can't hold back my laughter. The joy and excitement I feel whenever I'm with him is effervescent; I feel like a champagne bottle ready to explode. Everything about him makes me happy, and I'm a different person when I'm with him. It's like his presence in my life has given me permission to explore the parts of me I've kept hidden for so long.

As Kai approaches the foot of my bed, slowly peeling off his shirt and revealing the smooth skin covering his cut abs, my mouth goes dry and the laughter stops. Slowly he climbs onto my bed and doesn't stop until his long, lean body is covering mine. He stares down at me as if memorizing every curve and dip of my body.

"Do you have any plans after this?" His thick voice sounds as if the words are choking him.

I shake my head, unable to focus on anything other than the weight of his body on top of mine. "No."

"Good." He lowers his head, dropping featherlight kisses across the base of my throat. "Then I'm going to take my time covering every." Kiss. "Single." Kiss. "Inch." Kiss. "Of this body with my mouth."

I wish I could come up with something to say, some poetic words telling him I agree and appreciate this plan of action, but thankfully, the moan that escapes my lips says it all.

All I get in response is the feel of his lips parting against my neck before my shirt is over my head and my pants are thrown across the room. I lay spread out on my bed completely at his mercy under the heat of his intense gaze.

"Thank god I'm not a painter." His voice is a whisper and I can barely hear him over the sound of my heavy breathing. "Because I could never re-create anything as beautiful as you laid out in front of me, but I would spend every single moment of the rest of my life trying to chase this perfect picture before me."

His words, the ones he gives to me so freely, steal my breath away as tears threaten to fill my eyes. Luckily for me though, before my emotions take over, Kai's soft lips slowly graze my stomach with kisses until he settles between my thighs and proceeds to make good on his promise.

All day long.

If you're anything like me, Lovers, you like hometown dates because they are wholesome and adorable. Poor Noah and Theo are clearly there for the numbers only. They did what was expected and showed Delilah around their towns, introduced them to family, blah-blah-blah. Been there, done that, moving on.

For the real contenders, Drew was up first. If you've read my past posts, you know that the producers are working overtime to have viewers fall in love with him. He hit it off with Delilah on day one and they've been great together since. Even though he lives in Miami now, he brought her to meet his family in Ohio. Now, don't hate me, Ohio readers, but it was an immediate red flag for me. I love LeBron James, but Ohio? Not for me.

Drew's family seemed fine enough, and when they left, he took her to a barn/hotel/school? Again, Ohio, so who knows? After the barn date disaster earlier this season, Delilah's face looked like ours—abject horror, to be precise. But then they stepped inside and it was a goddamn fairy tale! Twinkle lights were everywhere, an entire HomeGoods' worth of pillows covered the floor, champagne, desserts. You name it, it was there. They started feeding each other strawberries, and when the cameras cut, it wasn't a fade to black, it was a hard cut. I think they both forgot the cameras were there and were going at it.

Now for the love of my life, Anthony. Anthony is a Chicago boy through and through. His grandparents on both sides were first-generation Americans and met in Chicago. My feelings on Chicago, you ask? Love the aquarium, Da Bears, weather is bonkers, also pretty racist. Giving it a five out of ten. Now, when Anthony brought Delilah to meet his parents, I didn't know what to expect. He's pretty laid back, but you can tell he came from some money. Well, I'm here to let you know that his mother, Dolores Alberti, is a freaking dream! Never in the history of *Real Love* have I fallen so hard for anyone. She was beautiful, she was funny, her food looked divine (homemade ravioli and tiramisu!), and she was smart. ADOPT ME, Dolores!

Oh, and her son did all right too.

After Anthony left his parents' house, at which I wept, he drove her into downtown Chicago. He made a very funny, very adorable joke about not getting carsick after the boat catastrophe, and then they pulled up to the Lyric Opera house. Apparently on one of their earlier dates, Delilah told Anthony one of the things she regrets is spending so much time working that she didn't explore other things she loved. She said she wanted to get more involved in the arts, especially ballet, which her late grandmother had loved. When dancers came out onstage, Delilah full-on sobbed—and Lovers, so did I.

Once the curtains closed, the pair couldn't take their hands off each other. It got to the point that they ran from the cameras and we just got subtitles from what their mics picked up. Spoiler alert: most of it was inaudible, but the only part anyone is talking about is when Anthony said, "I don't care, I can't wait any longer to be with you." The cameras cut to commercial and when we came back it was cocktail hour.

However, as much as Delilah loved spending time with both of these men, she's made it very clear that she wants to stay in Miami. Dentist Drew already lives there and is looking forward to merging his life with Delilah's. While Anthony, on the other hand, isn't sure about uprooting his life in Chicago. Just like Delilah does in Miami, he has deep roots in Chicago and a tight-knit relationship with his family. Could it be that what has drawn them so close together could be the thing that tears them apart?

Delilah did something different this week. Instead of dragging either Noah or Theo along to the final episode, she sent them both

home. This is a two-horse race and I've never been happier to have
a heroine who's over the games. Give us what we all came for,
Delilah! But with that elimination, the final is right around the corner.
Drop a comment below with your final pick for the winner!

XOXO,
Stacy

22

I STILL HAVEN'T heard from Ella and I'm starting to get pissed.

You would think she'd at least text me on my birthday or even email me an e-card. Anything would've been nice. But instead she's still acting like a toddler who won't admit she did anything wrong.

I did, however, hear from Vaughn.

He sent me a text message, but I didn't see it until well after midnight thanks to Kai. He asked to meet me so we can talk. I haven't responded yet. I don't know what to say.

My mom still thinks we're working on things and I don't know if I should listen to her or not. She is my mom and I often think she knows what's better for me more than I do.

I thought turning thirty would make things more clear to me, but I'm more confused than ever before.

A knock on my cubicle wall startles me out of my thoughts, and Greg pokes his head in.

"Hey, Maya." His voice is uncharacteristically quiet. "Would you mind chatting with us for a second?"

My stomach clenches and dread causes my toes to curl. Because of course. As if my life hasn't spiraled down far enough, let's add losing the promotion and take away the only thing I thought was safe.

Cool.

"Yeah, of course." I somehow manage to keep my voice from trembling and follow him across the crowded floor.

Unlike the last time I went back to their office to talk, this trip is devoid of all smiles and small talk. I mean, I guess this is good because it prevents me from oversharing about my life and what a total shit show it's turned into. It's also bad because the silence has allowed me to envision the worst outcome possible. I was nervous last time, I feel defeated now.

Marcus is sitting behind the desk when we walk in and he doesn't look any more excited than Greg does. I knew there was a possibility I wouldn't get the promotion, but I was so sure of myself. I know there's still a chance I can get the position in the future, but I really thought this was my time. The knock to my confidence hurts just as much as the disappointment.

I've worked so hard to become the youngest director in the company. Even if the rest of my life is in flames, I felt like this promotion would have been the first step in setting things right.

"Take a seat." Greg gestures to the chairs in front of his desk. I follow directions without saying anything.

"How are you doing, Maya?" Marcus asks.

Thankfully I've never been diagnosed with an incurable disease, but if I was, I bet this is exactly what the doctor would sound like before delivering the terrible news.

The truth is on the tip of my tongue. Maybe they really want to know that my sister probably hates me, the guy I like made me the most thoughtful gift I've ever received, my ex might want me back—which my mom would love because she wanted me married yesterday—and oh yeah, there's still this unbelievable prospect of *Real Love* lingering. Or maybe I should definitely keep it to myself.

"I'm okay," I say instead, because you know, social cues.

Nailed it.

"Good, that's good." Marcus rests his elbows on the desk and steeples his fingers beneath his chin.

"And how have things been since we last talked?" Greg picks up where Marcus stopped, and even though I know they're letting me down gently, I still have to marvel at what a good team they make.

"You know, things have been good." I try to sound nonchalant, but I'm pretty sure my voice is the highest it's ever been besides the one NSYNC concert I went to when I was a kid. "I've been working, trying to prove that I'm an asset to the team."

The truth is, I brought this on myself. I got too comfortable. I spent too much time with Ella and going out with Kai. I was having fun, but at what cost? It was sloppy and I can't blame them for not going with me.

Marcus and Greg look at each other, probably expressing pity for my pathetic behind with their eyes.

"We appreciate that, Maya." Marcus speaks this time, and I really wish they'd hurry up and get it over with so I can go cry in my car. "We really do want you to know that we think you've done an extraordinary job."

"Yes," Greg says, nodding in agreement. "Such an extraordinary job. We don't know if you're aware of this or not, but you are the youngest person who has ever been up for this promotion."

"Oh wow! Really? That's so cool." I feign surprise, not wanting their efforts to soften the blow of not getting the job to go to waste.

It's Marcus's turn to speak. "We want you to know that we were rooting for you, but ultimately who gets this job isn't totally our decision to make."

Oh good.

This conversation is finally almost over.

"It's okay, I'm grateful I was even considered for the position. I'll keep working so the next time the position is open, I'll be the only choice."

Way to go, Maya. That sounded mad professional. You definitely deserve a cocktail and a tub of ice cream after this.

I push my chair back and stand up, prepared to leave after that perfect parting line. Ending this conversation on my terms helps to soothe my pride enough to not have a full breakdown until I'm alone.

"There's just one problem with that." Greg stops me and ruins my boss exit.

I lower myself back down, my stomach clenching again. I don't say anything this time because there's nothing to say. Adding this to the dumpster fire makes me feel like I'm drowning.

Once I'm back in my seat, Greg and Marcus turn their attention to each other again and I'm convinced they communicate telepathically. They stare at each other for a few more moments before looking back at me.

"It's just that"—Greg pauses and takes a deep breath—"it's going to be really hard to apply for the job when you already have it. We only need you to say yes—you're the one that makes the final decision."

I hear his words and see the giant smiles lighting Greg's and Marcus's faces as they high-five each other, but none of it is making any sense.

"I'm sorry." My eyes shift between the two of them as my brain goes into overdrive trying to process what in the fresh hell is going on. "I'm not sure I understand what's happening here."

Greg and Marcus both stand and round the desk until they're flanking my chair.

"You got the job!" Marcus says.

"You, Maya Johnson, are Wright, Ghoram, and Degrate's youngest director!"

Once I'm sure this isn't some very cruel joke, I let their words penetrate and leap out of my seat. I throw my arms around them with the enthusiasm of a European soccer fan whose team just won the World Cup.

"Oh my god!" I bounce up and down, taking a giant step back once I release my bosses. "Are you serious? You're serious, right? Because I couldn't take it if you weren't."

Greg's cheeks are flushed pink and Marcus is adjusting the tie I messed up in my wild embrace.

"Not a joke," Greg says. "Congratulations, Maya, you earned it."

I bite back my intended response of *fuck yes, I did*, and opt instead for the much more respectable, "Thank you so much for this opportunity. I'm not going to let you down."

"We know you won't," Marcus answers for the both of them. "And since you just made Wright, Ghoram, and Degrate history, we insist on you taking the rest of the day off to celebrate."

"Thank you." Kai is working on the yacht today and Ella is still ignoring me, so I don't know who I'll celebrate with, but I don't argue. Time alone might not be horrible.

They both extend their hands, probably worried I'll accost them again, and congratulate me one last time.

I open the door and it becomes apparent we weren't as quiet as I thought. As I step onto the office floor, everyone is standing, clapping and congratulating me. I weave my way through thanking coworkers I've never spoken to before and feeling a bit like a rock star. When I get back to my cubicle, I look at my little decorations and the framed pictures scattered along my desk and picture them in my new office with floor-to-ceiling windows. I wish I could tell Ella.

"Maya!" Bailey barrels into my cubicle with Delilah hot on her heels. They nearly knock me over when they slam into me and wrap their arms around me. "Congratulations!"

I'm still low-key pissed at Bailey for inviting Vaughn to my party, but I haven't said anything to her. I can't tell if I'm overreacting because I do think her intentions, as misguided as they might've been, were good. Plus, no matter what, we still work together and I'm trying to keep any drama as far away from the office as possible.

"We know you might not ever trust us to celebrate with you ever again." Delilah at least has the decency to look contrite. "But can we at least buy you a drink?"

I want to ask her about Ella, but I manage not to.

Barely.

"Maybe come to my place for one this time?" I'm not prepared to go out with them again so soon.

"That sounds perfect," Delilah says. "I have to head out of town tonight for promo stuff and the reunion, but as soon as I get back?"

"I can't believe the season is already almost over." It feels like we just went to the premiere at Delilah's house. So much has changed since then.

"Seriously, it went by so fast," Bailey chimes in. "I can't believe it's between Anthony and Drew and that you still haven't told us who you freaking picked already!"

"Whatever." Delilah rolls her eyes. I don't think she even registers Bailey's comments about the show anymore. "You'll find out next week like everyone else."

Bailey opens her mouth to argue back, but I have the rest of the day off and I don't need to be here for this. "As much as I'd love to stay and rehash this argument again"—I open my drawer and pull out my purse—"I'm out of here. I have to call my mom and tell her the good news."

I talked to her for my birthday, but I kept it short. I've been avoiding her calls for weeks now and I can't wait to tell her the good news. She's going to be so proud that I've finally given her something she can brag to her friends about.

I barely check my rearview mirror as I peel out of my parking spot and the squeal of my tires bounces off the concrete walls. I take the corners faster than I ever have before and hit call on Mom's name as soon as I see the sun shining from the garage exit. If she sends me to voicemail, I'm going to be seriously pissed. I'm so excited to fill her in I'm about to burst!

Much to my surprise, she picks up on the second ring instead of the usual three.

"Maya? What's wrong?" She's out of breath and sounds a little unhinged.

"Nothing's wrong," I say, feeling terrible that in my excitement I made her worry. "I just have some really good news that I wanted to share with you."

"Oh. Okay." Her exhale echoes throughout my car and throws me off-kilter. "Good news is good. What is it?"

She doesn't sound like my always-put-together mother at all. Even when Ella broke her leg jumping off the back patio, my mom never broke a sweat. She never gives any hints of feeling anything other than capable and confident. She behaves as if she has control over the uncontrollable. It's equal parts inspiring and intimidating.

And probably a big part of the reason I never feel like I measure up.

"Are you all right?" I ask instead of sharing my news. "You sound . . . off."

Static fills my ear and it sounds like she's moving around a lot before it finally quiets and her voice comes across my speakers again. "I'm fine. I thought maybe you had talked to your sister."

"Ella? Why?" My palms start to sweat on my leather steering wheel as one worst-case scenario after another fills my head. I knew I should've made her come back to my place until we figured everything out. This entire fight was a giant misunderstanding and who knows what's happened to her now. "Is she okay? What's going on?"

"Maya! For goodness' sake, please relax." My mom, who is often stern, but never—and I mean *never*—raises her voice, screams from the other end of the phone. "Your father and I are having a little . . . hiccup and the university is going through a bit of a hard time, that's all. I'm just a little stressed out."

Again, my mom does not get stressed out, and if she does, she for damn sure doesn't admit it out loud. And suddenly I realize that's exactly how I described my breakup with Vaughn to Ella, as a "hiccup," and I know something must be truly wrong.

"What do you mean by a little hiccup, Mom?" I press the issue, something I would've never dared to do before. "What is really going on?"

I brace for her to scold me for getting involved in grown folks' business. Because even though I'm now thirty, my mom will never see me as an adult.

"Well, you know your father," she says on an exhale, surprising the hell out of me. "He's a wonderful man, but he's still a man. There are times where the stress of the hospital becomes too much and he . . . Well, he wanders. And of course, this would be when the university is having budget cuts and my department is on the line. It's not a great week. Now, why are you calling?"

I open my mouth to respond, but words don't come out.

I'm too stunned to speak. I turn into the nearest parking lot and idle because I cannot focus on driving after the bomb that was just dropped on me.

"Mom," I say, still trying to process everything. "Are you saying that Dad is cheating on you?"

My dad? My surgeon, uptight, doesn't even like the word "suck" dad is cheating on my mom? And my mom isn't chasing after him with a broom?

"Oh, don't be childish," she says, and even though I can't see her, I know she's waving me off. "When you've been married as long as we have, there are obstacles you have to overcome. Your father loves me, but men aren't perfect. We've been through this before and we'll get through it now."

I look out the window, inspecting the outside world, trying to find the glitch in the matrix because this can't be real. There is no way my mother, Professor Johnson, is sitting here and accepting it, and even saying it's happened before, instead of packing her shit and walking away. Aliens must have me or I died and went to the bad place. All of those options are better than the strong, brilliant, confident woman who raised me lying down and accepting this.

"Mom! Are you kidding me?" My head feels like it's going to explode. I can feel the pressure building behind my eyes. "Please tell me this is a ridiculous joke. I know you, there is no way you would stay with a man who cheated on you. Not even Dad."

I freaking love my dad. He was my hero growing up. But he worked long hours, and when he was home, he expected perfection from me but always gave me a reward for it. When I would get an A on a test or win a spelling bee, he drove me to get ice cream or bought me a new toy. He loved his girls and we loved him, but that doesn't excuse him from being a terrible husband.

"This is why I didn't want to tell you, Maya." She groans into the phone, sounding more annoyed with me than with her cheating husband. "What did you think I meant when we spoke last about accepting Vaughn for who he is? Did you think I gave that advice blindly? No. Absolutely not. No man is perfect, life is not perfect. But you chose him and you have to deal with it, just like I have."

For a split second, I'm pissed at her for even insinuating that I should accept a life where duty and expectations are more important than love and happiness. But before I can even say anything about it, my heart breaks. Because I know how she feels. I know the heavy acceptance that something is better than nothing, and that if you lower your standards you can be happy. I had been so dedicated to the idea I'd even been convinced that asking for crumbs from Vaughn was asking too much.

Then I met Kai and he showed me I was so totally wrong. I watched Delilah find love on a television show and start demanding more out of life. I spent weeks with my over-the-top sister who milks every drop of joy from everything she does, who loses her mind when she thinks—even for one second—that I might settle in my life for a relationship, home, or even job that I don't 100 percent love.

My heart crumbles in my chest for my poor mom, who doesn't think she deserves better and didn't have anyone in her life who never stopped trying to convince her that she did.

"I'm so sorry, Mom."

"Like I said, don't be sorry. Your father and I will be fine." The defensiveness I never realized she wielded like a weapon is back in her voice. "I have been Mrs. Johnson my entire adult life and that won't ever change."

"But what about when you were Deborah Mack? What happened to her?"

My grandma passed away years ago, but I'll never forget her looking over at my mom with a wistful smile, telling me stories about a version of my mom that felt so foreign to me they were like fairy tales. She'd tell me about my mom always ripping her jeans at recess and how her hair would be a disaster when she came home because she played double Dutch all day. There were stories about my mom's wild teen years where she snuck out more than she stayed in, and how once she got older, she found the focus she had never had before.

But now, listening to my mom, I don't think she found her focus. I think she lost herself.

"What kind of silly question is that, Maya? Are you going to tell me this good news or not?" I hear papers shuffling in the background; my mom is always busy doing something. "I have an appointment soon."

Telling her about my promotion is on the tip of my tongue. Even after hearing all of this, my first instinct is to do and say anything to make her proud. Which makes this so freaking hard.

"Oh, yeah." I try to think of any reason I could've called. "I'm thinking about renting my condo out like you've been suggesting."

This isn't completely true, but it's not a total lie either. While I don't think landlord life is the life for me, I have been tossing around the idea of selling.

"That's wonderful." She buys it somehow. "It's about time you and Vaughn started settling down more permanently."

My insides twist and I can't be sure if it's because I lied or because of her vision of my future with Vaughn. Either way, I know I have to get off this call.

"Well, I'll let you go, Mom." I wish there was something I could say to her to convince her to see herself the way I do, but I know I can't. "I love you."

"I love you too," she says. "Now go be great."

She disconnects the phone before I can tell her I already am great and that from here on out, I'm never going to forget it.

I move to put my car into drive, but think better of it and send a text first.

I might not know exactly what I'm going to do in life, but I for sure know now what I'm not going to do.

23

AS A TEENAGER, compared to most of my peers, I was pretty average. Compared to Ella, however, I was a freaking saint. Because of this, I was largely ignored. My parents trusted me to do what I needed to do and I never gave them a reason not to. Even with the freedom this granted me, I never took advantage. I followed the rules and did what was expected.

Which might be the reason that even though Vaughn broke up with me, part of me still felt guilty for liking Kai so much. I wondered if I was really interested in Kai, or just trying to make myself feel better while waiting for Vaughn to find his way back to me.

But now I know I wasn't.

Am I making the best life choices? I honestly have no idea. Maybe I'm not, but it's nobody's business but mine. Or at least it shouldn't be. And I decide that I will be making the decisions I want to make because they're right for me and no one else.

For the first time ever.

I enter the restaurant feeling equal parts nerves and excitement.

"Hi." The hostess greets me, oblivious to what a huge deal this is for me. "How many?"

"I'm actually meeting someone here." I take off my

oversized sunglasses, because as much as I'm feeling my-self right now, I can't be the person who wears sunglasses inside. "I think they might already be here."

"Great. You're free to look around." She aims her bright, friendly smile at me and it's no wonder she got the hostess job here.

For a second I wonder if part of my plans for Maya 2.0 include befriending polite hostesses. I have been saying I need new friends for a while, and this could be a great place to start. I bet she's not auditioning to be the lead on a reality show or inviting an ex-boyfriend to my birthday party. The only reason I don't shoot my shot is because I see Vaughn approaching out of the corner of my eye and I forget every-thing else.

"My," he says when he reaches me. He wraps his long, thick arms around me and pulls me tight against his chest. "How are you?"

Ugh.

This would be so much easier if he wasn't so freaking hot.

"I'm good." I try not to tense in his arms, the need to curl into his familiar warmth at direct odds with how good it felt to be in Kai's. I don't know how people have affairs. This is exhausting and I'm not even doing anything wrong.

The thought is an unwelcome reminder of everything my mom's going through and what I'm vowing to avoid to the best of my ability. From here on out, I'll know my worth and accept nothing less.

"I'm over here." He drops his arm and points to a table in the corner. He reaches for my hand to guide me across the restaurant, but I tuck it into my pocket. "I ordered you a Crown and Coke."

"Thank you." Oh wonderful. This is going to be even

harder than I thought. Leave it to Vaughn to wait until now to become considerate.

"Here we are." Vaughn stops beside a table for two and pulls out my chair . . . something he's never done for me before.

"Thank you." My stomach twists with his newfound chivalry.

"Soooo . . ." He draws out the word as I awkwardly fiddle around and avoid eye contact. "How have you been?"

"Good!" I really shouldn't have come. Avoiding situations like this has to be the reason they invented text messaging. "I mean, things have been really good. I actually found out I got my promotion today, so that's exciting."

"The director position?" He lifts his glass and says, "Congratulations! I know how hard you've worked for that."

"Yeah, thank you." I follow his lead and touch my glass to his. "I did work really hard for it and I can't believe it paid off."

"Well I can." He stretches a long arm across the table and squeezes my hand. "You're the most capable woman I know."

Okay. Yeah.

I'm gonna need him to stop being so nice.

"Thank you." I hold tight to his hand in mine and look him straight in the eyes for what feels like the first time in ages. "That really means a lot coming from you."

And it does.

No matter what we've gone through recently, Vaughn has been my best friend for over ten years. After my mom, he was one of the first people I wanted to reach out to. But in doing so, I think I realized what I haven't wanted to admit for a long time.

Vaughn has been my comfort blanket. I reach for him

out of habit, not because he actually makes me feel better. After spending time with Kai, realizing how sad my mom is, and watching Delilah go on this wild journey of self-discovery, comfortable won't suffice anymore.

"Have you been here before?" Vaughn picks up his menu and I know he's about to tell me to order something he wants . . . and in that moment I know what to do. "You should order th—"

I cut him off. "I can't do this." I was hoping we could have dinner together so we could have a nice send-off for our relationship, but I can't. "I can't do this anymore."

"You can't do what?" His eyebrows knit and his eyes narrow in concern.

"Us." I've never been the one to take control between the two of us and it shows. His mouth is hanging open and I think I've stunned him speechless. "You were right to end things. We aren't happy, and we haven't been happy in a long time if we're being honest."

"But I thought this was us working things out."

"No." I grab my drink and take a giant gulp. "There is no us to work out anymore. The person I was when you broke up with me is gone. I'm a sparkly cherry now and I'm letting my colors fly!"

I don't mean to yell, but I couldn't stop myself if I tried. Everyone in the restaurant is staring at me, but instead of being embarrassed, I try something new.

"I'm choosing to be happy!" I shout to the very confused patrons surrounding me. "Who's with me?"

Unlike in the movies, this does not garner the response of cheers and *hell yes, sister* being shouted around. But that's okay, because I didn't do it for other people. I did it for me.

"Have a nice life, Vaughn." I grab my purse and tighten

my grip on the leather strap. "I truly wish you nothing but happiness and love. I know you'll find it."

Just not with me.

And that's freaking wonderful.

I walk away from Vaughn without the smallest urge to look back. When I step out of the restaurant and into the bright Miami sun, I feel lighter than ever. I pull out my phone and hit dial before I make it to my car.

"Hello?" Delilah answers on the second ring.

"I know you're leaving tomorrow, but this is an emergency," I tell her without greeting. "My house, as fast as you can. I'll call Bailey, you bring Ella even if you have to sedate her."

"If sedation is required, then I know it's going to be good," she says. "We'll be at your place ASAP."

24

I PACE MY living room floor waiting for everyone to arrive.

And by everyone, I mean Ella.

When she arrived all those weeks ago—unannounced and uninvited, I might add—I never thought that I would spiral from spending a few days without seeing or talking to her. Between Vaughn and Kai alone, I have so much to fill her in on.

I hear voices in the hallway and run to swing the door open before they can even knock.

"Oh, it's just you two." My stomach falls when I see Delilah and Bailey, but no Ella.

"Just us? We rush over here and that's the greeting we get?" Bailey pushes past me and heads straight to my counter where I've set up a makeshift cocktail bar. "Oh! But at least you provided quality booze."

Heat tinges my face. "I'm sor—" I start, but Delilah places a gentle hand on my shoulder and stops me.

"Don't apologize." Her voice is so quiet and apologetic it causes my sinuses to burn. "I know you wanted to see Ella, but she left town this afternoon. I didn't know until I called her to invite her over."

The ground disappears from beneath my feet and the tears welling up threaten to spill down my cheeks. The sudden end to the hope I was feeling is like a punch to the gut and I don't know how to catch my breath.

"I really thought we'd fix everything before she left." The guilt I feel for making her feel as if she wasn't good enough, for not including her in my own life for so long, is more than I can handle. I wanted to make things right, to show her how much she means to me. I wanted to show her how much she's influenced the way I view myself and what's important. "I can't believe I let her leave without talking to her."

"I know you don't see it, but you two are so much alike." Delilah takes my hand in hers. "You're both so stubborn and set in your ways, but you also have the softest hearts and work overtime to protect them. Take it for what it's worth, but I think she's more upset about what she said to you than anything else."

I don't want her to be upset about anything, but this at least gives me hope that she's not still furious with me.

"Oh, come on. You're sisters, you'll get over it." Bailey hands me a mystery cocktail. I don't know if she means to be so dismissive or if I'm being übersensitive, but it kinda hurts my feelings. "Now are you going to tell us why you dragged us over here in such a hurry?"

I shake my head, trying to clear it of sad thoughts about Ella and remember why I called them over tonight.

"I wanted to tell you that I think I've been wrong about everything." I take a sip of the drink Bailey made me and start coughing when it damn near burns through my esophagus.

"What?" She looks at me with big, innocent eyes. "You said it was an emergency. I thought a heavy pour was necessary."

Delilah shakes her head and rolls her eyes, which is super out of character for her; she is the most patient person I know, but that might not being saying much considering my group of friends. I wonder if during all of my drama I missed something . . .

"What do you mean you've been wrong about everything?" Delilah asks before I can figure out what's going on between them.

I put the glass of liquid fire on the counter and wring my hands as I try to figure out where the hell I should even start.

"I guess I always thought I was laying the foundation to be happy, and now I'm realizing that being happy isn't a destination that you prepare for, it's what you're doing now." I don't know if I'm making any sense at all. I usually have a point to make and make it; blurting out my feelings is new for me. "So if I'm not happy in my job or relationship now, why would I be happy in ten years? Does checking things off my vision board guarantee success? Does success guarantee happiness? I've been focusing on trying to become someone I'm not instead of loving who I already am, and I'm missing out on everything."

Bailey and Delilah are both staring at me, saying absolutely nothing. I doubt I'm making any sense at all.

"Well damn, girl," Delilah finally says. "That was a whole fucking word. I know you didn't come to all of that just because of Ella. What's really going on?"

For a person who doesn't cry often, my tear ducts are working overtime. The wildest part is there's so much going on inside my head I can't tell if they're tears of sadness, relief, or joy.

Maybe a combination of them all?

"I don't even know where to start?" I mean for it to be a statement, but it comes out as a question. "My relationships, my family, my job? I don't know if I've ever been right about anything to be honest."

I've heard of a midlife crisis, but nobody warned me that I would turn thirty and lose control. This feels like a pivotal moment in my life and I'm terrified I might choose the wrong path.

"That's a whole lot to be worried about," Delilah says. "Why don't we break it down? You got the promotion you've been vying for and I thought you loved WGD; what's going on there?"

I listen to Delilah and all I can remember is sitting at that restaurant with her a year ago, being too scared to take a risk. What would've happened if I wasn't so afraid? What would this year have looked like for me if I'd decided to live my life by faith instead of fear?

"Are you happy?" I ask her instead of answering her question. "Because you used to say you loved your job too, but now everything is different for you. Are you happy with the decision you made?"

Even though I'm sure some would say I'm deflecting, I really need to know. I need to know if she regrets what she did and wishes life could be simple for her again.

"I've honestly never been happier." Her smile softens and she reaches for my hand. "But it was also the scariest 'yes' I've ever uttered. I regretted it immediately after I signed the contract."

"Really?" Bailey chimes in. "You never told me that."

"Me either." I don't know if this makes me a terrible human, but for some reason, knowing she struggled with making this decision makes me feel a little better about all of the indecision currently bouncing around the inside of my skull.

She's seemed nothing but confident and sure about the show since she was offered the lead. It was like she was pre-destined for it and she knew it.

"Oh yeah." She nods so fast and hard it's a miracle she's

not dizzy. "The day after I agreed, I thought I was going to die. And I'm not exaggerating. My body revolted. I spent the day alternating between throwing up and nursing a killer migraine. I think I had spent so much of my life making the 'right' choices that following my heart made my body go into shock."

And that's where I feel I am right now. My heart and head are going to war and I don't know which one to listen to.

"How'd you get over it? You didn't think it was a sign you should call it off?" A million questions run through my mind and I need the answers more than I need my next breath.

"I think it was the opposite—the big reaction was proof that I needed to do it. I needed to fight through the hard to get to the good. It's changed my perspective on everything. I'm going to put in my notice at work and just enjoy my life." Her voice drops to a whisper, forcing Bailey and me to lean in closer to hear her. "Because what I got is beyond good. It's the best I've ever had."

"I'm really happy for you." And even though these stupid tears are still falling, I love this more for her than I hate it for me.

She took the risk I was so afraid of and now she's on the other side, and I'm all the way back at the starting line.

"It could still be you," she whispers. "*Real Love* is still interested in you. I have meetings all this week; if you want the spot, I can talk to them."

Between everything that has happened with Kai and Vaughn, I almost forgot that this could still be a possibility for me. I could still have a chance to go back and take the route I ran away from, and I think I might actually want it.

"I don't know—" I say, but Bailey cuts in before I can get it all out.

"Not to be an asshole during this little moment," Bailey

says, and I brace for whatever asshole thing she is most definitely about to say. "But do we not remember that I was the one who made us all audition for *Real Love*? It was *my* idea. Neither of you even wanted to do it. No offense, Maya, but you said no. You lost your chance. I don't understand why Delilah is fighting so hard for you to go on the show and not me. Don't I deserve a chance at this too?"

Wow.

I braced, but I didn't brace enough.

"Are you being serious right now?" Delilah turns her full attention to Bailey and I wouldn't want to be on the receiving end of the glare she's wearing. "Please tell me you're joking."

"Why would I be joking?" Instead of reading the room, Bailey straightens her shoulders and doubles down. "It *was* my idea and Maya *did* say no. Neither of those things are untrue. But for some reason, you seem to ignore those facts. I don't know if it's because you're threatened by me or what, but it feels really crappy and it's not okay."

I feel like my eyes are about to pop out of my head and I nearly choke from the tension suddenly filling my little apartment.

"You think I'm threatened by you? Bailey, come on." Delilah starts to laugh, but there is absolutely zero humor in the sound. It's fucking terrifying. If I were Bailey, I would run.

But Bailey does not do the smart thing and run.

"What? It's a fair question. You have attention now, but let's be honest, I'm more of the typical lead for the show. If I were to go on next, you might not be the favorite anymore. I know that's why you're really doing this. You know Maya wouldn't overtake you as the favorite, but I would."

"Whoa, whoa, whoa. I'm going to need you to walk that

one back a little bit," I say, not appreciating the shade Bailey is throwing at my expense. "Not only are you being rude, but you're just plain wrong."

"Why are you even getting involved, Maya?" Bailey snaps back. The bitterness in her face causes her usually delicate features to scrunch up in a very unattractive way. "You already said no! Literally none of this concerns you."

I've never seen Bailey so worked up and angry, which is why—even though she's acting like a real asshole right now—I feel bad for wanting to laugh in her face. Having good sex with Kai has truly mellowed me out, because a few weeks ago, I'd be going off right about now.

"It feels like it concerns me since . . . I don't know . . ." I pause for dramatic effect and watch as Bailey's face changes from alabaster to bright red. "*Real Love* is calling me, not you?"

"And they wouldn't be calling you if Delilah wasn't so insecure and just told them I'm the best person for the show!"

Because none of my friends have had children yet, I'm not used to seeing temper tantrums. It's as fascinating as it is disturbing.

"Bailey, I *did* recommend you at the beginning of the season when they asked if I had any suggestions for future leads with promise." I've heard Delilah mad before, but her voice is so flat that I'm convinced the only thing holding her back must be Jesus himself. "They saw your tape and didn't think you'd be a good fit. I pushed for you for a while until all of your snide comments about me and my choices became too much and secrets I told only you ended up in the *Real Love* gossip blogs."

The. Way. I. Gasp.

I almost pass out as the world spins so fast and I have to hold on to the counter to stay in my seat. What in the world have I been doing that I didn't see any of this coming? I mean, Bailey does like to gossip and she did send me blogs every single week, but still. I never thought she'd sell out Delilah like that!

"What?" All of the fight in Bailey disappears. Guilt is written all over her face and I don't know if I feel worse for her or for Delilah.

"Bailey, I know you think you're smarter and far more clever than us, but I'm not an idiot." Delilah doesn't relent. This must've been building for weeks and she's finally snapped. "Why do you think I never let it slip to you who I chose? Not only did I not want to hear whatever insult you'd throw my way, I didn't trust you not to tell everyone. And if you think I didn't clock the way you invited Vaughn to Maya's party, you're dead wrong."

I was hoping to stay an innocent bystander in this massacre, but now that Delilah mentions it, I do have questions.

It never did make much sense. She knew we were separated and that things were going well with Kai. I was confused, but I didn't think her intentions were bad, just sorely misguided—likely by her complete lack of interest in anyone but herself.

Until now.

"She has a point. Why did you invite Vaughn?" Even though Ella and I clearly have issues we need to talk through, this fight we're in could've been avoided if Bailey hadn't stuck her nose where it didn't belong.

"Because!" She throws her arms in the air and her southern accent explodes full force. "This thing with Kai is never going to last. I mean, come *on* Maya. He's a globe-trotting artist and you're an uptight finance boss. Get real, it's obviously just a fling and it's not going to work out. No way would you be able to be with someone as free, someone as cool as him. I figured if I got you back with Vaughn and you were on track again for your perfect little 2.5 kids, white-picket-fence life, you wouldn't care about *Real Love* again and Delilah would finally think about *me!*"

Woof.

Listen, I'm not saying lying is acceptable, but if I were Bailey, this secret would've gone to the fucking grave with me. No way would I ever admit to being such a conniving asshole. And the way she pretends like she's trying to look out for me while simultaneously insulting me every step of the way is mind-boggling. I'm actually stunned into silence.

"And there it is." Delilah sits down and deflates onto the stool beside me. "I didn't want to be right about this, Bailey. It's why I didn't say anything. I hoped I was being a little paranoid and seeing things that weren't there. During this entire process of *Real Love*, I had to learn to trust myself. I think I'm most upset that I let you make me question myself again."

"I didn't mean . . ." Bailey says, seeming to understand the gravity of what she's done. "I didn't want to hurt you. Either of you. I really do love you, you've been so good to me. I just wanted to be included too."

"But you *were* included." I think back to all the time we've spent together, and Bailey was always there. "You didn't want inclusion, you wanted superiority. You didn't want to be friends with *us,* you wanted friends who would inflate your ego."

All of this sucks.

25

AFTER BAILEY LEFT my place with her tail between her legs, I told Delilah about everything from Vaughn to Kai to my parents. I also gave her my blessing to put my name in the hat for *Real Love* and then immediately started to think I'd gone a little cuckoo for Cocoa Puffs.

"I know it's scary, but I promise you won't regret it." Delilah must notice the fear written across my face. "I don't think I ever told you this, but after I signed the contract to go on *Real Love,* I almost called a lawyer to help me back out."

"No, you definitely never told me that story." My memory might not be the best, but I'd remember lawyers. "What made you decide to go through with it?"

"Well, besides the thought of being sued for breach of contract by a major television network, I decided I had to trust myself. The entire reason I signed up was because something deep down inside of me was telling me I belonged there. I—" She cuts herself off and I can almost see her mind working out a problem. "Say it's God or the universe or whatever you want to call it, but I think I was being pushed to meet Anthony."

Now I've always considered myself somewhat of a skeptic, but hearing Delilah tell me that she picked Anthony makes my heart explode inside of my chest.

"I knew it!" I jump off the stool and wrap my arms around my gorgeous, happy, and in-love best friend. "From the first episode, I knew you picked him!"

Maybe from the first episode is a bit of a stretch, but I called Anthony from the very beginning. The way that man looked at Delilah, as if she hung the moon and stars, was not something that could be faked.

"And he's so amazing, Maya. I can't wait until you can meet him." The same look I saw in his eyes on TV is in hers now and I could not be happier for her. "But what I'm trying to say is that if you really sit with yourself, you already know exactly what you want. Maybe it's *Real Love* and maybe it's something different. I just want you to make a decision that you're basing on faith and not fear."

"That's so much easier said than done though." I've been told my entire life that being dutiful is superior to all else and that success is found by pleasing others. "I don't know if I can trust myself. I'm not like you and Ella, people don't just fall in love with me."

"Don't talk about my friend like that. You are the most capable, lovable person I know." The ferocity in her voice knocks my breath away. "You changed my life in ways I could've never imagined and I won't allow you to doubt yourself."

I start to squirm beneath her praise. It's funny that as much as I crave it, I also struggle with accepting it.

"So does this mean you're moving to Chicago now?" I attempt to shift the focus off myself, not even caring that I'm giving away the fact that I've not only been watching the show, but I've also been paying very close attention. "Who am I going to talk through all of my issues with?"

"Actually . . ." She drags out the word and a smile I don't trust pulls at the corners of her mouth. "I think I know the perfect person."

* * *

Even though work is usually the one place I do my best thinking, I call out for the next two days. I'm attempting not to overthink every decision I've ever made in my entire life, and having to run into Bailey and even Delilah was too much of a distraction. I needed to follow Delilah's advice and really sit with myself for a couple of days. Luckily, being a workaholic means I have an abundance of PTO and might take the entire week off.

I'm watching the United Kingdolls perform "UK, Hun?" for the thousandth time when I hear a key unlock my front door.

"See you've really brightened up the place since I left." Ella waltzes into my apartment, lifting her chin in the direction of the empty Lucky Charms box on my counter, judging me within less than a minute of being in my presence.

I really need to apologize for doing that to her for the last twenty years.

"Shut up." I drop the remote onto the couch and run to my sister. Instead of the fight we got into the first time she showed up unannounced at my apartment, when I reach her, I stand on tiptoe and wrap my arms around her. "I'm so glad you came back. I'm so sorry that I was such a bitch to you."

"I'm sorry. I saw Vaughn and flipped out. I didn't even give you a chance and then I attacked you." There's no sarcasm in her voice, and this might be the first authentic apology Ella has ever given me.

I can't believe how much we've grown.

"I might not have deserved it that night, but I did deserve it." All of the regrets I've been ruminating on since I saw her last float to the surface. "I've been so hard on you and it wasn't fair. Also, I talked to Mom and holy shit. You were not wrong to run as far as possible from her expectations."

"She told you about Dad?" she asks, and my head jerks back so fast I'll probably have to find a chiropractor to fix it. "Our parents are insane."

"How long have you known?"

"Since I overheard them fighting about it when I was sixteen. I asked Mom and she told me to mind my own business, but I was able to crack Dad when we went golfing one day."

"Ella!" Since she was sixteen? So many things start to fall into place. No wonder she always scoffed when I brought up our parents' marriage and living according to Mom's expectations. "Why didn't you tell me?"

"And break your heart? I don't think so. That was going to be on them." She walks to my fridge and grabs one of the bazillion drinks she had left in there. "I might meddle with certain things, but no way was I drifting into that lane. No way."

That was probably a good call. I wouldn't have believed her anyway. It's still hard for me to believe, and Mom told me.

"Speaking of things I've been right about, I heard Bailey showed her entire ass," she says, and all is right in the world again.

"You heard?"

"Duh." She rolls her eyes and clicks her tongue. "You do realize that Delilah and I talk a lot, right? She called me as soon as she left."

"Hmph." My arms drop to my side and my bottom lip pokes out . . . something I'm sure is the exact opposite of cute. "I thought you were out of town! I wish you would've been here to see it. It was wild."

"I was technically out of town. I spent the night in Palm Beach." Ella grabs her phone out of her purse and walks over to the couch. "But if you want to see something even crazier, boy do I have something to show you."

"I'm not sure anything could top the rant Bailey went on," I tell Ella, who's busy tapping away on her screen. "She was saying that she deserved to be on *Real Love* and Delilah was jealous and only cheering for me because I wouldn't steal her spotlight—"

"Here it is." Ella cuts me off, clearly not interested in anything I was saying, and shoves her phone in my face.

"What?" I ask as my brain begins to process what I'm seeing. I grab the phone out of her hand and look even closer. It's Bailey's Instagram feed and she tagged Victory, one of the clubs Vaughn worked with a lot. "Is that . . . it can't be. Is it?"

"Is that Bailey at Victory, smiling and laughing next to Ralph?" Ella says what I didn't think could be true. "It definitely is."

Well then.

Any pity I had for Bailey goes up in flames.

" 'Fun nights with new friends! Seeing a lot of good times in the future.' " I read her caption out loud and almost fall when I see Vaughn comment with a winky-face emoji. "An emoji? He always made fun of me for texting emojis!"

"Listen," Ella says, and takes her phone back. "I'm not saying you have terrible taste in friends, but I am saying that you trust people too easily and you should run all future prospects by me for approval."

In the past, I would've scoffed at this suggestion, but now I'm honestly not even really opposed.

"Do you think . . ." I don't even know how to finish the question because I don't think I want the answer. "Do you think they've hung out before?"

Do I think that Bailey sucks? Yes. Do I think she would've slept with my boyfriend before I was aware that she sucked? No. At least, I hope not.

"I don't think so. From what I got out of Bailey when I did still talk to her, she didn't really go to the clubs Vaughn worked at." She tosses her phone onto my table and sinks down on my couch. "I think they ran into each other, and since they both are terrible, they hit it off and posted because of said terribleness."

Oddly enough, that makes me feel much better.

"You follow Bailey on social media?"

"Please." She grabs the remote and starts scanning through the streaming channels. "I would never give her the pleasure. This is a fake account that I use to occasionally stalk people who have wronged me in case I accidentally like one of their pictures."

I have social media, but I'm terrible at handling one account. I'd be hopeless at two.

But I guess this is what sisters are for.

"I appreciate your dedication to staying informed."

"I know you're not going to look, so I do what I can." She finally settles on the newest season of *Housewives*. "Plus, hate scrolling is my favorite pastime."

"Oh. That makes sense I guess." Ella's favorite part of *Mean Girls* was the burn book, so her enjoying hate scrolling adds up. I lean into the couch and my stomach growls, reminding me of exactly how long I've been watching *Ru-Paul's Drag Race UK*. "By the way, I ordered a ton of food if you're hungry."

She follows me into the kitchen and takes stock of the overabundance of delivery, as I've already ordered today.

"Were you expecting company?" she asks as she looks into the five—yes, five—boxes on the counter.

"I was planning on stuffing my feelings down, thank you

very much." I open the box of sweet potato fries and she swipes one before I can stop her.

Why did I want her back again?

"What?" she asks when she sees how I'm looking at her. "You asked if I was hungry and you know how I feel about sweet potato fries."

They are the superior fry.

"Whatever." I roll my eyes, but my heart's not in it. "At least get a plate."

"So what else is new?" she asks once we've piled our plates with more food than we'll ever eat. "Delilah told me you had good news, but wouldn't tell me what."

Considering they are new best friends, that was nice of her.

"I got my promotion." I'm prepared for her to groan because of her constant jabs about my job. But to my surprise, she drops her fry-and-mozzarella-stick-covered plate and runs around my counter to hug me.

"You got the promotion? Congratulations!"

"Thank you." I hug her back, so grateful that we're not fighting anymore.

I might be 100 percent an introvert, but even introverts need genuine human connection. Yesterday was a lot. Having my sister be so happy for me, even when—no, scratch that—*especially* when she doesn't necessarily agree with the trajectory of my life means so much to me. She may be my polar opposite, but I couldn't love her more if I tried.

"You were up against two guys, right?" she asks.

"Yeah, it was me and two men in the running," I confirm. "There aren't a ton of women in the industry."

"Look at you, bringing down the patriarchy." She lets out a long, slow whistle that I still to this day cannot do. "Good for you, Maya!"

"Thank you." I beam under the praise I would've brushed off a few weeks ago and I know that's more about me than it is about Ella. "But . . . and you're partially to blame for this . . . I don't know if I want to accept it."

I feel like anyone else would at least pretend to be sad hearing this news. I mean, I did just spend the last decade of my life working to get here. Throwing away all of that work is pretty depressing.

But not my sister.

Nope.

"Oh my god!" She bounces up and down and her smile grows about a hundred sizes. "Yes! Quit! I'm going to go to Brazil! You can come with me! It will be so much fun. Me and you, exploring South America. Tasting the food, experiencing the culture, lounging on the beaches."

As far as pitches go, this isn't a bad one. Some time in the sun exploring with Ella does sound pretty appealing. And Brazil? I'm not sure it gets much better than that.

I'm about to tell her about Delilah and *Real Love* when there's a knock at my door.

"Did you order food too and still take my fries?" I look at her and aim an accusatory glare at her full plate.

"If by ordered food you mean invited Kai over, then sure." She walks to the door, looking at me over her shoulder with an expression I definitely don't trust. "It might not be takeout, but I have a feeling he's eaten quite a few things here."

"Ella!" I shout, my cheeks heating as the memories from all the nights (and mornings and afternoons) spent with Kai flash to the front of my mind.

I'm not even able to gather my wits before she swings the door open and Kai is standing inside my apartment looking as handsome as ever.

"My dude!" Ella high-fives him and somehow still manages to look cool doing it. "You're just in time."

"Am I?" he asks her, but he's looking at me. And even from across the room, I can feel his gaze drifting down my body.

"You are." Ella locks my door and practically shoves him until his butt is in the stool next to me. "Because I was just trying to convince our girl here to move to Brazil with me for a year."

His eyes do that thing again that causes him to resemble a really cute cartoon character. "You're going to move? What about your job?"

"She's not—" Ella begins to say, but does a zipper motion across her mouth when she notices the death stare I'm aiming at her.

"I got my promotion. I was going to call you, but then my world promptly caught fire." I spare him the gory details. "Now I'm not sure this is what I *actually* want as much as it is what I think I *should* want . . . if that makes sense."

"Total sense." Kai is the polar opposite of Ella's chaotic energy. His calmness is contagious as he skims his hand down my arm. "The cherry. It's spreading."

Tears spring to my eyes and I try to blink them away.

"Your cherry is spreading?" Ella's horrified shout breaks the moment. "What kind of freaky shit are you two talking about?"

"Oh sweet lord." I hide my face in my hands. I thought I'd dealt with enough recently that I could at least feel comfortable in my own home, but apparently that was too much to ask for. "Somebody kill me now."

Kai's warm laughter washes over me, but not enough to force me to show my face again.

"Get your mind out of the gutter," he says. I spread my

fingers and peek just in time to see Kai pointing to the present he made me. "I gave her that for her birthday. The color on the cherry is spreading throughout the pie."

"Aw shit, Kai! I forgot you had a deep, talented artist soul on top of slaying in the kitchen."

I don't know if Kai absorbs some of my humiliation, but when I drop my arms to my sides, his face is bright red. I guess it's all about balance when it comes to being around Ella.

"Oh my god!" Ella jumps around some more. "I heard there's a great art and food scene in Brazil! You should totally come with us. Like the three amigos, but you two can bang."

"I hate you." I love her, but I also hate her. "What are your motives right now?"

"Motives? What are you talking about?" She does the puppy dog eye thing she used to get away with everything in high school. Luckily for me, I'm immune to all that shit.

"Oh no. No, ma'am. I'm not falling for any of this nonsense." If I'm going to spend a year with her, we need to be completely open with each other. And that includes the little games she finds so much joy in.

"There is no nonsense. It's just that . . ." She trails off and confirms to me that there is, in fact, nonsense.

"It's just what?" Ella is never one to beat around the bush with anything in life. If she's hesitating, maybe I want to wait until we aren't around company. But it's too late for that.

She's quiet for a moment, and then she finally says, "You're nicer when you're taken care of."

"What are you talking about?" The fire that blooms so easily in my sister's presence ignites. No offense to Kai, but even though I know he's successful in his own right, I'm willing to bet that the savings account I've been steadily contributing most of my salary to for the last ten years would take care of me better than he could. "I don't need anyone to take care of me. If you haven't noticed"—I gesture to the empty and slightly depressing apartment we're standing in—"I've done a pretty great job at providing for myself."

When I look to Kai for backup, his eyes are creased at the corner and he's chewing on his bottom lip like he's trying not to laugh.

"Oh my god, Maya!" Ella throws her hands into the air. "I'm talking about sex! You're much nicer when you are getting some good D on a consistent basis. It's how I knew Vaughn was trash years ago. You got mean."

Oh.

My.

God.

"You did not say that." I'm just going to go to my room now. I'd much rather die in my comfy bed than in front of company.

"I was trying not to, but it's true." She shrugs and tosses a fry in the air and catches it in her mouth.

"Well," Kai says before I lose my mind. "As much as I would love to be the third cast member in what is bound to be an epic comedy adventure, I'm afraid I can't."

Even though I still haven't decided whether I'm even joining Ella, hearing Kai turn down the offer is equal parts relief and disappointment.

On one hand, I really like him. Like a lot. Like so much that I wouldn't be upset exploring South America with him and my sister. He's so thoughtful and talented and hot and I think I'm a better person when I'm around him.

And did I mention hot? Because he's hot.

But on the other hand, part of me is afraid I'm jumping

into something with him to avoid being alone. I like who I am with him, and I'm nervous I won't like who I am by myself. And even though I still haven't called my therapist, I know that's not okay. I don't want to latch on to him because I think I need to. I want to choose him because I want to.

And what if this fast and hot whirlwind romance is all we're supposed to have? I don't want to ruin the magic of our time together by not walking away when I should. If we part ways now, I can keep the memory of our time together saved and untouched by the drama that inevitably comes with life.

"Oh bummer," Ella says after she finishes chewing, because she might be a little savage, but she's not a monster. "Why not? I thought you were getting antsy in Miami and looking to leave."

Well that's news to me.

"I was . . . I mean, I am." A smile like I've never seen on anyone lights up his gorgeous face and takes him straight to mythological levels of hotness. "My work got commissioned for a gallery in Seattle. They are going to provide me with a place to live and studio time to create an interactive and interchangeable exhibition for a year."

"What?" I don't hesitate before I turn to hug him. "That's amazing! Congratulations!"

I loosen my grip on him, and when I pull back, he's looking at me the way he did the first night we were on my couch together. There's longing and appreciation and excitement.

"Do you mind if we go talk on your balcony?" he asks before shooting a rueful grin Ella's way. "No offense, Ella."

"None taken." Ella shoves a handful of fries into her mouth. "Go be alone, profess your love to each other."

I almost apologize for her, but luckily Kai is already an

expert in dealing with my sister and I don't have to say a word. One more perk of being with Kai.

Once we slide the glass door behind us, we settle onto my balcony overlooking the same ocean where we first met.

"So . . ." He turns to me, his strong hands immediately finding their way to my hips. My body lights up beneath his touch, reminding me that I'm not ready to part with it yet. "It seems like you might be leaving Miami. I didn't think that was really an option for you."

I lean into him, not overthinking anything for once and just allowing my body to take what it needs. "It wasn't, but I've made a few friends who've convinced me that maybe it's time to consider expanding my horizons."

"Friends, huh?" His grip tightens against my hips. "Am I one of these so-called friends?"

"Would it be okay if you were?" I regret the question as soon as it leaves my lips. I know better than to ask something I don't want the answer to.

"Yeah, I want to be your friend." He nods his head, the reflection from the sun making his eyes look impossibly blue as he looks at me, and my heart that's yearning for so much more shatters just a little bit. "But I'd also like to be your partner. I want to explore with you, create with you, grow alongside you as we both continue to discover who we are. I know Seattle is about as polar opposite from Miami as you can get, but if you wanted to come, I'd love to have you there. I don't want you to feel pressured at all—I've loved watching you start to come into your true self these last few weeks and I would never want to get in the way of that. But if you *are* looking for a change, maybe we can brave the gray skies together and switch our boat dates from yachts to ferries?"

His hands slide around me and my slight fear of heights

are the only things preventing me from falling over right now. All of my breath leaves me in a whoosh and I think I hear Ella screaming from inside, but I'm not sure.

I've spent the last thirty years playing by the rules, following the safe, predictable, boring path. Now, in the span of twenty-four hours, I have four different paths to choose from, and I'm not sure any of them are bad. I could keep pushing forward in my job and climbing the corporate ladder; I could go on *Real Love;* I could travel to Brazil with my sister; or I could risk everything for a guy with kind eyes in Seattle.

So many choices. So little time.

I know there are no promises for any of them, but I am sure that for the first time ever, I'm going to live my life the way I want to.

I'm just not quite sure what that means yet.

26

ELLA ONLY STAYED for a week this time around.

She found a great deal and flew to Brazil to scout places for her year of adventure. She's been FaceTiming me every chance she gets to show me the cute apartment she found or the view of the beach I just have to see. I still don't know if I'm going, but I'd be lying if I said it wasn't very tempting.

On the other hand, Delilah has been obsessively texting me each morning with a "Fun Fact of the Day" where she tells me another reason I should commit to being on *Real Love*. These range from quick pictures of something she thinks will persuade me to novel-length stories about new opportunities coming to her every day. These have been fun and pretty stress-free until last night when she texted me, informing me that the producers moved up the start date. I'd had a few more weeks before I had to give them an answer, and now they need it by tomorrow.

Everyone is waiting for me to give them answers I don't have.

Except for Kai. Of course my sweet Kai isn't pushing at all, just checking in and reassuring me that whatever decision I make will be right and he'll support me no matter what I choose.

I don't know what I'm going to do, but I do know what I'm not doing.

My chest hurts, my head is killing me, and I haven't been able to eat a full meal since I made my decision. It wasn't an easy choice and a lot is still unknown, but I'm relieved to finally take something off my list. Even if it means I feel like I'm being trampled by a herd of elephants.

I knock on Greg's office door. His head shoots up from whatever document he's studying and a welcoming smile crosses his kind face. "Hey, Maya." He gestures to the chair I've become so familiar with over the last few weeks. "Come on in. Take a seat."

"Thank you." I eye the trash can in the corner of his office in case I need to use it. I'm sweating profusely and my stomach feels like it may turn on me at any moment. I take one step in and, just as fast, nearly pivot on my heel and run back to my desk to stay there forever . . . where it's safe and predictable and boring.

But I don't.

One foot in front of the other, I cross the small space and sit. I have no idea what I'm going to say. It's the first time I'm making myself a priority and it's so scary. It's so much easier when I can blame my problems on other people.

Will my parents be eternally disappointed in me? Possibly. Will I squander all my money, become unemployable, and end up moving in with Delilah? Also possible.

I've lain in bed every night for the last week going over every worst-case scenario. But even as bad as they were—one fairly dark one was that the news would cause my parents to both have heart attacks—one thing was abundantly clear: I have to get off this merry-go-round. I can't keep doing the same things and expecting a new outcome. That is, after all, the very definition of insanity.

I think about the salary I'm giving up and consider the very plausible idea that I'm not thinking clearly at all and this might be a mistake.

"So what can I help you with?" Greg asks when I sit in silence for a few moments too long. "Is everything okay?"

"Oh. Um . . . yeah, everything is totally fine." *Oh? Um? Totally fine? Get it together, Maya!* I close my eyes and take a deep breath. "Yes, everything is fine." My voice is strong and steady even though I still feel like a wreck inside. "I'm so grateful to you both for giving me the opportunity to become director. It was all I wanted for years, and I can't put into words how much it meant to reach that goal."

Greg is watching me intently, his welcoming smile transforming to a sad one as I speak.

"I feel a 'but' coming soon," Greg says, confirming that he's read my intention correctly.

I nod, certain my expression matches his.

"But lately I've come to realize that as much as I thought this position is what I wanted, it's not what I needed." Every ounce of hesitation and fear I had going into this conversation disappears and is replaced with relief so stark it brings tears to my eyes. "I'm sorry for such late notice, but today is going to be my last day. I have compiled all of my information on my clients and given them to Julie. She's up-to-date and ready to provide them with a smooth transition, and I think either Leon or Jackson will make a great director."

"Wow." He sits straighter in his chair, and even though he knew what was coming, I can tell the suddenness of my departure has thrown him for a loop. "Is there anything I can say to convince you to stay?"

"Probably," I say honestly. "But please don't. Even if this turns out to be a mistake, it's one I need to make."

"Well then." He pushes his chair back and stands. "We're going to miss you, but I have a feeling this won't be a mistake. Whatever you do, I know you'll succeed."

"Thank you." I shake his hand, and when I walk out of his office, I feel like I could fly, and it's all the confirmation I needed to know this was the right decision.

So instead of walking straight to my desk and packing up the few little trinkets I have, I take a small detour.

Bailey's long hair looks as beautiful as ever as she sits in her cubicle, focusing on the monitors in front of her. She's usually busy flitting around the office, catching up on and spreading gossip, and I don't think I've ever seen her sitting like this. I knock on the cubicle wall and she spins in her chair. The bright smile on her face falls as soon as she sees me.

We have avoided each other since she left my apartment. Even though she said some pretty messed-up things, I'm not mad at her. I understand better than most what it feels like to not feel good enough and be overlooked. And I know hurt people hurt people. Do I love her budding friendship with Vaughn? Not really, but I hold no ill feelings. I hope she'll come around and see that.

"Hi?" she says, but it sounds more like a question. I don't miss her eyes as they shift around and I can tell she's planning her escape.

"Hi. So listen." I dive right in. I'm not here for small talk. "I want you to know that even though some of the things you said really hurt my feelings"—she opens her mouth to defend her herself, but I continue—"I'm not mad at you. I understand that you wanted what Delilah had, but I hope in your future friendships when you're feeling like that, you speak up and tell them that you're hurting. You were trying to compete with people who weren't running the same race as you. This didn't have to happen. You could've won without making us lose."

"I'm sorry," she says, and I believe her. "I hope I can make it up to you."

"You don't need to make it up to me. I'm not mad." I used to carry things with me for so long, but this feels so much better. I thought about asking her what was going on between her and Vaughn, but then I realized it's not my business and I don't care. "I put in my notice with Greg and today is my last day. I only came over here to tell you that I really hope you find your happiness one day and I'm grateful for the good times we did have together."

All traces of sadness leave her face and shock takes over, which is fair seeing as I've shocked myself. "You're leaving?"

"Going to pack up my office now." Saying it out loud for the first time causes the reality of what I've done and the opportunities in front of me to set in. I thought this would feel like panic, but instead I feel like I could fly. Like the entire world just opened up for me.

"Where are you going to go?" Bailey asks.

I tell her the truth. "I'm not sure yet. But I know it's going to be good."

My little cardboard box filled with frames, highlighters, and a pencil holder is sitting on my dining room table right next to my laptop. I have two missed calls from Ella and three from Delilah.

A website with flight tickets is on the computer screen. Prices for options to Brazil, Los Angeles, and Seattle are on three separate tabs I keep clicking between. For once, numbers aren't saving me. Flight numbers, prices, and departure times all blur together until I give up and slam my computer shut.

I walk through my apartment, acutely aware of how empty it is. Unassembled boxes and rolls of duct tape lean against my bare walls. I push aside the unopened packages of packing paper cluttering my counters and pull out a glass to make a Crown and Coke.

"If any night calls for alcohol, it's this one," I say to nobody at all.

The sound of the Coke can opening goes off like a shot in the silence as I top off the uncharacteristically heavy pour of whiskey. I raise the glass to my lips, and when I do, the glimpse of the pie Kai made me catches my eye from the corner of my kitchen.

I put my glass on the counter and walk over to my favorite, and currently only, piece of art. I let my fingers gently trace the stem of the cherry, marveling at how Kai made something so beautiful and strong out of something delicate and mundane. I inspect the glitter now encased in glass, tucked in tight but still giving the effect of spreading throughout the pie. I remember how happy I was in that art class after Sofia shared her precious sparkle with me. How even though I objectively failed, I accomplished everything I came for.

Certainty spreads through me like color through clear glass.

I sprint across my apartment, my feet slipping on the smooth wood floors, and I race to my computer, afraid that I'll talk myself out of it at any second.

I enter my password and the screen filled with flight options comes to life.

I exit out of two screens and choose my one-way ticket. I click through the pages as fast as I can, only scrolling down to pick the perfect window seat with extra legroom . . . it's not a short flight after all. My fingers fly across the keyboard as I fill in my name and credit card information until the confirmation number appears on my screen.

I close my computer, gently this time, and walk back to my full glass. I lift it and offer a toast to no one and everyone before I bring it to my lips and drain every last drop.

Well, Lovers, another season has come to pass and I don't know if I'm thrilled or devastated that it's over. Our girl Delilah came, saw, and conquered the hearts of America, but also the heart of Anthony Alberti. It was the love story of the ages and I loved every single second.

There are a lot of people who are upset she didn't pick Drew, and while I understand that we develop feelings for the couples, I think it's important to remember that we weren't there for the entire journey and we only saw what the producers allowed us to see. There are only two people who have to live with this decision, and that is Delilah and Anthony.

In the finale, the producers were still editing it to heavily favor Drew, and I'd be lying if I said I didn't begin to think about switching away from Anthony. They almost got me. But there was one moment that sealed the deal for me. And that was when they showed the men before the final decision and Drew was Mr. Chatty, discussing all the ways this process was so hard on him and that he didn't know if Delilah was ready. He was so nervous about Anthony and wouldn't stop discussing him. Then they cut to Anthony. I know they wanted it to seem as if he was too nonchalant and not invested, but they left in the part where he said, "I've never been more excited about my future. Sometimes you just know. And no matter what she had with Drew, I love what she has with me."

And you know what? Just freaking swoon.

He knew what they had. He didn't pressure her to tell him anything about her relationship with Drew. He accepted her and didn't need to prove it by constantly pounding his chest. He proved it by the way his eyes would go soft when she walked into a room, when he listened to every word as she spoke.

Yes, Anthony is a lawyer with a heart of gold, but more important, he's a man who's won the heart of a good woman. And I know he won't mess that up.

Until next season . . . where rumors are ALREADY swirling!

XOXO,
Stacy

27

"CALL ME AS soon as you land." Delilah loosens her arms around me and I'm able to breathe again. "I'm going to miss you, but I'm so proud of you for doing this."

"I'm going to miss you too." I swipe away the stupid never-ending tears with the back of my hand. "Are you sure you don't mind handling the moving company?"

In my rush to hurry and buy my ticket, I booked a flight before I hired a moving company. They weren't available until a week after I left. Thankfully for me though, I have an amazing friend who stepped up right away.

"Are you kidding me?" She looks at me like I've lost my mind. "You know how much I love your pool, and now that the world knows I chose Anthony, this is going to be our honeymoon pad until the attention dies down around my house."

"Turning my apartment into a sex dungeon? Good for you!" I wiggle my eyebrows. "But seriously, if you need anything, just call."

All of the nerves that were nowhere to be found when I took the plunge and booked my ticket have been slowly returning in the days since. Ella and Delilah have been calling me daily to remind me I'm doing the right thing, while my mom has called me every day to try to talk me out of it.

I stopped taking Mom's calls.

"All set." The Uber driver slams the trunk on my suitcases that are packed to the brim with brand-new dresses, jeans, the cutest rain jacket and boots ever, and not an Ann Taylor item to be found.

The dormant butterflies in my stomach go wild and Delilah pulls me in for one final hug.

"You got this," she whispers in my ear. "It's going to be the most amazing experience ever and I can't wait to hear all about it."

I return her embrace with more force than necessary, not letting go until the Uber driver rolls down his window and clears his throat. "I don't mean to interrupt this touching moment, but traffic isn't great and I wouldn't want you to miss your flight."

"The sarcasm is noted, sir. She's coming," Delilah says over my shoulder. "Okay." She grabs me by the shoulders and looks me straight in the eye. "You are about to go on the adventure of a lifetime, so please don't miss out on a single second of it, okay?"

My throat turns thick with unshed tears and I can only nod in response.

"Now go." She spins me around and shoves me into the car. "And don't forget about me."

Like that could ever be possible.

Owen, my driver, was not wrong about the traffic. With every passing moment sitting on the stagnant Miami highway, the knots in my stomach grow. By the time we arrive at the airport, I have him blasting the air-conditioning, trying to counteract the nervous sweating I can't stop.

"Thank you so much." I take my second suitcase from him after he drops it on the sidewalk.

"My pleasure." He looks like he's holding back laughter. "And have fun on your trip."

Owen was not only a superb driver who never forgot to

signal or say thank you when he was allowed to merge, he also talked to me the entire ride once I started to freak out and gently told me he wasn't going to turn around when I demanded it in the middle of the freeway.

He's definitely getting a massive tip.

My sweaty palms struggle to grip the metal handle before I finally gather my composure and head into Miami International Airport.

The line to check in is blissfully short and doesn't give me the opportunity to run back to Owen and beg him to bring me back to Delilah.

A woman behind the counter waves me down to her station and asks for my name.

"Maya Johnson." I hand her my ID before I load my suitcases onto the scale.

"Perfect." She pulls her red-painted lips into a bright smile I'm sure she gives to every traveler who passes through her line. But for me, it feels like a good omen, like she too can tell that I've made the right decision.

She tags my suitcases and throws them onto the conveyer belt behind her before handing me my boarding pass. "Have a wonderful trip."

I'm not sure if she can see my hand shaking as I reach for the ticket, but she doesn't say anything if she does. I take the ticket from her with a grateful smile, words evading me as the weight of the journey ahead of me weighs down on me full force.

But as soon as I look at the ticket and my destination looms large at the top, excitement and a sense of peace I've never felt before come over me.

I don't know what the next year is going to bring, but I know that no matter what, I will never regret this.

For once, I'm following my heart and I'm excited to find out who I really am instead of who I thought I wanted to be.

Acknowledgments

I DO NOT even know where to begin so I will just start with a general THANK YOU. There is no way to remember every possible name and individual that allowed this moment and this book to happen. So I want to thank those that have supported me, believed in me, prayed for me, and trusted me in writing this book. This is something that I could have never done by myself, and it took a village of people and support to get here. I am forever grateful for your dedication, love, and encouragement.

In life we make certain decisions that set us on a path that determines the rest of our time here on this earth. My life changed entirely when I simply said yes to doing a reality television show. I often wonder what would have happened if I'd said no. This book evolved from that no. This book is fictionalized from the fear and doubt that would have held me back from what I was ultimately destined to do. When I think about where I was six years ago and where I am now, I am incredibly grateful to be soaring from the mental cage I was trapped inside. I hope this book resonates with you and encourages you to take chances and live fearlessly and freely. Thank you to everyone and everything that inspired this book. I hope this leads you to find peace and *Real Love*, whatever that looks like in your life.

I want to of course thank God for guiding and ordering

my steps as I stumbled across this thing called life. I may struggle with faith and question you at times but trusting and leaning on YOU has never led me astray.

Bryan. My dear, patient, kind, and overwhelmingly supportive husband. Thank you for your forever love and support.

Thank you, Alexa Martin. You are absolutely amazing, funny, and inspiring! This was not possible without you. I connected with you from the first time we spoke, as we share a love for so many of the same things in this world. I knew that you would understand and appreciate the vision, and you brought this book to life. I learned so much from you in this process and am grateful to call you a friend.

Thank you, Maryssa and Lauren: You changed my life forever.

Thank you, Hilary Teeman, Caroline Weishuhn, Anthony Mattero, Alex Rice, Ballantine Books, and Penguin Random House for taking a chance on me and believing in the vision of this story.

REAL LOVE

RACHEL LINDSAY

RANDOM HOUSE
BOOK CLUB

Questions & Topics
for Discussion

1. When the novel begins, we see Maya turn down the opportunity to go on the incredibly popular dating show *Real Love* as the lead because she already has the life she wants. If you were offered a similar opportunity, would you take it? Why or why not?

2. Maya has worked incredibly hard to give herself what many would consider "traditional" success: a high-powered job, a long-term partner, and a glamorous apartment in a big city. In what ways do you think Maya was fulfilled by this success, and in what ways do you think she was not?

3. What did you think of Maya and Vaughn's relationship at the beginning of the book? Did they seem happy? Why or why not?

4. As Maya watches Delilah's big decisions play out on *Real Love* as well as in real life, she reflects on her own life. Have you ever had a friend do or try something that made you think about something in a new way?

5. When Maya meets Kai, there's an instant connection. What do you think attracted her to him, even though they seem so different on paper?

6. Throughout the novel, Delilah and Ella (and even Kai)

push Maya to step out of her comfort zone, and often-times she finds she's all the better for doing it. Has any-one in your life ever encouraged you to try new things?

7. Where Delilah made some very sudden, very big changes to her life, Maya is starting a bit smaller and just trying to find some new passions, like art. Have you ever made a small change to your life that made a big difference?

8. As Maya and Kai grow closer, we see that the dynamic between them is quite different to Maya and Vaughn's relationship. In what ways did you notice this?

9. Maya's birthday party is a pivotal scene in the novel and a pivotal point in her relationships with many of those around her. What did you think of how Maya handled herself and the decisions she made as a result? Did you agree or disagree with her choices?

10. As we reach the end of the novel, we discover that Maya has a very big choice to make. Would you have made the same choice she did in her position, or would you have chosen something different? Why or why not?

A Q&A with Rachel Lindsay

Q: You are an incredibly busy woman: You are an attorney, TV correspondent, podcast host, and now an author. What made you decide to start writing?

A: I have actually been interested in creative writing for a long time. I dated a guy in high school who was an actor and into poetry, and he opened my eyes to a whole new world. I started writing poetry here and there, and then I started writing in journals. But as usual, life got in the way at a certain point and legal writing took priority. It is such a rigid and structured way of writing that I really began to yearn for ways to express myself creatively through the written word. Once I decided to prioritize creative writing again, it was easy for me to first start writing about my own experiences, and then start writing my blog during the pandemic—that eventually led me to this space of fiction writing.

Q: While you also authored a collection of essays, *Miss Me with That, Real Love* is your first novel. What made you decide to write fiction? How did the experience differ from writing nonfiction?

A: There were certain experiences that I was too afraid to write about in my collection of essays, and I thought it would be interesting to take those and explore them in a fictional story. In the same way, ever since I said yes to

The Bachelor, I've had this ever-present feeling of what would have—or could have—happened if I had said no. But since that is not my reality, I wanted to explore the idea in a fictionalized setting. This experience was the total opposite of writing nonfiction, because there is so much more freedom in fiction. I didn't have to worry about hurting anyone's feelings or sharing too much, and there was no limit in where I could go with this novel. That made writing it even more exciting, interesting, and mysterious.

Q: In the novel there is a reality dating show called *Real Love*—is it safe to assume that the reality show depicted in the novel was inspired by your time on *The Bachelorette*? Was anything else in the book inspired by your life?

A: Absolutely! Maya is watching her best friend enter a world she declined to join. This story is loosely about the other side of the coin of my own life . . . what if I had said no to *The Bachelor* and continued the life path I was on? What would have happened, where would I have ended up? But while the reality show was directly inspired by *The Bachelorette*, not much else too closely resembles my life. After all, this novel is an exploration of a path not taken!

Q: Have your views on love or success changed over time the way Maya's did? How did they change and what did you learn?

A: My outlook on success has always been the same foundationally. Life and time, however, have taught me that success does not have to be linear; I believe there are core attributes that contribute to one's success, but the path to achieve them does not always have to go exactly according to the plan you originally set in motion.

I have realized that learning from mistakes and accepting surprising twists on your journey can lead you to the exact space and success you are meant to have. And I think I can apply those same lessons I learned about success to love—I was rigid in the way I looked and believed I would find love. Once I was willing to see something different, I felt something different, and it has been so beautiful to experience. This is exactly Maya's journey.

Q: Did you learn anything about yourself while writing this book? Is there a message you want readers to take away from it?

A: I didn't necessarily learn anything new about *myself*, but publishing this book has taught me that I can accomplish any dream. This book coming to life is a creative dream—but one with a message. I do hope readers can see themselves in Maya or any one of the characters in this book. Maya is so many of us—she is at a crossroads and desperately trying to determine which path is the best for her in love and life. We are often faced with a crossroads and truly must look within and trust ourselves to make the best decision for us. It is scary, it is exciting, and it is worth it.

Q: And for the final question, something just for fun! If *Real Love* were to become a movie, who would you want to see cast as Maya, Kai, Ella, and Delilah?

A: I would love to see *Real Love* be a movie or a television series. It truly deserves one! Tika Sumpter or Coco Jones as Maya, William Levy as Kai, Meagan Good or Serayah McNeill as Ella, and Eiza González or Adria Arjona as Delilah.

About the Author

RACHEL LINDSAY is an author, attorney, media personality, podcaster, and speaker. She is currently a correspondent for *Extra* and cohosts The Ringer's *Higher Learning* podcast and *Morally Corrupt* podcast. Prior to her media career, she practiced law at Cooper & Scully, P.C., in Dallas. Lindsay has an exclusive newsletter called "Honestly, Rach" on Meta Bulletin where she talks about love, life, careers, friendships, and social issues. Last year, Lindsay authored a collection of essays titled, *Miss Me with That: Hot Takes, Helpful Tidbits, and a Few Hard Truths*. An avid sports fan, Lindsay enjoys music, dancing, exercising, reading, and spending time with her husband, Bryan Abasolo, her dogs, Copper and Brownie, and her extended family. Lindsay is also an ambassador for the College Football Playoff Foundation and a member of the University of Texas at Austin College of Education Advisory Council. She lives in Los Angeles.

@therachlindsay

About the Type

This book was set in Walbaum, a typeface designed in 1810 by German punch cutter J. E. (Justus Erich) Walbaum (1768–1839). Walbaum's type is more French than German in appearance. Like Bodoni, it is a classical typeface, yet its openness and slight irregularities give it a human, romantic quality.